AN EMBARRASSMENT OF RICHES

CAROLYN KINGSON

Lirio Publications

Published in the United States of America

Lirio Publications
Box 113
Dixon, New Mexico 87527

Cover and author photos by Douglas Fir

ISBN-13: 978-0615541228
ISBN-10: 0615541224

Table of Contents

For Jonathan
Everything I have is yours.

AN EMBARRASSMENT OF RICHES

CAROLYN KINGSON

PART ONE

HENRY LIONEL ASHE

CHAPTER ONE

On his last day, Hank asked for the sloop to be provisioned for lunch. As he hung up the phone, Juliet moved her legs to make room for him on the bed, but he didn't notice and headed toward the side of the room where open shutters revealed the sea, the deck, and the breakfast table that held the remains of omelets, pastries, fruit, and juice.

"Do you want some more coffee, Juliet?" he called as he refilled his cup.

"Is it still hot?"

He sipped. "Not really." He returned to the bedside phone, punched the button, tapped his foot, ran his hand through his thinning hair, and around the back of his neck. "Yes. We'd like some more coffee. Thanks." His slim, pedicured feet rocked impatiently as he spoke, but his voice was quiet and polite.

The scene was a large thatched-roofed pavilion built out over a cove on the west coast of Thailand. The complex had a sitting room where the furniture was teak and the cushions were covered with white and beige silk. Planters behind the sofas contained purple, yellow, and white orchids; elegant, minimalist flower arrangements around the room kept to the same color scheme; wooden statuary, antique chairs and tables were arranged on the gleaming floorboards. Along an interior wall, a carved unit of shelves, drawers, and desk held a library of music and movie CDs and DVDs, along with equipment connecting the suite to the world with satellite television, phone, and internet. Outer walls had shutters that could be raised to catch the breezes and the perfect views. In an alcove separated by a screen of carved flowers and winged deities was a round table and eight chairs, generous seating for what was intended for, and was at the moment being used as, a honeymoon cottage.

A door in the sitting room led to a half-bath, another led to a kitchen—well stocked—and several rooms for staff—unoccupied. The honeymooners had brought no one with them, except for the plane crew; resort staff for their personal use were, however, hovering nearby.

The focal point of the sitting room was the antique carved doors and ornate peaked doorframe that led to the bedroom. Beyond were the hot tub, and massage table, and His and Her showers, tubs, toilets, sinks, vanities, and walk-in closets.

Juliet rearranged her pile of silk pillows on the enormous bed and leaned back as she watched Hank pace. Their two weeks at the resort were ending; Hank had likely not stayed in one place for so long in years, and she suspected he was finding it a little frustrating to pretend to be an ordinary man on a honeymoon with his wife's body more than enough to occupy his full attention. Not that her body had been neglected, but there was no pretending that Hank was an ordinary man with ordinary interests. Juliet smiled with affection, watching his quick movements telegraph the restlessness of his mind. He crossed his arms, ran both hands through his nearly-grey hair, adjusted the louvers on the shutters, and peered intently at the mechanism and workmanship. His features were sharp—thin lips in a narrow face and a straight nose with delicate nostrils. He looked both patrician and appealingly fit.

"If there's enough wind, let's go out to Ko Luang." He squinted in the direction of the large island whose top was just visible over the bright water.

"How long will it take to get there?"

"Oh, I guess an hour. A little more. Doesn't look as though there's any wind today either."

"Harvey told me that 'no wind' is the literal meaning of *nirvana.*"

"Really? Add another to the list of unfortunate boat names. Remember *Permanent Wave* that was berthed next to the *Elan* in Florida?"

Juliet laughed. "I love it. And *Refried Dreams.*"

"How about *Passing Wind.*"

"You gotta be kidding! Where did you see that?"

"I think it was Sydney."

Juliet's laugh turned into a yawn and stretch that Hank watched fondly. She was small and trim and her limbs were shapely with muscle under her smooth skin. She looked like a compulsive exerciser, though it was purely the vigor of youth that gave the effect. Actually, she was one for curling up in nooks with good books; even now she looked longingly at her e-reader on which *The Elegance of the Hedgehog* awaited her. She began to reach toward it, but stopped, reminding herself to keep her attention on her husband. There would be plenty of time to read on the boat while Hank swam or fished.

A gentle knock sounded from outside the door to the bedroom. A young woman wearing the graceful Thai costume of tight tube skirt and long-sleeved blouse in

7

iridescent-green silk—the uniform of the resort—smiled and ducked her head modestly as she entered the bedroom. She bowed to Juliet and Hank, murmured, "With permission," placed the fresh coffee tray on a low table in the sitting area, and asked if it were convenient to clear the breakfast table. "Later," Hank said, and in a moment they heard a door close softly. He poured a cup for himself and made an inquiring look toward Juliet. She smiled and shook her head. He could drink ten cups a day.

Juliet knew Hank was yearning to be closer to his staff's time zone, closer to the action. Though he had financial and legal teams costing him millions, he micro-managed their every move with preternatural energy; he had been on the phone with San Francisco from midnight to one-thirty that very morning. Two weeks in Thailand had stretched his patience with inactivity, and this wasn't even the end of the honeymoon.

To follow after Thailand, he had arranged a week of wine tasting around France and a visit to the vineyard in Portugal that was the ancestral home of one Agostinho Teixeira who had come to the U.S. and begun planting grapes in the Napa Valley in the 1920s. Juliet's father, Sheldon Pierce, was employed as vintner at the winery he had founded there—Quinta da Agostinho—and Hank was its half-owner, its silent partner. Juliet had, not so long ago, taken off a year from university to work and learn at the Teixeira vineyards in Portugal, and was devoted to the family. She had hoped to follow in her father's footsteps. Now, to find herself one of his employers, was a twist of fate that she could hardly grasp. In addition, there would be a stop in Antibes to look at a yacht Hank was considering buying. Tomorrow the Dassault Falcon would take them to Europe.

The multi-leveled deck outside the bedroom held all

the accoutrements of indolence: the table with its large white umbrella, an infinity-edge pool, a staircase descending into the ocean, a thatched pavilion with lounge chairs beneath it, and a dock beside which bobbed the neat little sailboat, *Nit Noy*. The resort was well known as a luxury port-of-call for yachts and megayachts, with adequate berths and full chandelling services—not to mention villas, spas, and restaurants that often tempted the most pampered yachtsman onto the mainland—but if you had not come with your own boat, one could be provided. The sailing had disappointed Hank however; he preferred the challenge of near-gale force winds. Here, sailing hardly seemed to involve anything so extreme as wind. It was as though the sloop was wafted by air currents stirred by the wings of the butterflies that accompanied them to the little islands scattered around the bay. Juliet thought it was just right.

She rearranged her lacy silk gown, wiggled her toes and contemplated their polish. She had recently had her colors done and had been pronounced a "Summer;" she never should have allowed that orange a pink. Her hair—the light brown sort that bleached in the sun—was frosted so skillfully that no beach hours were required for her California-girl look, and was cut into permanent wind-blown casualness. Her bright blue eyes and pink cheeks that cried health and vigor continued the theme, but the rest of her face—her elegant, straight nose, subtly curved lips, and graceful jaw and neck—gave her the sort of classic beauty that might be expected of a woman occupying such a suite.

She was enjoying her honeymoon even if it was something of a mad dash. Besides their sailing days, they had helicoptered to an elephant preserve, shopped in Bangkok's Siam district, flown to Siem Reap for a two-day visit to Angkor Wat, and attended a dance performance at the royal palace as guests of the king's cousin. They had even hosted a dinner party.

Juliet was discovering that rich people had many friends—at least Hank had many friends—and one of these happened to be staying at the resort. Not such a coincidence actually. The very rich didn't have *that* many places to go. They had to be secure and hyper-comfortable. Their resorts and spas had to have the proper cachet, with nearby runways for their jets, and accommodations for their preposterous yachts. They were always running into each other at their approved hotels, restaurants, and events, which was of course the idea. Perhaps the unexamined life was not worth living; perhaps it was, but for the rich, the *unobserved* life—unobserved by those few who could truly appreciate the outlay involved—was definitely not desirable. Packing in so much rare opportunity was exhausting without regular quaffs of the elixir of others' envy.

Hank's friend was George Dubose, there with his yacht, *Viridian*—thirty-eight meters of sleek luxury—and four fortunate guests flown over to join in a run from Thailand to Hawaii: around Malaysia, along the east coast of Sumatra and Java, past Bali and Australia, through the Solomons, and up. Hank and George had crewed together at a regatta off Cape Cod a few years before, and were happy to see each other. The other men were Haver, Pete, Harvey, and Alex. They had been the dinner party guests.

Giving a dinner party simply meant having the attentions of the suite's staff manifest in your dining room. Juliet thought the compliments she received somewhat ironic, seeing that she had done nothing more than approve the menu and select the wines—she had the most wine expertise of the newlyweds, young as she was—but it had been her maiden voyage as Hank's hostess, and even with the services of the resort at her disposal, she had been slightly anxious. She was not yet accustomed to attending rich people's parties, much less planning them. She was not yet accustomed to being rich.

Juliet watched Hank again top off his coffee. "You're getting ready to go home, aren't you. Are you going to be able to enjoy France and Portugal?"

"Ah, you read me, huh," he smiled at her. "I *was* thinking about that sale. But give yourself credit. If the Nibels fuck it up, so be it. I'm completely happy to be here with you."

"You've talked to them every day. They're going to have mighty little time between phone calls to do something wrong."

"Yeah, you're right. I shouldn't think about it. No, sweetie, I'm going to love tasting fine wines. We'll be back soon enough."

In many ways, Juliet was still poised on the edge of her new life, not quite daring to take the plunge. She had only just finished her last semester at university when the courtship had started. It had not been a happy time, those college years. Her mother's death and her father's remarriage had left her feeling doubly bereft. Meeting Hank, experiencing his head-long pursuit with its over-the-top luxury—private jet, spas, charity balls, screenings, yachting . . . . It had been orchids from the day they met, her daisy life left behind, with trepidation.

Hank was very dear. They made love well and often; he had chosen the most beautiful spot on earth for their honeymoon. But, on the immense bed with sheets like petals of the plumeria blossoms for which the suite was named, in the dancing light reflected from the ocean to the bamboo and palm thatch cathedral peak, and back down to their entwined bodies, Juliet could see the beginning of a sag in Hank's neck and the thinness of his hair. She did not worship her husband's body. It did not inspire her to kiss or caress each part, as hers did him. There was shame— deep down and vigorously suppressed—that she had agreed to marry a man so much older, and especially so terribly rich. The shame rose a few fathoms when she saw the eyes of Hank's friends, narrowed, appraising. It had come perilously near the surface when she was accosted by Hank's sister, Louise—a debacle of which Hank had still not heard.

But largely, Juliet had made peace with her choice. Her husband was a force of nature; she was lucky to even know such a person. His name wasn't exactly a household word, but the company his father and he had built—Home Base—certainly was. Its record sale eight years ago had made it possible for him to go from the stratosphere to the troposphere of wealth, as virtually all his investments insisted on coming up roses. And for some reason he was laying it at her feet, wanting to make everything possible for her: her dreams of owning wineries, of studying and making fine wine, of children—though he already had two, Paige and David, neither of whom she had met—and of supporting good causes, as well. Hank had promised that he was nearly ready to move into philanthropy, claiming to be tired of an exclusive focus on increasing his wealth. When Juliet had made a doubtful face at him, he'd laughed. No, no. He was serious. The sky was the limit, and she loved him. She *did* love him—just in a sane, calm sort of way.

Palat and Tai arrived with a picnic basket, cooler, and linens. They boarded the *Nit Noy* and arranged the provisions while Juliet put on a white bikini, sarong, and dark glasses, and Hank donned his blue trunks and a polo shirt. He brought out his new speargun and handed it down into the boat where it was stashed with fins, snorkel, and mask. Palat and Tai—boys, teenagers, young men, it was hard to tell—slipped the sleeves from the sails and lofted them while the motor idled. They had prepared to cast off when Juliet came out with her reader and camera, and stepped over to the sloop's deck. Hank clapped Tai on the shoulder as he boarded.

"Tell the kitchen to be ready to cook fish tonight," he said.

"Don't bring grouper, sah. Too many bones."

"We ate it last time. It was good." Hank raised his eyebrows.

"I think they gave you other fish, sah," Palat laughed. Hank had become a favorite with the staff.

"You lie, Palat."

"Yes, sah. I lie. Or maybe not. You want me take a picture?" He made clicking motions on an imaginary camera.

"Yes, please," Juliet said, extracting the camera from a waterproof case and handing it to him. Hank pulled her down beside him on the bench. They arranged themselves this way and that as Palat clicked. She retrieved the camera, looked through the pictures, and took some shots of Palat and Tai as they mugged in turn. Tai tossed the line, and Hank coiled and stashed it under the cushioned seat in the stern. They motored away from the dock.

"Do you think that's true about the fish, Hank?"

"Ach, maybe. I felt like big stuff bringing in a fish that was larger than me. A shame though if it wasn't edible. I'll look for yellowtail this time. I don't know if those boys were putting me on or not." Hank killed the motor, hauled the sail close, set the jib, and set off on a tack to the island as Juliet slathered sunblock on her skin. In a moment she got up, sat beside Hank at the tiller, and began applying it to his arms.

"There's an exercise in the closing of barn doors," he said, kissing her cheek. His arms were deeply tanned and the skin mottled from exposure on the sea. It might not be healthy, but it was very appealing, very manly, saving him from looking effete with his elegant grooming.

This outdoor enthusiasm was the first thing Juliet had learned about Hank. They had sat across the table from each other at Quinta da Agostinho on that September day four months ago, at the winery's harvest celebration. Hank had told her how, almost at the last minute, he had been made part of the three-man crew in the U.S. Soling entry in the Barcelona Olympics. A team member, a friend, had had a heart attack a month before the games, and Hank had been able to step in. He was very funny about his crash fitness program, though it had been hard to believe this wiry, lean man had ever been out of shape. And they had taken the bronze! It was the proudest event of his life he had said, smiling into her eyes.

Like this honeymoon, the wooing had been water-borne. Hank had taken Juliet sailing off San Francisco and Palm Beach on yachts so enormous they required a crew. This svelte sloop and calm bay were an entirely different order of experience, and much more to her taste than holding on for dear life on the frigid North Pacific while the professionals moved around the deck in an intense ballet.

The resort had required an initial supervised sail that Hank accepted graciously for Juliet's sake. Palat, with his excellent English, had taken them out on the bay on their first day at the resort.

"The crew—" He had nodded to Juliet. "—stands

by the jib line when the captain—" He indicated Hank. "—
says 'Prepare to come about.' " They practiced until Juliet,
the earnest student, had it down. Sailing was a large part of
the package she had accepted with her husband.

If they went out at midday, the resort packed a
gourmet lunch; if at sunset, their hors d'ouvres and wine
went with them, or Martinis, or margaritas—whatever they
might desire. As an opulent bower for love, their well-
appointed sailboat lacked only rich fabrics trailing behind in
the water like a doge's barge. And that water was
breathtakingly beautiful. Where the bottom sank away, the
color was a luminous turquoise; in the shallows, over rocky
outcrops or coral, the water was so clear it was impossible
to believe it held any potentiality of color. Sometimes a
school of little fish passed, sometimes a larger presence.
The shadow of the boat side-slipped along the white,
rippled bottom.

They reached Ko Luang a little before noon, made
a pass around it that took nearly another hour, and chose a
pretty cove for an interlude. Karst formations marched out
into the water, looking a bit like ice cream cones of stone,
with sprinkles of vine and shrub on top. Birds flew from
islet to islet. As Juliet took pictures, Hank lowered the
anchor, and furled the sails.

"Are you hungry, baby?" Juliet asked. Of course
Hank was hungry. His metabolism was fierce; he was an
oven in bed. She opened the basket without waiting for his
reply. "Let's see what we have today. Looks like glass
noodles with sauce." She dipped a finger. "Peanut sauce,
naturally. Rambutans. Chicken satay. What's this? Little
spare ribs . . . umm, tasty. Do you want Singha beer or
wine? They've given us a French chardonnay—Intime,
2002. That should be good. Remember we had some
Intime at the club in Palm Beach? I think that was a 2003."

15

"How do you remember that, sweetie?"

"I don't know. I seem to have a wine lobe in my brain, I guess. You can remember the wind conditions each time you went sailing for the past thirty years."

"Oh, well," Hank laughed, "that's entirely normal."

They decided on the chardonnay. Hank uncorked it and poured into the bottom-heavy stems that rode the waves well—not that there was anything worthy of the name out here, just as there was little wind. The wine and food made them feel sleepy and sexy. They went below to the bed wedged into the prow, made love slowly as the boat rocked, and fell asleep to the soft slap of the water a few inches from their ears.

Hank was awake almost immediately, eager to get in some spearfishing while Juliet slept. He readied his new speargun, put on his fins, adjusted his mask and snorkel, strapped a knife to his thigh, and slipped over the side. He was swimming easily some distance from the boat when Juliet came up on deck with her e-reader. She piled up pillows and leaned against the cabin, twisting her shoulder-length hair on top of her head, and securing it with a clip. Almost immediately, Hank gave a whoop and held up a large, thrashing fish on his spear. Juliet stood and cheered. His competency really was a delight. Dropping her sarong, she jumped overboard, and swam toward him.

"I'd give you a kiss if you weren't so heavily armed. Is it a yellowtail? Right on!"

"It's the third one I chased. They didn't like the looks of me. I dare the cook to turn his nose up at this!" Hank grinned like a kid showing off for his mom.

"Maybe we should make sashimi!" Juliet treaded water and pushed some strands of hair off her face.

"I'd worry about parasites. I think we should cook it."

"Ew, parasites! I can't wait to see it on the table tonight."

Hank laughed and swam to the boat. He put the gun and fish in first, then heaved himself over the side. Juliet swam slowly, thinking that it must feel like this in the womb—warm, caressed in buoyant saline, calm. Something brushed her toe, and she looked down to see a school of multicolored fish inspecting her legs. Their beauty brought a surge of physical delight indistinguishable from happiness. She swam to the ladder affixed to the side and began to climb. Hank helped her on board.

The yellowtail was a beauty. Its sleek, silver body was touched with canary on the head and fins, as well as the tail. Subtle bands and spots shimmered. Hank had already gutted it, and now threw the bits over the side. He washed the residue into the bilge with a little bucket, and put the fish in the cabin, out of the sun.

"Were there lots of other fish besides those yellowtails? I saw parrotfish, I think." Juliet tried to release some water from her ear. Hank had opened a beer and was holding the bottle toward her. She shook her head.

"Not so many. I saw a small grouper, lots of oscars, an octopus."

"Can you tell if sea life is declining? You've been diving for a long time, right?"

"Since the time of the triremes, at least. Absolutely, yes, and the coral is bleaching. I was in Bintan last year—I'd been there, I think, fourteen years earlier. It was heartbreaking how few fish there were and how much dead coral."

"What do you think, baby. What do you think you—we—will do when we start the foundation? Environment? Human health?" Juliet stretched on the deck, her hands behind her head. "Hand me my sunglasses,

17

will you, sweetheart?" (She was, somewhat awkwardly, trying out terms of endearment.) She put on the glasses and continued: "They say infant mortality is the key to population control. The more infants that survive, the fewer parents feel the need to have. It seems like everything comes down to overpopulation, really. Don't you think, Hank? Maybe we *shouldn't* have a baby."

"You can have your one or two. The world needs to find a way to prevent the families of five, ten, twelve."

"What do you think about a campaign to get the millions of women who have had abortions to speak out so it wouldn't have such stigma?"

"Have you had an abortion?" Hank looked at her sharply.

"Well, no. How would you feel if I said yes?" Juliet sat up, frowning a little.

Hank ran his fingers through his hair, around his neck. "Uncomfortable, to be honest."

"But I have had sex. I was just lucky that my birth control worked. Does the sex make you uncomfortable?"

"No . . . but it's different."

"How? Do you think every time a woman conceives she has to have the baby?"

"I guess not." Hank looked out of his depth.

"Well, I don't think the earth needs a single unwanted child. I'm sure the wanted ones are plenty to do the planet in," Juliet said in preachy mode, sounding sure of herself, but feeling a chill. How had they gone this far without discussing abortion?

"No, no, I agree," he said at last. "Humans have reproduced 'til we're a dime a dozen. But you have to be careful if you go up against the ideologues, Juliet. There are some projects better funded surreptitiously."

She relaxed. "Oh, Hank. It gives me such a thrill to

think that we could make a difference."

"We'll do it. I just want to get through the restructure. There will *really* be some money to work with in just a few more years, and you want to get your Masters. But we can start soon, if you want, planning strategies so we can be ready to go when it's time. Philanthropy isn't easy to do right."

Juliet leaned forward to offer a kiss that Hank hoisted himself up and over the deck to receive. "I'm happy, sweetheart," she said when their lips had parted.

"See? This was a good idea. You shouldn't have made me beg."

"I love to see a big, strong man beg."

"Juliet, I'm begging you to go back to the resort."

"Awww."

"Nope. Time to get back. I want to make that call to the Nibels. Ach. I'm sorry. I'm trying not to call them the Nibels. But you have nothing to worry about. You're my one and only. And my savior." He kissed her mouth again, then her nose.

Hank had been divorced for just over a year when he met Juliet in the golden afternoon light on the terrace above Napa Valley, and fell head-over-heels into new hope. His wife of twenty-three years, Blaire, had left him, as it was later revealed, for her personal trainer. The divorce had been beyond ugly. Hank had had no will to fight, but his two sisters, Louise and Evelyn, had made up for his lack of intestinal fortitude, and more.

Blaire's passion had for many years been the San Francisco Opera; its doors likely wouldn't be open without her—Hank's—money. The first opera in Wagner's *The Ring of the Nibelung* was *Das Rheingold* in which gold, stolen from the Rhine maidens at the bottom of the Rhine River, is guarded by dwarves called Nibelung. Blaire gave the name

"Nibelung" then "Nibels" to the financial team who watched over the Ashe gold, and the name stuck. Juliet hated the reference because she was impressed by its erudition. *She* wanted to be the well-educated, well-read, well-informed one, not the unspeakably greedy Blaire.

Hank went to the bow and flipped the switch on the anchor winch. It had gathered chain for only a moment before the tone changed and the deck began to dip toward the surface.

"I think the anchor is fouled," Hank said, shutting off the winch, and looking over the bow. Dark dentation rose from the white sand. "There're rocks down there. Must be hung up on them." Hank pulled the chain up and down, trying to work with the drift of the boat to release the anchor, but it wouldn't budge.

"I'll go down and get us loose." He went back to the cockpit and put the mask and fins back on.

"How deep do you think it is?" Juliet asked as he outfitted himself. "I didn't dive down."

"Oh, not very. I don't think there could be more than ten feet of chain out, probably less. I'll be right back. Watch this technique." Hank grinned at her and rolled backwards off the edge of the boat. Juliet applauded him as he swam around to the anchor chain and dived. She scooted to the bow and leaned over to watch, but making out little in the turbulence of his kicks, she went down to the cockpit to pack the basket. As she began to slip a wineglass into its holder, the boat jerked sideways as though some great baby god had kicked his bath toy. Her hip hit hard, and the glass flew out of her hand and broke at the stem. When she raised herself and looked toward the bow, she saw the anchor chain jerking against the edge of the boat. Something terrible was happening. She crawled across the deck and peered over the edge.

Blood. Blood. There was blood in the water.

Screaming Hank's name over and over, she grabbed the chain and pulled. At first it ripped at her palms as it jerked, then it suddenly slackened and allowed her to lift it a foot out of the water. There! Hank's hand appeared clutching it in a white-knuckled grip. The increasingly opaque water heaved and boiled. Time slowed, seemed nearly to stop, even as her brain ran in frantic circles around the idea that Hank was being attacked by a shark. The blood thickened until the roiling water was crimson; the sea rose in an unnatural peak that erupted in the next instant and drenched her. Startled into action, she leapt toward the winch switch, threw it. The rising chain would surely pull Hank from the water and out of the creature's reach, she thought excitedly. And this time the motor *did* lift the chain smoothly, and Hank's arm *did* emerge from the hellish redness. She flopped to the deck and made a grab for him. Her hand circled his wrist for a brief moment before his arm was wrenched away from her grasp. Juliet watched in disbelief as, with a regal oscillation of his wrist, his arm sank beneath the surface. The anchor came up without him.

Time reversed speed. In an appalling burst, Hank's torso and limbs broke the surface. An actual shark—sharp-nosed, colossal—came with him. Over and over, his body was tossed forward and back as Juliet lay at the edge of the deck, staring transfixed at his somehow-graceful accommodation to the wild attack. A glimpse of his face— where was his mask?—revealed total, frowning concentration, eyes squeezed tightly shut.

She must shoot the shark with the speargun! She crawled back toward the cockpit to get it, but first encountered a gaff bracketed against the side of the cabin. After nearly falling overboard as she wrenched it free, she

21

scrambled back to the tumult that was wetting the deck with bloody water. Crouched behind the railing, she lanced at the mottled head with all her might, as in the distance it seemed someone was screaming in time with each blow. The gaff hit the shark again and again, but made as much intrusion into its flesh as it would had the creature been made of hard rubber.

Suddenly the shark stopped its movement. A thick stillness froze Juliet with gaff still raised. Rolling slightly, the creature fixed its sight on her, eye to eye across millennia of species divide. Pure evil? No, less comprehensible than evil. This was a blank, mechanized, indifferent stare. The shark watched her, calmly preparing a lunge that would mean her own death—Juliet could see it clearly. But it turned slowly and undulated away, as though the whole episode had been a complete bore.

Hypnotized, chilled, trembling with adrenaline, Juliet waited almost too long to pull Hank's drifting body toward the boat with the gaff. Flat on her stomach, hanging so far over the edge she nearly unbalanced herself, she just barely succeeded in bring him to the surface and getting a hold on his wrist.

He was so clearly dead. The arm that she held above the water was bloodless beneath the pink drops that clung to his flesh. The ocean slowly cleared, the red stain washing back toward the mainland and the resort.

Passing his wrist from hand to hand, she worked her way around the supports of the railing. She scanned the water again and again for the shark, terrified that it would return to carry out its plan to drag her from the boat. It took all her courage to place herself so near the water. When she had Hank's body alongside the cockpit, she could see the jagged wound near his groin where the flesh had been removed to the bone. The cavity did not bleed.

His swimsuit was gone, except for the elasticized waistband; his tanned flesh had turned blue-grey. His penis bobbed gently, shrunk with shock. She gazed at his flat, vacant eyes and peaceful face, at his limbs that moved at the whim of the sea.

Juliet dashed her tears to focus on him—Hank, her husband. Strange thoughts surfaced and sank. "Full fathom five thy father lies." The watery grave. The drowned Phoenician sailor—wasn't that a card in the Tarot?

She had to get him on board; the shark could return at any moment. Juliet tried for a grip under his arms, but didn't have the strength to get even half his chest out of the water. She leaned her head on the wood, bumped her sunglasses, pulled them off. Twice more she heaved with all her might, but lifting him was beyond her.

Would she have to sail back with him still in the water? How *could* she sail back? She couldn't all by herself—but maybe she could start the motor. Did it possibly hold enough gas to get all the way to the mainland? She'd have to tie him to the boat somehow. Letting him drift away would be like him dying all over again. Would people from the resort come looking for them? Not for hours. She had to stop crying and think. The rope Hank had stowed under the seat was on the other side of the cockpit out of reach. The gaff was on the deck . . . but what good was the gaff anyway. Hank had tossed her sarong below when he cleaned the fish. Her bathing suit: that was it.

Juliet unhooked the top with her free hand, shook it from one arm and switched her hold on Hank to slip it off the other. With immense concentration she tried to picture making a tether using just her free hand. She would have to double the strap, get it around his wrist and push the bra through the loop. No, she just had to lay the strap over his wrist and bring the rest under and through.

She draped the strap over his arm, but it slid off when she moved the suit. Twice more the same thing happened. Finally, she hauled his arm onto the rail and held the strap in place with her chin, pushing down hard. With her free hand, she fed the rest of the bra through the loop. She tightened the tether fiercely around a cleat, and tested the hold again and again before slowly raising her chin. Now, she could let go of his arm. Was that true? The logistics seemed so confusing. Her fingers were stiff and clawed from her desperate grip; they opened slowly and Hank's wrist remained securely bound. Heaving a huge sigh of relief, she thought for a sweet moment that her life hadn't fallen off a cliff. Then it was clear again that it had.

Hank's body drifted down; only his gray hand and wrist were visible above the gunwale. Again Juliet scanned the water looking for the shark. Was that a tremor in the water? Was it? Terror rose so sharply that her bowels turned to scalding liquid and she had to dash below to the head.

It took all her courage and strength to get back up to the cockpit. The sea was calm. Hank's hand waved gently. Cowering on the bench opposite, she stared at fingers that seemed slowly to straighten. His wedding band gleamed. It brought her eyes to her own rings, her star sapphire and diamonds. The engagement ring was a little loose; she had lost weight before the wedding, and they hadn't yet had it sized. It was a wonder it hadn't come off in the water. Now her hand was cold and shriveled and it was looser yet. The rings had to be reversed so the wedding band would keep the sapphire from slipping off. With shaking hands, she took each ring from her finger, first the sapphire and then the circle of emerald-cut diamonds, and tucked them under her thigh. What do you do with your

24

rings when your husband dies? When do you take them off? My God, not now! She fumbled her finger first into the sapphire ring followed by the wedding band, and looked toward Hank's hand guiltily as though *he* had observed and judged.

She became aware that her breasts were uncovered. The sarong was below. Juliet lurched toward the hatch; her legs gave way at the top of the ladder; she skidded down and banged her knee on a bench. After a long moment— like a baby who has hit herself with a toy—her lower lip began to tremble and she burst into tears. She wailed and rocked with her hands around her knee. A little blood seeped through the abrasion; she bent to lick it off between sobs.

Eventually, after staggering to her feet, and still heaving from her cry, she found the sarong, knotted its corners above her breasts, and hauled herself back on deck. Hank's pale hand still waved back and forth.

The breeze was fresher—an evening breeze. She'd have to get back to the resort. And the anchor was up; the boat was drifting. She swung around to see if she was in danger of washing up against any of the karst islets, and was startled to see the colossal *Viridian* looming a distance away. George, Alex, Pete, Harvey, and Haver were leaning over the side.

"Juliet!" George called distantly. "Ahoy! Is everything all right?"

She shook her head and opened her mouth, but nothing emerged.

"Do you need help? Where's Hank?"

She shook her head again, and raised both arms like a child begging to be picked up. She could hear George calling back and forth with the captain. Apparently the yacht could come no closer. After a bustle of activity on the

25

swim platform, a small tender was launched toward the *Nit Noy*. As it motored alongside, it made the sloop dance and Hank's hand beckon. George, Alex, and Haver jumped onto the deck, leaving one of the *Viridian*'s crew in the boat. They froze as they saw the spatters and streaks of blood on Juliet's face, shoulders, and arms.

"What's happened?" Alex said. "Is Hank below?" He took hold of her arm and looked around; his eyes fell on Hank's hand reaching from the sea.

"There," she said blankly. Can you pull him out? I can't do it."

The men's eyes met in shock. George leaned across the bench, worked his hands down Hank's arm to his torso, leveraged his body to the surface. Hank's head lolled. Juliet whimpered.

"Can you loosen that tie, Alex?" George said. "We could pull him in by his arms." Alex struggled with the cinch Juliet had put all her strength into, but finally undid it. He and George each took an arm and heaved Hank's upper body over the gunwale. As the wound came in view, the men froze again. Finally, Haver pulled the intact leg in, and gingerly, the other.

"He lost his fins, too," Juliet said.

"What on earth? A shark?" Alex asked.

"He went down to release the anchor. It was big. I hit it but it was too big. It was as big as the boat."

"A shark?"

"Yes, a shark."

"Juliet. Juliet." At the sound of the sympathy in George's voice, she collapsed on the bench, hugged herself, and made low keening sounds as she rocked. George could bear it only by taking charge. "Let's get her aboard the *Viridian*. Alex, help her into the boat and take her over. Joe, get someone to help you sail the sloop and come back for us."

"Yes, sir!" The young man looked anxious about rising to the occasion.

Alex took Juliet's shoulders firmly to lift her to her feet. "Come on now," he said gently as he walked her across the deck. He swung her over to Joe and jumped aboard behind her. When they reached the aft platform of the *Viridian*, Harvey was waiting. He and Alex helped Juliet aboard and up the stairs.

"Jesus, look at that leg. It's barely attached," George said under his breath as he and Haver lifted Hank's body onto a tarp and wrapped it around him. When the tender returned, they and the two crewmen transferred Hank's body to it. The young sailors boarded the sloop to sail it back to the resort. George and Haver motored back to the *Viridian*, sunk in silence beside the canvas shroud.

With effort, Hank's body was brought up to the dining area in the stern of the yacht. Harvey draped a blanket over Juliet's shoulders; Alex sat beside her on the bench and held her hand. She stared into space, seeming not to know that anyone else was there. No one spoke. George sat across from Juliet with his head in his hands. The chef came up with warm milk; Juliet was still shaking so much that Alex had to hold the mug. Another sunset spectacle was coloring the clouds with vermilion and gold as the *Viridian* approached the dock.

CHAPTER TWO

By the time Juliet gave up trying to sleep the next morning, the Gulfstream carrying Hank's sisters, Louise and Evelyn, and his daughter, Paige, had already re-fueled in Hawaii and was nearing Tokyo. David, somewhere in Italy, wouldn't be learning of his father's death until he checked his e-mail and called his mother. Also onboard was Fred Goldman, Hank's attorney, with a computer full of documents. Fred was Hank's age, rather overweight and lumpy in a suit that was going to be too heavy when they reached Thailand.

Even with the shock of Hank's loss—a loss not just of a client but a friend—Fred had acted with his usual efficiency. He had copies of the will containing the details of the division of the estate between Juliet and Hank's children, as well as the prenuptial agreement. He had not been eager to see Louise's reaction when she heard it only concerned divorce. Even a possible remarriage after Hank's death would not limit Juliet's share, and when he told the sisters this news, their grief indeed was considerably distracted by the painful awareness of how wealthy Juliet would be.

Louise considered, and reluctantly rejected, a challenge to the will on grounds of incompetence. But there was another possibility.

"It must be said—" Louise fell silent as the attendant approached, cleared the half-eaten meals, and placed glasses of sparkling water on the table.

"I'll have more wine," Paige said, putting her fingers over the flared bottom of the glass to keep it from being removed. The attendant retrieved the bottle from a serving table and poured.

"That will be all," Louise said coldly. The young woman moved forward to her seat near Louise's assistant.

"As I was saying, we must consider that we may be dealing with something other than a shark attack here. Or that the shark may have attacked Henry after he was already dead."

"Christ. I knew it!" Paige threw her napkin to the floor.

"Let's not get ahead of ourselves, Paige. I'm only saying that the matter has to be investigated. I'm certainly not going to see that girl getting away with so much money if she had anything to do with his death—not getting away with her freedom either. Henry was such a fool. I told him—but oh no." Fred took off his glasses and pressed his thumb and forefinger to the bridge of his nose.

"Fred, how are we going to get the proper assistance in Thailand? Can we get him out of there and back to the U.S. for an autopsy?"

"Of course we'll repatriate his body, but we can't do it until it's been seen by an examining magistrate. He'll do an autopsy if the death is suspicious." Fred had already done his research.

"Well, he must do an autopsy then," Louise

asserted. "We'll want a proper one done in the U.S., too. Shouldn't she be held by the police until these autopsies are done?"

"It appears the police will require that she remain in the country during the Thai investigation, but certainly on her own recognizance. We'll have to see what's happening with that when we arrive. Hank's body will be examined in Bangkok. Juliet will surely be allowed to stay at the resort." Fred could see this was going to be beyond awkward. He was the representative of Hank's wishes, and now, his heirs' interests. Unless Juliet had indeed murdered Hank, which he didn't believe for one minute, she would be well-endowed. Not being of one mind with Louise was an uncomfortable position, and Fred soon begged off to go to sleep.

Juliet sat in the shade of the thatched pavilion on the deck, looking out to the bay. Her face, which sometimes appeared pert and pretty and sometimes calm and classic, today was ready for a tragic role. The skin under her eyes was so dark it looked as though it was smudged with mascara, and there was a sagging of her cheeks and mouth that indicated where lines would someday form. Even in normal times she could be unsure of herself and melancholy. What had happened was going to weigh her down; it was going to hold her under; it was going to be more than she could resist, and she was afraid.

Her eyes were turned, without really seeing, to the boats filling the bay—boats from up and down the coast, of all sorts and sizes. Everyone was looking for the shark. Understandably, the staff of the resort was in a state of barely restrained panic. A U.S.-trained doctor had been summoned to offer tranquilizers and sleeping pills while silk-clad girls brought special teas and small treats. They had decorated the suite with sandalwood flowers, appropriate for mourning. The *Nit Noy* was not in evidence.

The previous day, Hank had been taken away so quickly that Juliet was having trouble grasping what had happened. When the *Viridian*—preceeded by radio notice of the accident—had entered the marina with Hank's body, a large and respectful coterie had been waiting. Juliet had been escorted to the suite by two of those perfect girls, put in a hot shower, and dressed in a black evening dress whose scanty top had been made modest with a shawl.

The manager had brought her to a small event room where Hank was already laid out between banks of white flowers. He was partially covered with a pink silk cloth woven with gold and wore his own shirt, tie and navy blazer. When had they taken the things, she wondered. While she was in the shower? He looked so small it seemed as though his spirit had made up half his physical presence; how could that creamy silk collar that had fit so perfectly now buckle at his neck? She had stared at it while she sat with George and his friends. Strangers came and went, took her hand, murmured things. Clouds of sandalwood incense competed with the sickening sweetness of the flowers.

She was taken into an adjoining room where officials presented papers for her signature. George and the manager examined them, conferred, and decided she should sign some and not others. One document she did sign gave permission for Hank's body to be transported to Bangkok where it would remain until she took him home. Shockingly, that meant that he was to be taken away, *then* in the middle of the night. Juliet was escorted back to her villa.

George spent the bulk of the night at the satellite phone, quietly suggesting calls and extracting names and numbers from Juliet's memory and Hank's telephone and

Skype contacts. The first call had been to Fred Goldman, who had subsequently notified Hank's sisters and daughter, the financial team, and Mr. Peters, the household manager. Mr. Peters called to offer Mrs. Ashe his condolences, and to say that he would come immediately to help; Juliet declined his offer. Fred called back and talked at length to George.

Juliet's father promised to be there as soon as he could. She had surprised herself by how much she wanted to see him, and had told him to get Mr. Peters to arrange his flight. Others of Hank's and Juliet's closest friends were told, among them everyone at Quinta da Agustinho. Between calls, Juliet paced, lay sleepless on the bed, or sat looking into the night, while the hotel staff, the doctor, George's friends, tiptoed in and out.

Local police arrived while the maids were trying to tempt Juliet with breakfast. An audience had attended her interview with them. There had been disagreements over the interpreter's translation and tense exchanges with the resort manager. The men of the *Viridian* glanced anxiously at each other, and were not reassured when they too were interviewed, each separately. Later, Tai and Palat had come and bowed and cried. Juliet had finally fled to the deck, asking to be left alone. Whenever she glanced back toward the living room, she saw anxious faces looking her way. Federal police would be here soon to question her again. She had agreed to remain at the resort pending . . . something. She wasn't clear what.

By ten-thirty in the morning the first call had come in from the press. George, who had slept no more than an hour, and that on the sofa, said only that Henry Ashe had died in a boating accident. There would be no statement from his widow, who was devastated, no other information at this time. George quietly conferred with the resort

33

management. No calls besides those from Sheldon Pierce, Fred Goldman, or Mr. Peters would be routed to Juliet's suite. The office would log all other calls; George would screen the list until Fred arrived.

Juliet's mind was a riot of scenes from her brief life with Hank, alternating with the attack and her pitifully inadequate reaction. The speargun . . . if only she had gone for the speargun and not used the worthless gaff. What would people say when they realized there had been a speargun nearby? Why had she left the prow when Hank went down for the anchor? If only the anchor had just come loose. *Could* she have stopped the shark with the speargun? What if she had missed and shot Hank! Did you cock it? How? Where was it? It must be still in the *Nit Noy*. Everyone would know there had been a speargun.

Hovering behind the details of the attack was the terror of dealing with Hank's complicated life, about which she had not even the foggiest understanding. Businesses, foundations, holding companies, family, possessions . . . the Nibelung. They would eat her alive.

Alex appeared in the door to the deck. "May I sit with you, Juliet?" he called out. Perhaps he would distract her. Yes, she nodded.

Alex was blond and tall—he towered over her—and had the commanding chin of a movie star. Too handsome, Juliet had thought when she'd first met him, but he had been very kind, very sweet.

"I brought your camera and sunglasses."

"Thanks." She looked at the glasses. Five hundred dollars—in her life with Hank, a throwaway. She put them on, wondering what it would cost to be truly enclosed in anonymity. The camera contained the last scenes of her former life. She looked at the stored pictures: The yellowtail. More yellowtail. Juliet on the deck. Juliet swimming. Clouds. Patterns of light and shadow on the sail. Karst formations… She hadn't taken a picture of Hank. There was none of him until the ones taken by Palat. At least he looked happy.

"When will Hank's family get here?" Alex sat on the edge of a lounge chair, looking at her with concern.

"I don't know. Soon. They're on the way. Hank's lawyer called and said they had refueled in Hawaii. We haven't heard anything since that. Look at all those boats."

"I hope they get revenge," Alex said.

"I keep seeing that shark's eye. I have this terrible feeling I'll see it for the rest of my life."

They were silent for a time. "This is so strange," Juliet said. "Now, I feel I hardly knew Hank. We only met four months ago and hadn't even told all our stories. I'm not looking forward to seeing his sisters. I don't know if his children are coming. I've never even *seen* them except in pictures. They were all completely opposed to the marriage; didn't come to the wedding. They thought I was marrying Hank for his money. I don't know what they'll think now." Juliet fell back into silence, remembering the horrible interview with Louise.

"What are you thinking?" Alex finally asked. "His family can't believe you didn't do all you could."

"His sister Louise actually offered me money not to marry Hank. She had nothing but contempt for me. I think he proposed to me the first time after we'd known each other for a month, and it wasn't very long after that I got a note from Louise. God, how did she even know? I never asked Hank what he told her. I . . . I never told him about it at all. You see? I never even had enough time to tell him things. Though I probably wouldn't have told him about that, ever."

35

"What did she say?" Alex asked gently.

"She had me come meet her at this restaurant. She's his oldest sister, in her sixties I guess. She looked spectacular, so slim and regal, you know, with her streaked hair, kind of grey and blond, pulled back to her nape with a ribbon draped across it, like rich women wear their hair. And she had immense South Sea pearls and elegant manners. She shook my hand and thanked me for coming. Then she let me have it." Juliet laughed without humor and fell silent again, remembering:

"Juliet, let me come to the point. The family—that is I, my sister, Evelyn, and Henry's children, Paige and David—feels that your marriage to Henry would be ill-advised. Of course, Paige and David know very little of these things, how men of a certain age can act so foolishly and with such great impropriety. It will be so unfortunate if they must be estranged from him. I, and my sister as well, have more experience of the world. We are aware of the temptation of Henry's wealth, and that you can hardly be expected not to *try* to secure a position as his wife. We have only Henry's interests at heart, and we cannot sit idly by and watch as he moves toward an act that can only make him unhappy. He couldn't stand going through a debacle such as he has suffered again."

Alex let Juliet stare unseeing over the water until she finally remembered him.

"She said Hank was acting foolishly and that his children wouldn't accept a marriage between us. She said he was still devastated from his divorce. He had been divorced a little over a year." Juliet began speaking faster. "It's true. She was right that he was still upset, but he didn't love Blaire anymore. I'm sure he didn't. It was a bad divorce, a big fight over money. But it was really Louise and Evelyn who made it so complicated, at least that's what he said— or hinted at. He didn't say bad things about people, even Blaire who . . . well, there was another man. I think he just wanted out."

A young woman approached with a tray holding two glasses of tea. Juliet motioned her forward and stared toward the boats while glasses, napkins and a dish of some strange tidbits were arranged on the table between her and Alex.

"Let us not be dishonest," Juliet remembered Louise saying, her lip in a sneer. "Henry is hardly a romantic icon. Women must not be fools in this world and I can see that you are no fool. My sister and I are prepared to make it, as they say, worth your while to let Henry go. You can have your reward and will not have to put up with a husband old enough to be your father. I don't know if Henry has made you aware as yet that you will be required to sign a marital agreement, so in any case, you will have limited recompense for your effort."

Juliet brought her hand to her sunglasses, squeezed her eyes shut. Louise had been so sure of herself, so cold, had knocked her off balance so easily. Was it she who convinced Hank to ask for the prenupt? Juliet remembered signing with a flourish. There! That's how much I'm not like what Louise thinks! But then she had never told him what Louise thought, as though saying those terrible words might have given Hank pause, as though those words contained some small measure of truth.

"Juliet, have some tea," Alex said, reaching over and touching her arm lightly. "You should try not to think about his sister."

"Yes. You're right. It was *awful*. I jumped up and ran away and I felt like such a fool. I had to get away before I started crying and then after I got on the freeway I thought about how I hadn't paid for my tea or tipped the valet who brought my car." She laughed bitterly. "At the time, that seemed the most humiliating thing. I was shaking so badly I had to pull over."

Was it all true, she thought. Did I marry him for his money and my vineyards? Did I love him enough? Was any part of it that I wanted to spite Louise? Oh, it was more than she could bear to have to see her just now. How delicious it would have been for the years go by and for Louise to still be *wrong, wrong* about her motives. It flooded back: Hank's embarrassment about the prenup; it had been only about divorce—after so many years, so many children—and generous even so. But it was from some world she had never imagined, and in truth, it had shown that he hadn't *really* trusted her. He had been afraid that she was what Louise said. He must have been. How ugly money was! Of course she'd told no one. She'd tried to pretend it had never happened.

The guilt and self-doubt—she had nearly escaped it. The honeymoon had been going so well! She was happy with Hank. She hadn't thought, "What have I done?" Not even once. She didn't think he had either. He was so kind. She had been going to show everyone that she was no fortune hunter. He'd have been happy! Of course he would have been sixty-seven when she was forty, but forty was pretty old, too. And Hank would have died first, probably, but she'd have had their foundation and her vineyards. Oh, my God, Quinta da Agostinho. She already owned one of the preeminent vineyards of Napa, and not because she'd gotten a degree and started small and produced truly fine wines and grown—as her fantasies had run before Hank—

but by fiat of some finger pointing from the heavens and choosing her to be rich, rich, rich, and a widow.

"Oh, Alex. I just realized I'm a widow."

It was a word that had already occurred to him.

Alex knew that there was money, a great deal of it. George had surmised that it might run into the hundreds of millions, even billions, as the men of the *Viridian* sat talking over the tragedy after their police interviews. Not that George really knew anything of Hank's finances, just rumors—though the rumors mentioned lots of zeros. The boat Hank had been talking of the night they'd dined in the suite . . . . George had Googled it—$2,600,000. Not that much as boats went, but not nothing. And there had been Home Base, after all.

"But he sold Home Base, right?" Alex said. "Why do you suppose he did that?"

"I think he got an offer he couldn't refuse. Didn't it go for nearly forty billion?"

"God. Does Juliet inherit something like that?"

"Who knows? Apparently there are two sisters on the way over here. The company could have been jointly owned. I think Hank had children and there's no telling what sort of marital agreement he had with Juliet. Anything's possible, but I bet he'll have taken care of her."

George had proposed they delay their trip to see Juliet through this. For Harvey, whether or not he could go on to Hawaii depended on how long this took. He had to be back at his practice in a month, but he was concerned, and told George that his constraints were not to be considered. Haver had plenty of time—not that his wife completely agreed—and wanted to be sure Juliet got proper treatment too, and Pete was content if he never got beyond Thailand.

Alex had listened with a mind already full of plans. He had decided to try to become someone Juliet could lean on. He was divorced and having a tough time keeping up with his richer friends. Who knew? He just might win the beautiful widow, especially if he made use of this vulnerable period. He would gladly give up island hopping.

He knew he'd make a better match for Juliet than Hank had. He believed as well that she'd already taken note of him at the dinner party a few nights earlier. Hank and George had been talking yachts and the big boys—who was selling, who was buying, which sheik or Microsoft prince. It had been galling to sit there with no toys of his own to brag about, but worth it with Juliet at his side, smelling fresh and clean and rich.

The raised shutters around the pavilion had invited in an ocean breeze that distributed the sweet scent of the plumeria flowers around the table. There had been five courses; the ramekins that had contained a passion fruit crème brûlée had just been cleared away. Two graceful girls were alternatively refreshing the wine and retreating to the far side of the room.

"Hank wants to stop in Antibes to look at a Dutch boat. Who is that designer, darling?" Juliet had asked.

"It's a 76-foot Jongert ketch. I need something more comfortable than my old Columbia for Juliet. We hit a gale one time out and I'm just waiting for the post-wedding announcement that she's through with sailing," Hank said.

"I might consider getting very busy on land, but then I'd never see you. I think the real problem is the North Pacific. I'll sail with you here any day."

When the conversation veered into engines and auto-pilots, Juliet gestured to the girls, quietly asked for the wine to be left on the table, and for brandy, snifters, and the cigar humidor from the sideboard to be brought. Afterwards, she dismissed them. When they were gone, Alex, with a flourish, brought out a plump joint and waved it under her nose.

"Thai stick," he said with a suggestive lift of his eyebrows. I got these for four hundred baht apiece. Probably a rip off, but it's first rate. Shall we?" he addressed the table as he lit and inhaled. "Be careful," he said in a choked whisper as he handed it to Haver.

"I thought Thai stick had gone with the hippies," Harvey said, sniffing at the ascending blue-gray ribbon. Where did you get this?"

"One of the waiters clearly had me pegged," Alex said with a smoky snort of laughter. Juliet watched the marijuana make the rounds, wondering if Hank would participate. When it came to him, he took the tiniest sip, and she accepted that as permission for her to do the same. That was all it took to make her giggly and voluble. When Alex leaned in to ask where she and Hank were going to live after the honeymoon, she told him at considerable length about their California life, about Quinta da Agostinho, and her desire to get a degree in winemaking. Soon she had caught the table's attention with her bright jokes and happy laughter. Somehow, her husband had not taken offense at her special attention to Alex—as Alex perceived it. Hank had beamed over her.

"Alex, what did you think you were doing, taking that orchid from behind her ear? Can you *believe* the elegance of these girls?" Juliet was talking about the female hotel staff. "They just couldn't have their full compliment of internal organs, they are so slim. They must be required to give up a gall bladder, half a liver, and several feet of intestine before they can get a job. And those elegant silks! Oh, they are the most beautiful girls I've ever seen."

41

Had she been trying to call attention to herself, slim as youth could make a woman whose breasts and hips curved so generously, clad also in Thai silk—carmine woven with gold, he remembered—and beautiful in a homegrown way that made her eminently suitable for his accustomed fantasies?

"I think they are much more attractive than the men, don't you?" he had flirted back. "The men are just as slim, just as lacking in internal organs but it doesn't suit them. Or—you tell me, Juliet, do the men turn you on?"

"You are talking to a girl on her honeymoon, and I have nothing to say about other men turning me on." But even as she had held her husband's eye at the other end of the table, she had laughed. Alex was sure he knew how to read the signals.

And Aimée? The woman back in New Orleans who had good reason to believe she might be Alex's next wife? When it came to millions, she had no need of the plural. It had seemed sufficient until now.

Yes, Juliet was a widow. Alex leaned forward in his lounge chair and spoke with tender earnestness. "I'll make sure they don't hurt you."

"Thanks, Alex. Please forget all that stuff I said. I shouldn't have talked about Louise like that, or Hank. I don't know what I was thinking. Please don't repeat any of that."

"I wouldn't dream of it."

The events that had led Juliet to the pavilion with the cruel sea lapping at its pillars, the sea whose secrets had proved so dark, had begun in Napa at a house on the second tier above the orderly rows of trellised vines—a Tuscan-replica mansion with roofs at various heights, rising even to a bell tower. The sunset colors of the stucco and tile seemed to suspend the life of the house at the magic hour. A grand terrace overlooked the impeccable rows and held a pergola, easily forty feet long.

The beams topping the pergola were covered with vines that cast dappled shade upon a long table—the sort of table where a European family of at least five generations might gather to drink to the joy of the newly married couple, or celebrate the baptism of a child. Where looks of inter-generational love would linger over the rims of glasses . . . as the name of the vineyard appeared on the television screen and music swelled. No commercial was being filmed that afternoon at Quinta da Agostinho, though the scene looked as though an award-winning set designer had been at work.

The table, covered in white cloth, had stretched the length of the pergola. It was set with bright Portuguese majolica, flashing crystal and flowers. Beautiful people had smiled and laughed over their arugula and goat cheese and roast lamb. And the bottles of wine! More than a score had waited open and breathing for the guests to fill their own and their neighbor's glasses, and then their own again, as conviviality rose into the fresh Northern California air. It had been harvest time, but of course it was not that year's harvest that was being drunk, but those of three to five years earlier with the occasional even-older treasure. Among the family had been special friends and neighboring winemakers who had brought their own prized vintages to crowd the bottles of the hosts. And there had been Juliet's father without whom Quinta da Agostinho would not have been so lavished with awards.

Juliet had been placed across from Hank, who was looking lean and tanned and at his best. Her light brown hair fell in casual waves; her smile was intimate. Hank had learned that this darling creature was Sheldon Pierce's

43

daughter, that she was just back from university, and that she wanted to be a vintner herself. As he sought to entertain her, Juliet had listened to his stories and laughed at his jokes.

"Don't you think, Hank, wine is just about the loveliest cultural tradition we have?" Juliet had asked as the afternoon slipped into evening, leaning forward to ring her glass against his. Her blue, blue eyes were soft and fond, and they met his in wine-induced harmony. Hank had dared to dream that his life was not yet over.

And so in those four months to follow he had courted Juliet. Yes, she hesitated with the twenty-seven-year age difference, with the disparity of wealth, with her middle-class upbringing. She'd had no clue how to live in his style. How did you treat servants? Did you thank them for their endless attentions? Tipping—a mystery she had hardly known existed outside restaurants. Where did the household manager, the pilots, the guards, the masseur, fall in the scale of things? On a visit to one of his houses, Hank had offered her one of the staff as a personal maid, and she had realized that a woman of his acquaintance might have been traveling with her own. Did one compliment the décor or act as if the opulence was too ordinary to mention? What was she to talk about with Hank's friends— his Republican friends?

Ann Teixeira, who with her husband Mike, was the other owner of Quinta da Agostinho, had cautioned her: "Don't feel obligated to him, Juliet, because he's entertaining you lavishly or giving you gifts. The money is nothing to him, remember. He's awfully nice. I love Hank, but you have to understand there are differences between you, and not just age."

Juliet's father had felt constrained. Father and daughter had been through a difficult time, and were only just feeling their way together again. Juliet's mother had died of cancer; Sheldon had been caught in an affair before the end. Juliet had reacted with grief and insult rolled together, and now he was afraid that anything he said would be taken amiss. Other friends had also wondered whether to advise caution. Those that did were gentle with it. After all, Hank had powerful attractions, and they all were fond of him.

On their third "date," Hank had taken Juliet for a week to Palm Beach, to Las Ventas, his Florida estate. That was when she had first met the entourage: the pilots and cabin crew of Hank's plane, Mr. Peters—the household manager—and Ms. Edwards—the cook—both of whom had already flown out, and the staff of Las Ventas. The place was so clean and polished the rooms looked like real estate photos. Hank showed off his Olympic bronze in its glass case; hardly any other personal touch was in evidence. With its curves of stucco, vast expanses of glass, marble, tile, and the occasional incongruous Corinthian column, no house had ever looked less like a home. It contained a ballroom, a twenty-foot fish tank, an indoor pool, and ten bedroom suites. Outdoors, there was another pool, a pool house, a nine-hole golf course, a helicopter pad, stables— empty of horses—and accommodations for staff. When Juliet got out of bed to pee in the night, she'd been lost for a good while in the master bath complex.

A pretty ketch moored in the marina required more employees—a crew of two who lived in the gatehouse and served as part of the security team. Mr. Peters and Ms. Edwards had accommodations over the four-car garage where there were also rooms for the maids.

They had sailed each of the days and dined on Ms. Edward's meals on the glass-enclosed terrace, at extraordinary restaurants, or at the club. Juliet was encouraged to spend time being pampered in the club's spa—hairstyling, French tip manicure, doctor-fish pedicure, scrub, oiling, soaking, and massage—of muscles that had never yet known an ache.

Mr. Peters had procured clothing for her to choose any or all. He had apparently discerned not only her size but her psychological profile, the clothes were so appealing. He was in his late thirties, slim, balding—with a pleasant, friendly face and a warm manner. He was apparently gay, at least to Juliet's eye, and exuded impeccable sensitivity to the style suiting Ashe wealth and social status. Half-delighted, half-guilty, she chose an elegant pink batiste spaghetti-strapped dress for evening, white duck pants for the boat, some up-scale tees. Dress sandals. The rest remained in the bedroom reserved for her private use, and most found their way onto her back by the end of the visit, at which time they were all packed and sent off with her.

Never mind what Ann had said, Juliet knew that the decision to agree to the Florida trip must be to agree to sex. Hank had made it easy and very pleasant. He was definitely attractive, beautifully dressed and groomed, but with an appealing roughness from life spent so much on the sea. He'd worn a beard then, perhaps to assert that his outdoor life was his real one, perhaps in some gesture following the divorce, like Al Gore after the election debacle, but at any rate, he'd soon shaved it, likely because it was too gray. Medium height and slight, he'd probably had trouble finding a woman of his age who didn't outweigh him, she'd thought, until she'd found out that the women of his class were thin as concentration camp survivors.

In a half-apologetic tone, Hank had asked her at breakfast the fourth morning if she wouldn't mind going to a charity ball that night. He warned her that they were perfectly horrible events, which he had given up since his divorce, but tonight was a benefit for Sudanese lost boys, the pet charity-objects of a friend to whom Hank owed a favor, and a donation. Since he was in Palm Beach, he really should attend. She had nothing to wear to a ball, Juliet protested, but it appeared that Hank had already taken the liberty of arranging for her to be properly dressed.

Mr. Peters showed her a pale blue sheath of spiraling and undulating silk ruffles and silver Jimmy Choo sandals. The dress was the most beautiful thing she'd ever seen. It was couture work, hand sewn with built-in bra, as delicate inside as out. Light as a feather, it seemed to be in constant, floating motion around her. A seamstress had been on hand to make adjustments, but none were needed. And when she was coifed and dressed that evening, Hank asked if she would do him the honor of wearing his mother's diamond and pearl necklace and earrings. From a circle of square-cut diamonds, nine large pear-shaped pearls hung from diamond bows. Like the dress, the necklace was youthful, elegant, dazzling. Even larger pearls dangled from the diamond bows of the earrings. The velvet box that held the ensemble said Harry Winston. Almost as an afterthought, her wrists were adorned with simple diamond bracelets, and an aquamarine ring was slipped on her third finger, right hand. Hank, Mr. Peters, and the maid, Corazon, had looked at her with considerable pride of accomplishment. They gave her a round of applause as she mimed a trip down a runway with hips forward and a bored expression she was unable to maintain.

At the ball, it was all Juliet could do keep her chin from dropping in amazement. With her Baccarat champagne flute in hand, she met a stream of men in evening dress, and women in coruscations of diamonds and colored stones who looked at her with sharp curiosity when Hank introduced her as his special friend, Juliet Pierce.

Their eyes flicked over her attire, and she blessed Mr. Peters, or whoever had been responsible, as she saw it pass inspection, though it was hardly a social event at which she felt comfortable.

But the trip turned out to be fun even if everything was out of her league. Juliet liked Hank's mastery of his world. He didn't speak much of his financial life, but when he did it was with obvious confidence. He looked so deeply joyous out on the water, calling for the adjustments of the sails, taking a slap of spray with gusto, enjoying the company of the crew, that Juliet found him endearing.

He kept up a pleasant patter at their breakfasts, reading bits from *The New York Times* and the *Wall Street Journal* to her. He was a little too fond of the editorials in the latter for Juliet's taste, and they had some discussion on the subject that remained good-natured. He seemed flexible.

From that time in Florida, Hank hadn't let a day go by without seeing Juliet or phoning at length. She had been both flattered and confused by the attention of such a man-of-the-world, and when the casual gift of a Patek Philippe watch shocked her into declaring a no-more-gifts rule, Hank offered his first proposal.

"Juliet, let me love you. Let me take care of you. I'm sorry I'm so much older. I only wish I'd met you . . . but what's the use in wishing that? Won't you please marry me anyway?" he begged. "I'll try to give you your heart's desire."

"My heart's desire?" she had mused evasively. "Well, I want children, Hank. I always thought two."

"I'm ready to start this minute," he had said, nuzzling her neck.

"I wouldn't want to turn a child over to a nanny."

"No, I can see you wouldn't, sweetheart. But you'll

enjoy having a little help with a baby."

"I suppose . . . ."

"This is sounding hopeful! Come on, Juliet. Fly away with me. Make me happy."

"Can we be happy, Hank? Can we stay happy?" Juliet had put a hand on his chest, half-caress, half-demand that he stay back until there was a satisfactory answer.

"Ay, girl. What can I say to that? It's a big question. But I'll promise to be good and faithful, and I'll spoil you every way I know."

Juliet had thought how he didn't have a clue about the music she liked, and didn't seem to like any of his own. He had attitudes toward politicians of whom she had barely heard, and her friends went silent in his presence. He didn't read books, either. He made money and sailed; he certainly wasn't likely to attend any more opera. But then, it was fun to be doted upon, and she enjoyed fussing over him too, learning his likes and feeling necessary to his happiness. He was really very sweet. Juliet was sure she could lure him away from his conservative politics when she had the chance to work on him. Mightn't love come? She had delayed an answer. He had continued to propose.

One gift Hank had offered was irresistible. There was another dearest wish—her own vineyard. She wanted to go back to school, learn everything about wine-making, and try her hand. With the modest inheritance from her mother, and what she could save, she thought she could eventually buy a small vineyard, slowly expand. Hank dangled the possibility of skipping the intermediate steps. Of course, she knew he had a half-share of Quinta da Agostinho, not that he involved himself in the details of the winery, and not that Juliet would wish to crowd her father. But she learned that he owned vast vineyards in Mexico too. *There* was a possibility so exciting she tried not to even think about it. His friends the Teixeiras had proposed those purchases a few years ago, though for Hank it was only one investment out of many, and he'd only told Juliet as an afterthought.

At a party with his middle-aged crowd one night, with the women all worked and botoxed into a simulacrum of youth, Juliet had overheard someone say that maybe she and Hank would be like Sophia Loren and Carlo Ponti, and might have a long and happy marriage despite the age difference. Yes, she thought. Did marriages always work when people married for head-over-heels love? Obviously not. But what if love came along and it wasn't Hank? And what if she rejected Hank and a better love never did come along?

Hank's friends acknowledged that Juliet was no bimbo, not arm candy, not *apparently* a fortune hunter. She was a very smart, very vivacious—well, a bit of a lefty. The two of them might do some vote canceling, but she'd grow up and come to her senses. They liked her, and not just the men.

If some thought they had a chance at a good marriage, there was, of course, Louise, who did not. When a mutual friend reported to her she'd seen an obviously besotted Hank *three times* with a much younger woman, Louise had thought it necessary to take her little brother in hand.

"Henry, what do you think you're up to?" she had demanded. "Are you going to risk everything all over again? Blaire hasn't offered enough gold-digging for one lifetime?"

"Now, Louise, don't be offensive. You really have no call to speak of Juliet that way. She hasn't agreed to marry me, but what if she did? Don't you have enough money of your own that you can let me do what I want with my money and my life?"

"You are hopeless, Henry. Your marriage barely cold—"

"Let me assure you, Louise, my marriage was cold long before the divorce."

"But what about Paige and David?" It was embarrassing that David was a few months younger than Juliet.

"What about them?"

"What if you married her and had more children? How would they feel about that?"

"Louise, I love Paige and David. They will have more money than is good for them even if I have a dozen more children. And that's even though they haven't been particularly attentive since the divorce. I can't live my life for them, or at any rate, I won't. I'm going to marry Juliet if she'll have me." He felt more sure of his decision the more Louise badgered him.

"At very least, protect yourself with a marital agreement. Spare this family another court battle and our name in the papers."

"Here's a bone for you, Louise. I will ask her to sign one. I suppose my faith in my fellow man, and woman, is shaken enough for that."

In the end, Juliet said yes. She and Hank were married on the sun-filled terrace at Quinta da Agostinho where they had met. She wore a slim gown of bias-cut satin with a low back, and carried calla lilies. Hank's sisters and children had not come, but the long table, and two more, had been filled with guests. There were laughter, tears, toasts, and good wishes. In a couple of days, they had flown off on their honeymoon—beginning with the two weeks in Thailand.

The second evening after Hank's death, Juliet was

about to lie down for her first real attempt at sleep when a gentle knock came at the door of the suite. The manager, all apologies for disturbing her, thought she might wish to know that her relatives had just arrived at the resort. Juliet felt a stab of fear, and stammered out something about how they were surely tired from traveling so far, and how it would be better for her to see them in the morning.

An interview with Louise, if anything like the last, was a horrible prospect. With Hank dead she felt undermined, any moral superiority gone. Louise would have had, ultimately, to accept the marriage if she had taken care of Hank and made him happy, but she had let him die. Hank was not there to insist on her position, and that position now felt as illegitimate as Louise believed it to be.

The meeting with the federal police that afternoon had not been pleasant either. Through a translator they had asked if Hank was conscious when he entered the water, if he had hit his head on anything, if he knew how to swim. Had they had any disagreements that day? Was the marriage happy? Alex, who had been with her, had told them it was entirely outrageous to question her in such a way when she had just lost her husband. And what is your connection with Mrs. Ashe, they asked, turning toward him suspiciously. Of course only Juliet had seen the shark attack. Others could testify to the apparent sincerity of her grief, to the husband and wife's loving interaction, to a wound on Hank that would surely have severed the femoral artery—that was all they knew.

Around eleven the next morning, the manager returned to tell Juliet that her family requested her presence in their suite. He would drive her over in the cart if she wished.

Juliet was admitted into the salon of the four-bedroom complex by a young woman who introduced

herself as Mrs. Esterbrook's—Louise's—assistant. She led
Juliet through to the pool area, where a breakfast table was
being cleared. Fred Goldman rose and came forward to
greet her. He wrapped her in his big embrace, and took her
to the table where the sisters and Hank's daughter, Paige,
remained seated.

Evelyn extended her hand and introduced herself.
She looked smaller and plumper than Louise, but not much
warmer.

"And you must be Paige," Juliet said to the young
woman, who avoided her eye. "You look so much like your
father. Hello, Louise."

"Sit down, Juliet," Louise said. "We have a great
deal to discuss."

"Yes. You want to hear how it happened." Juliet
barely got the words out before her face crumpled. "Awful,
awful . . ." was all she could say for a time, but when Paige
choked on a sob, Juliet reached out a hand to her. "I'm
sorry, Paige. I'm so sorry."

Paige moved sharply away. "For him to die so far
away from us all! It's . . . it's tragic!"

Juliet hugged herself with the rebuked hand, slowly
gathered her composure, and began the story. "We had
sailed out to an island and when we were ready to come
back, we found that the anchor was caught on some rocks.
Hank couldn't get it loose, and he decided to dive down
and release it."

"Why wouldn't Henry just have abandoned the
anchor?" Louise said.

"I don't know?" Juliet looked up, surprised. "I wish
we had. Can you do that? It was on a chain."

"Of course you can, and Henry would have known
it. And? What next?"

"He dove down by the anchor chain. Suddenly the

boat kind of heaved, like it had been shoved or pulled, and I went to look down, and I saw blood in the water."

"How long was he down before the boat *heaved*?"

"Thirty seconds? I guess he had reached the bottom and freed the anchor because I tried at one point to raise it and it came up."

"Why did you raise the anchor?"

"Hank's hand was around the chain. I almost got hold of him. The water was filled with blood; I couldn't see." Juliet took a deep breath. Tears rolled down her cheeks. "The shark was shaking him and I grabbed a gaff and tried to fight it off. It was no use, but the shark did finally notice me and let go of Hank and swam away. I pulled Hank to the edge of the boat . . . but he was dead."

"You were sure he was dead? You kept his head out of the water so he could breathe?" Louise demanded.

"He was dead, Louise. His eyes were so dead. And the water cleared, and you could see he had just *bled out*. There was no blood coming from the wound. It was a terrible wound. He was dead. I'm so sorry. There was nothing I could do."

Everyone was silent. Evelyn touched a handkerchief to the corner of her eye. Paige made a grimace of grief. Fred shook his head over and over.

"We'll know more after the autopsy." Louise took a sip of her coffee.

"We're having an autopsy?" Juliet asked.

"It's customary when there's any question about the manner of death."

"What question?" Juliet looked around the table at each face. Everyone avoided her eyes.

"Well, Juliet," Louise said, "we have nothing but your story to go on. Oh, likely there was a shark involved— at the end—but, really, we don't know why Henry was in the water. There's an anchor *on deck*. There's no proof it ever was fouled. Why would Henry hesitate to leave the anchor behind? You stand to gain too much, Juliet, for us not to want to see if he drowned or not. If he had a blow to the head—you see my point."

"But I loved him. I had everything I could want and him too when he was alive. Fred? What's happening here? Am I actually being accused of murder?"

"No, no, of course not." Fred took off his glasses and massaged his nose where they bit.

Juliet had known the meeting would be bad, but not like this. She rose unsteadily, looking from Louise to Evelyn, to Paige, none of whom looked back. At last Fred stood, took her arm, and accompanied her across the patio and through the salon.

"Juliet, I'm sorry. Louise is . . . well, you see. I think she's distraught, in her own way. I want you to know that I'll see to it that you get a fair hearing. We'll assume it will all come out well with the autopsy and the police. Are you doing all right?"

"Fred, how could I be doing all right?" Juliet cried. "Is Louise trying to get me accused of murder? Is she going to pull every Ashe string? Are you going to be on my side?"

"Oh, Juliet. Please don't worry about what Louise said. An autopsy will certainly clear up her questions."

"I'm going back to my room," Juliet said, looking around, half-frantic. "Oh, I wish my dad were here already! Excuse me, Fred. I have to go." She pulled her arm from his and ran across the pool and restaurant area head down, and nearly collided with George.

"Juliet! What is it? What's happening?"

"George, I'm going under here. I've just seen Hank's sister—his sisters and daughter—and his sister thinks I might be responsible for Hank's—and there's going to be an autopsy and what if someone does think—Did I sign permission for an autopsy?"

"I think it's customary, Juliet. It doesn't mean there's any suspicion."

"There's plenty of suspicion, believe me."

"I'm so sorry. Hank's sister! What kind of person is she! Look, it's going to be clear that Hank was killed by the shark. He's not going to be found to have been dead when he went in the water, is he now. Here, sit down."

"No, he must have drowned during the attack. He'll have water in his lungs . . . but what if it was from loss of blood? He might have been unconscious from the pain. What if he hit his head on the boat or something and it looks as though I hit him and pushed him overboard?"

Alex had joined them. He put his hand on Juliet's shoulder. "You don't stop breathing even if you are unconscious. And who's going to believe that you tried to drown him and a shark just happened to come along and take his leg half off. Doesn't make sense."

"Oh, Alex." Juliet sagged.

"I'm sorry, Juliet. I'm an idiot."

"I don't know if I'm coming or going. I keep thinking Hank wouldn't have let this happen to me. But there's no Hank!" she wailed. The men exchanged glances in awkward silence. Several other guests looked her way and whispered together. "I've got to get out of here." Juliet jumped up and ran across the patio. Alex waited only a moment before sprinting to her side.

"Let me go over with you. You've got to calm down." He put a supporting arm around her, and she slumped against him. "All right," she said weakly.

They walked along a path of black and white pebbles set in an undulating design. At intervals it branched to other suites hidden behind walls of foliage. Someone dove into a pool; swimming in the ocean had lost its appeal for the resort guests. Huge plumeria trees arched over the walkway and framed the vista of the bay beyond the rows of umbrellas and lounge chairs. Boats could still be seen dotting the water. Juliet stopped and stared at them.

"Don't you think all those boats will just scare it away?" she asked.

"They're out there with bait. They'll get him. We're heading out to look today. We were just talking about it. George wants to go farther out. We have some grouper for bait and he's been Googling shark fishing in Thailand, and thinks he has it figured out. There's a drop-off just beyond the island; apparently tiger sharks like to hang out where depth is changing. He thinks it had to be a tiger shark." Juliet turned away with a shudder. They reached the causeway that connected the suite to the land.

"Let me come in and be sure you're all right. May I?" Alex asked.

"Thank you, but I need to be alone," Juliet said, shaking her head.

"Juliet, you do *not* need to be alone."

She gave a long, groaning sigh. "All right. Come in."

Inside, Juliet wandered through the sitting room, looked out to sea, and came back to one of the sofas. She lay down with a pillow cuddled to her chest, and closed her eyes.

"Can I call for some lunch for you? Juice?"

"No, I couldn't eat. Maybe some hot tea. Could you make me some, Alex? If you go through that door there you'll find the kitchen. There's an electric kettle."

"Of course."

While the water came to a boil, Alex looked in the refrigerator. It was stocked with wine, fruit, chocolate, a fancy cake in a plastic container, and wrapped sandwiches. None of it looked like comfort food. Hot soup would be the thing.

Juliet sat up and sipped the tea, which Alex had heavily sweetened. She held the cup in both hands and dipped her head towards it. "This is good," she said gratefully.

"I want you to eat something, Juliet. I'm going to get them to bring that sweet and sour fish soup. Okay? Do you like it?"

"Yes, I like it. All right."

Alex called to place the order and joined her on the sofa. She sipped her tea. "Thanks. I guess I did need this. What do you do, Alex? You seem like a nurturing type."

"Oh, I don't know about that. I do try to take care of New Orleans. My family's been there for generations. Lemoine—L-E-M-O-I-N-E. It's an old name. I have various projects—Katrina relief stuff mainly. Summer jobs for kids. I have a foundation—Rebuild New Orleans. It's kind of like Habitat for Humanity."

"Really? That's wonderful. How old are you?"

"Twenty-eight. How old are you?"

"Twenty-two. At least I was yesterday. I feel somewhat older now." Juliet shook her head. "How did you get to be friends with George?"

"Oh, I've known him forever. He's a family friend. My father's banker."

"That's lovely, you being involved with rebuilding New Orleans."

"It's the least I can do. Those to whom much is given, you know."

With a soft tap at the door, three girls sheathed in green silk entered with table settings, covered bowls of soup, French bread, little salads, and sparkling water. They arranged the food on the deck table. One inquired in charmingly accented English if anything else was required. Juliet shook her head and thanked them. They backed from the room bowing, hands together.

"There's some chardonnay in the fridge, if you'd like," Juliet said.

"Do you want some?" Alex asked.

"Maybe I will. I'll try a nap after lunch. Maybe it will help me sleep. I usually fall asleep if I drink during the day."

"Have you been getting any sleep?" he asked when he returned to the deck with wine and glasses.

"Not much. I had horrible dreams every time I closed my eyes last night. Not about . . . but awful, incoherent stuff. I tried sitting up and watching the moonlight on the water but it made me think about the shark swimming around out there—and about Louise waiting for me. Then I watched part of *Across the Universe*, but the Beatles' songs all made me cry."

"Any time you want company, you know where to find me. You could call, day or night."

"Thanks, Alex. I do feel a little afraid to be alone. I hate my thoughts. And now Louise turns out to be as bad as I feared." She put down her porcelain spoon and stared into the distance.

"Eat, Juliet," Alex said softly.

She smiled vaguely and picked up the spoon. "So, tell me more about the summer jobs."

Alex told of black teens apprenticing in restaurant kitchens, assisting in restocking libraries, learning carpentry on the sites of homes in restoration. He could see she was impressed and warmed to his tale, making it sound as though he were modestly understating his philanthropy. Alex was nothing if not a clever liar. He'd have to play this fish carefully, he thought. A grieving widow. How delicious.

Juliet's face looked very tired, the skin under her eyes still had a purple tinge, and even so she was gorgeous. Alex struggled to keep the awareness out of his eyes.

Her soup half-eaten, her glass of wine half-drunk, Juliet thanked him for his company and said she'd lie down for a while. Could he send over a masseur, he asked? No, she thought she could sleep. Wouldn't she join the *Viridian* crew for dinner? Perhaps.

"I really appreciate your company, Alex. It's a help. I'm going to go crazy waiting for this magistrate to decide if I can get out of house arrest, though I couldn't tell you where I want to go. And what if there's a question? Sometimes horrible things happen in places like this. Well, anywhere, really."

The sounds of shouting reached them. Juliet's face froze. "Listen! What's happening? What now!" Alex left the deck, crossed the living room and stepped through the carved doors to the causeway. A man was running up the path under the plumeria trees.

"Madam! Madam! Shark caught! Shark dead! Tell Madam!"

Juliet had come up behind him. "I can't look at it, Alex. Will you go?"

Alex gave her a quick hug and hurried down the causeway, intercepted the man, and hustled off with him. He would find the shark split open with the stomach gaping by the time he arrived at the marina. George, considerably disappointed that he hadn't made the catch, was bending over the contents, pulling out shreds of blue nylon. He held a fragment toward Alex.

"Got him," he said grimly.

After Alex called the room to tell her that it appeared to be the very shark, Juliet stared out over the ocean. It was something, she supposed, something for the resort anyway, but it made it all the more real that there was a creature that really had killed Hank, that it was not going away, all this horror. Finally, she lay down and slept for an hour, slept hard and woke feeling groggy. She decided to have a bath. The tub, the size of a small dipping pool, had a bowl of flower petals beside it, and as she idly dropped them into the rising water, she heard a knock on the door. Wearing the resort's robe, she opened it and found Fred Goldman outside.

"Come in, Fred. Did you hear they caught the shark?"

"Yes, everybody in the province seems to know that. I talked to the magistrate and he knew about it in Bangkok. Juliet, I wanted to tell you that Louise and Evelyn and Paige are moving to the Intercontinental in Bangkok to wait for the autopsy and to take Hank's body back. I'll stay at the resort with you. May I sit down?"

"Please." Juliet excused herself to turn off the bath water.

"They can't have his body, Fred. I'm the next of kin," she said when she came back to the sitting room.

"Well, Louise wants an autopsy in the U.S. even if the one here shows the cause of death was the shark, and I'm afraid she's already gotten a court order to that effect from Judge Oster in San Francisco. The embassy has given her and Evelyn permission to transport the body. I think you may as well let it happen. The chargé d'affaires at the embassy is an old friend of hers, and the paperwork has already been done."

"What did the magistrate say?"

"It's not clear to me if the autopsy has been done or not, but he did admit that a preliminary inspection of the body didn't show any trauma other than to Hank's thigh, so it's probably going to be ruled accidental death. I don't want you to worry. It's true that Louise is bringing what pressure she can, but the magistrate seems like a good man. I believe they are going to let you go soon. You may have to go up to Bangkok for a hearing. I'll attend with you, and I've hired a local attorney. He's going to come down to see you tomorrow. I think he's very good, but if you don't agree for any reason, just say so."

"Thank you, Fred. I guess that's okay. I don't feel like I'm thinking very clearly, so I'm going to have to let you do the thinking. I know Hank would have trusted you to take care of me."

After Fred excused himself and Juliet returned to her bath, she was interrupted again, this time by the telephone. She turned off the water once more, as though the act were heavy labor, and dragged herself into the bedroom. It was a call from her father who told her the distressing news that he hadn't left California. A sore place in his leg had been diagnosed as a thrombosis; he had been forbidden the many hours in the air. But he could lie down on the chartered plane, she insisted. The doctor felt that pressurization was a problem, he said apologetically. Juliet had a flash of resentment that she knew to be unfair. She didn't tell him how much she had been wanting him, or about the accusations coming from Hank's family and the magistrate. Kindly, she assured him that there were friends of Hank's here helping her through the paperwork and taking care of her, and that the embassy was arranging the return of his body. She was okay. He must take care of himself and not worry. She would call tomorrow.

Juliet sat in the perfumed water and cried. She had really wanted her daddy, and hadn't felt that way since before her mother's death. Crying turned to sobbing; sobs turned to something like gasping laughter. It was some horrible black comedy. Hank dead, possibly at her hand. Louise playing the wicked witch. And she hadn't even taken a picture of Hank! She went on until she scared herself, until her eyes ached, and she nearly threw up. She climbed out of the tub, rubbed herself with a towel so thick and plush it was barely absorbent, and put on the silk robe.

On the bed, she stared up at the beautifully crafted ceiling—the coiled liana that held the bamboo armature in place, the complex pattern of the palm leaf thatch, the white silk globe of the lantern that hung from the peak. She had opted for a life of luxury where every whim was catered to and, to be fair, a chance to do good or exciting things, but it had all crumbled in her hand. Perhaps she would spend the rest of her life in a Thai prison; perhaps she'd have to endure a trial in the U.S. And now she was let down again by her father. There was nothing in the world she wanted to do and her own company was the last she wanted to spend time with. As the sun set, the phone rang again, but she didn't answer it. She refused the dinner she was offered; she eyed the sleeping pill—the single pill in its plastic jacket that the doctor cautiously allowed her. Maybe it would keep her from dreaming.

At eight-thirty there was a soft knock at the door. It would be the maid wanting to turn down the bed. Juliet let her in, smiling automatically. She wondered if she was on suicide watch the staff checked on her so often. And what must the Thais think about the family abandoning her after the brief visit? Before the maid was gone, Fred appeared at the door. He was sorry when he heard that her father wasn't coming.

"Yeah. I'm pretty lost here. It's strange. Hank made me feel as though nothing could ever hurt me again, and here I am under house arrest."

"I'm so sorry, Juliet. I should have brought my wife

to stay with you or brought one of your friends. I wasn't thinking."

"I probably should have let Mr. Peters come. He's a nice guy. But, it's okay, Fred. You're a great help. And George has been wonderful. His friend Alex, too. I'll be all right, don't worry. And I feel pretty tired. I think I can sleep."

But she slept very poorly. She went out to swim at dawn, at first descending toward the ocean by the steps from the deck, but fear and revulsion arose when her feet touched the water and she chose the pool instead. Later, she walked a jungle trail around the periphery of the resort, with a member of the staff following discreetly behind. Did they think she'd make a run for it or throw herself into the ravine? She had a massage in her room. It relaxed her into another crying jag, and by afternoon she was afraid to be alone. Fred had gone to Bangkok for the day. Perhaps Alex and the crew would come to dinner. She called the *Viridian* and asked for George or Alex. It was Alex who came to the phone.

"Hi, Juliet. I was just coming over to check on you."

"I wondered if you all would keep me company for dinner tonight."

"I don't know where they all are at the moment. Let me accept, though."

"Great. If you see—"

"Sure, I'll tell them. Where do you want to eat?"

"I don't feel up to anything public. Would you like to come to my suite? About seven? They'll make us something."

"Okay, I'll be there." Excellent, Alex thought as he hung up. George came up from his stateroom.

"I'm going to give Juliet a call and see if she wants

to have dinner on the *Viridian*."

"I just spoke to her and mentioned that. She begged off."

"God. Poor kid. I hope she'll be okay."

When the time came, Alex bathed, shaved, put on a sad and sympathetic face, and left for Juliet's suite, without being noticed. She poured him a glass of wine as they looked over the menu. She chose shrimp; Alex, Kobe beef. They would share an hors d'oeuvre platter. Alex made the order, and they went out to the deck to watch the sunset.

"I had another blow yesterday," Juliet said.

"What happened?"

"My father won't be able to come out. He has a blood clot in his leg and can't fly. I was so disappointed. I just wanted to dump all this on him and curl up in bed."

"I am so sorry to hear that. Your mother?"

"She died four years ago. She had cancer." Juliet's eyes welled.

"Oh, Juliet. Don't cry, please. No, no, cry if you want. God, I'm such an ass. I keep saying the wrong thing."

Juliet gave a little laugh and tried to dry her eyes. "What's the right thing? Who knows how to deal with people like me? Nothing's going to make me feel better. You're sweet, Alex. Maybe you *are* making me feel better."

"I'll try to put my foot in my mouth on a regular basis if it will help."

Over dinner they talked again about New Orleans. Alex's house in the Garden District had been spared in the storm—it was in one of those neighborhoods along the river that were on high ground.

"We never knew what was high and what was low until the levees broke and the canal was breached. New Orleans had always seemed dead flat. I had stayed on—

don't ask me why I did such a crazy thing. The poor weren't the only ones who couldn't picture real trouble, but I was glad in the end that I had stayed. I was able to be of some use. Remember when Sean Penn came down and found a boat and started rescuing people? Well, that was my boat, and we did what we could, and saw things that are hard to talk about. He's a great guy. We've stayed in touch and he's been very generous in helping the city.

If I get out of this with some money, Juliet thought, I'll help too. Hank had wanted her to have a good life, a life she found meaningful; perhaps he would make it happen after all. Alex seemed to have the right idea—jobs, roofs over heads. Juliet thought perhaps she too could have that kind of clear vision and do philanthropy as well as he did.

"Tell me about your family, Alex."

"My dad's in oil and gas. I guess you'd have to say we have a strained relationship. I was too much of a playboy when I was younger. I flunked out of Tulane I'm sorry to say, and I ran through quite a bit of money. It can be a curse, you know. My dad can't seem to see that I've turned around—well, I think I have, anyway. I've invested and things have gone well. I've decided to try to get a law degree. You can imagine I have some make-up to do after blowing my college record. At least I waited until the last year to mess up and my grades ended up recorded as incompletes. Family strings, you know. I'm not proud of it, but it will help in getting into law school. I want to do civil rights law, work with the poor. I'm lucky I can afford to have a pro bono career."

"And your mother?"

"She's always hung in there with me. She's really responsible for my deciding to get real. She does work with prisoners: counseling, helping them get representation, jobs when they're released. She would have me come along to interviews, and I began to understand what those guys are up against. The deck is totally stacked against 'em."

Alex distracted Juliet for a couple of hours with tales of money well and unselfishly spent, of ideals upheld. Perhaps the day would come when she could find another partner who would share with her a compassionate and generous path. The money—the money Juliet knew would be hers, if the Thais let her go—the money loomed like a minor planet whose gravity seemed to increase by the moment. It would take all her effort to turn it to good.

They parted with a chaste hug. He cupped her face with his hand. "You're very brave, Juliet. I'm so happy to have gotten to know you. Sleep well."

Alex's step was light as he returned to the *Viridian*. Sean Penn. That was a good touch.

Juliet almost slept through the night. About six, she climbed out of bed and wandered around the suite. She found herself staring into Hank's closet. The resort valet had arranged the jackets, shirts, underwear, and shoes on the hangers and shelves, and had kept everything clean and pressed. In the mirror she looked to herself like a little girl spying on the world of grownups. There was the faintest smell of Hank's soaps and scents, and of rich fabrics and leathers. She would have to have this packed and taken to the plane. And then? Disposed of someday like the rings that still flashed and gleamed on her finger. Would David want his father's clothes? She didn't even know what David looked like, what size he was. Did rich people do things like pass on clothes? Mr. Peters. She needed Mr. Peters who was paid to know what to do, what was appropriate, to keep her from making humiliating mistakes. She retreated and closed the door, feeling as though she had trespassed.

The shutters in the bathroom area were raised. An

insidious breeze brought the sound of the waves lapping at the pavilion's pillars. The sea was out there under her all the time while she tried to sleep or think. She should have moved to one of the villas on land and never even looked toward the sea. There could be sharks swimming round and round under her this minute. That was it: She would move today if another villa was available. Something small. There were some up the hill; you could get glimpses of them through the trees. Yes, maybe it was the sea. She had to get out of the pavilion, go to the restaurant where they served breakfast, talk to the management, not be alone. She threw on a cotton sundress and applied a dash of lipstick, but peering into the mirror, she saw a face still haunted. She hid as much of it as she could behind her sunglasses.

A maid tapped so lightly at her bedroom door that, if she had been sleeping, she wouldn't have heard it. She had come to say that Mr. Dubose hoped to see her at the restaurant beside the lagoon. Yes, George was who she needed.

But when she arrived at the large table where he awaited the others, she had to hold on to the chair to keep from falling. Her head swam and she felt she was being sucked into a dizzying vortex. Far away, George was looking worried and talking to her. His hand was reaching for her arm. A breeze blew in from the bay, fountains splashed and blossom-weighted branches of bougainvillea nodded, while a specter of cold death interposed itself between her and the brilliant color and dapples of sunlight. She looked at the menu, the flowers in the center of the table, the steaming coffee poured into her cup as though from a great, silent and terrifying distance.

What was George saying? He was asking what was happening, and she heard herself speaking: "Fred told me that there's been a preliminary examination of Hank's body and it didn't show any . . . you know. He thinks the magistrate will clear me and let me go, but Hank's sister has arranged another autopsy in the U.S. Did I tell you that?"

"Hank sure wouldn't have wanted this." George shook his head sadly.

"My Thai lawyer is coming down from Bangkok today. He's supposed to go with me to the hearing with the magistrate—Fred too—and someone from the embassy. They haven't even contacted me yet. Do you think I should be worried about that? There's someone there who is Louise's friend."

"Do you think you need a lawyer from the States, I mean besides Fred? I've got a friend in the State Department. Do you want me to give him a call?"

"I think Fred can take care of me. And I'm going to ask to move to another suite—something smaller. On land. I don't want to stay out there on that water anymore." Remembering the plan to move cleared her head. "I'll be better in another suite. How long will you be here? What are the plans?"

"If worse comes to worst, we're going to stow you in the bilge and get you out of here on the *Viridian*."

"Great. International Fugitive. But thanks, George. I really appreciate it." Juliet managed a weak smile as Alex and Pete arrived, kissed her and took their seats.

"Do you feel up to dinner on the *Viridian* tonight?" George asked." We were sorry we missed you last night."

"Oh, Alex said—"

"Yeah, we got our signals crossed," Alex hastily inserted. "Come tonight."

"I will. Thanks."

Even while the staff was still moving Juliet's belongings to a new two-bedroom suite, which she could share with Fred, Juliet's legal troubles began to unwind. Her local lawyer arrived and was kind and reassuring. It appeared the autopsy had already been done and showed nothing suspicious. The magistrate was prepared to speak to her by teleconference in just over an hour. She, the Thai lawyer, and Fred went over the story together before the call came into the resort's business center.

Fred was of the opinion that all was going their way. He said that if the magistrate released her the plane could be ready to leave the next day and, if he could fly with her, they could use the time to start familiarizing her with her affairs. Did she want to leave tomorrow if all went well?"

"When would Hank's body be going?" she asked.

"He'll be released when you are. Louise would likely want to leave immediately too."

"This doesn't feel right, Fred."

"I know, I know, but just hang in there. There's only so much harassment Louise can pull off."

That turned out to be true. The magistrate listened to Juliet's story and offered her his deepest sympathy. He hoped that she would someday be willing to return to Thailand, and that she felt she had been treated well. Fred completed the arrangements for them to leave the next day. The resort insisted on not charging for the honeymoon suite, but Juliet insisted on paying. Fred took care of the $52,000 charge, and the envelopes for the staff. Hank's belongings were packed and moved to the plane.

At dinner, George announced that the *Viridian* would also depart the next day. They drank to Hank; George and Fred told stories about him. Juliet managed not to cry. Before she and Fred left the *Viridian*, Alex took her aside. They leaned against the rail overlooking the marina and a hillside that twinkled with lights. They could faintly hear the gamelan that accompanied the nightly dances.

"I'm hoping we can keep in touch, Juliet. I'm going to want to know how you're gettin' along. I hope that someday the grief will be behind you and that you'll have a happy life."

"Thanks, Alex. You've been a real help. And I'm going to want to hear about your wonderful projects, and to help, too." He pressed her hand as Fred came out of the dining salon to look for her.

When they were gone Alex stayed on deck to enjoy the night breeze. He had a very good feeling about his chances.

Louise had done her worst and it had proved wanting. The U.S. autopsy found no reason to stay Hank's cremation; Juliet was questioned as gently as in Thailand; the will was not even going to probate. She was informed that the memorial service would be at Grace Cathedral in San Francisco. She was not included in the planning, and sensed her presence would be barely tolerated. It was humiliating, but losing Hank made that unimportant.

The cathedral was packed with San Francisco's business and political elite along with its yachting community. Dressed by Mr. Peters in elegant black, Juliet was escorted to the front pew by Fred, Sheldon, his wife, Shirley, Aunt Ava, and Ann and Mike Teixeira, but had to be abandoned there next to Louise and Evelyn with their husbands and children, and Paige and David. David was gracious enough to stand, shake her hand and introduce himself. He was much bigger than Hank and his head was shaved.

Hank was warmly eulogized. The story of the Olympic bronze was told with humor and affection, and no one had the bad taste to say he would have wanted to die at sea. Hymns were sung and the sure and certain hope of the resurrection intoned as Juliet sat in sorrow and loneliness. Afterwards, she stood in the receiving line for nearly an hour listening to Louise whisper to the elect to join the family at her home. Juliet was not invited. Before Louise left, she had her say.

"It appears you have had things your way, Juliet, and I'm sure you know I'm not happy about it. I just want you to know what you have achieved for yourself. You are now in a position where you will never again know if friends and lovers care for you or for Henry's money. And I hope it tortures you."

Juliet went rigid as Louise wheeled and walked away. It was as though the wicked fairy had come to her christening and predicted that she would someday prick her finger on a spindle.

PART TWO

ALEXANDER GAUDET LEMOINE

CHAPTER THREE

Since her return from Thailand, Juliet had been surrounded by a loving cluster, including Mike and Ann from Quinta da Agostinho, her aunt, and her father. She had seen the *Chronicle*'s obituary lauding Hank and numerous previous generations of San Francisco Ashes, and filled with information about him that was new to her. However, she had been shielded from the tabloid stories—"Child Bride, Child Widow," "Death on a Honeymoon," "The Shark and the Widow"—and the pictures, one taken with a telescopic lens of her at the resort with Alex, the other at the airport, as she, her clothes too elegant and her sunglasses too "Bvlgari," boarded the plane with Fred. Shielded, that is, until someone mailed a collection of the clippings to her. The insinuations of foul play and the breathless speculation as to the size of her fortune soon drove her to antidepressants. She spent a lot of time staring into space, grappling with the implications of what had happened. Four months of some insane dream, insane for both her and Hank. She'd hardly had a moment to think amidst the travel and gifts, the crazy luxury, and the promises. She'd been drawn through the membrane of the shimmering, iridescent bubble that surrounds the very rich and she was trapped inside with the oxygen failing. Had Hank wooed her, or had he bought her? Had she sold herself, or responded to a warm and needy man? Had she loved him?

Hank had wanted to start over, hadn't he? He had said he wanted children. He wanted to be young again; if nothing else, she'd had that illusion to offer. And he had pledged so much: her winery, good works. How sordid it seemed now that he was gone. How undeserving she was of all he left behind. Somehow the marriage counted as a failure. It just did. Not that it made sense, but it was the logic of her lightning-struck brain.

She could hardly bring herself to say it. Killed by a shark? On their honeymoon? How could such an absurd plot twist be believed? Surely she'd wake up from this embarrassing dream. She wondered if she should tell people he'd had a heart attack—those people she'd meet someday who wouldn't know the story. But he'd cared so much about being fit. Maybe an aneurysm? Were aneurysms shameful? The *Chronicle* had said only that he'd met with an accident in Thailand—Fred had taken care of that—but what good was it after those tabloid stories? There would never be a day when his death wasn't somehow suspect, or recalled with a snigger. It was like dying on the toilet or in the arms of a mistress—a joke of an end. Hank deserved better. She would never tell the story. She'd never say it. Never.

Between leaving university and getting married, Juliet had lived in a cottage behind the big house at Quinta da Agostinho, and had returned to it after the funeral. Her father's office was just across the patio. Ann and Mike also wanted to keep an eye on her while she got back on her feet. Mr. Peters, whose apartment was at the Ashe Mansion in Pacific Heights, checked in on her often. He would sit with her for a while, ask if there was anything she needed, tell her this or that about her properties. He and Juliet had liked each other immediately. She was grateful that he made sure that her social faux pas were small and far between.

Juliet had been left three houses: two in California—the mansion in San Francisco and a "cottage" on the Big Sur coast—and the house in Palm Springs, where a tree had fallen on the pool house while she and Hank were in Thailand. Mr. Peters reported when the repairs were completed. And as he gave her a new set of keys to the Ashe Mansion, he explained that the locks had been changed because of a sensitive problem: Miss Ashe—Paige—had been encountered there removing several paintings from the wall. Her excuse was that they had been her grandmother's favorites and should stay in the family. Mr. Peters had told her that, regretfully, he couldn't allow her to take Mrs. Ashe's property without first discussing it with her. He left out Paige's reaction. Which paintings? The four Tuscan villa scenes by John Singer Sargent. Surely Hank would have wanted Paige to have them, Juliet said. Wouldn't he? Mr. Peters hesitated.

"Frankly, Mrs. Ashe, I don't think so. They were ones her mother tried to get in the divorce settlement, and Mr. Ashe particularly refused to give them to her. To tell the truth, I think Mrs. Ashe—the ex-Mrs. Ashe—is still trying to get them. If you want to give them to Miss Ashe, it might be best to wait until she's more settled."

"What was she like? Mrs. Ashe. Blaire."

"I've only had this job for four years so I only knew her at the end of the marriage. Things were pretty rough."

"What was she like to work for?"

"She certainly put all my training to the test.

77

Carolyn Kingson

Exacting standards would be an understatement. She entertained constantly and made frequent use of all the homes. She might go to Florida for an event, want the house full of food and flowers, and go to Southampton a day later—where she'd want the house full of food and flowers. Two days after that be off to Italy. She and Mr. Ashe were seldom together. I was glad to see him so happy with you, Mrs. Ashe."

"You didn't get to see much of it, did you."

"Not nearly enough."

"Will you handle the painting thing for me, Mr. Peters? I don't know what to do. Is Paige close to her mother?"

"When it suits her. How to put it? Both those children seem to have been ill-served by all the wealth, and if the ex-Mrs. Ashe was like she was when I knew her when the children were young, I can't imagine she let them tie her down to anything as dull as mothering. I think Mr. Ashe blamed himself for paying more attention to Home Base than to his family. He said as much one time when he and Mrs. Ashe were discussing some scrape David had gotten himself into. Mr. Ashe was always trying to take David sailing, but he wasn't interested."

"Hank didn't have many other ways to relate, did he."

"You can't get into enough trouble on a sailboat to suit David."

Juliet smiled. "Where is Blaire now?"

"She has the Southampton house and the New York apartment. She asked me to go with her after the divorce, but it was an easy choice to stay with Mr. Ashe, even though he warned me he wouldn't be keeping up the social scene."

"Do you miss the challenge of all those houses and

parties? I can't imagine I'll be hosting any charity benefits either."

"I'm content here as long as you want me."

"What's your first name?"

"Sean."

"Can't we be Juliet and Sean?"

"It's not done, Mrs. Ashe. But rest assured I'll be on your team."

As Juliet stayed on at Quinta da Agostinho—not even trying to recover—she let misery recall misery. Brooding on the terrible time around her mother's death, with the horrible collapse of her body and her discovery of her husband's unfaithfulness, she winced at the memory of the unhappy marriage ending on the worst possible note. She thought of how she had turned her back on her father when she'd fled to Portugal. They'd hardly spoken for a year as Shirley moved in and transformed his life. She had attended the wedding, but had been cold, shamefully ungracious, as though she was her mother's representative, there to remind the assembly of her culture and intelligence and to contrast it with Shirley's. Shirley, this plump widow, so proud of her son-the-lawyer, and of Sheldon too, gazing on him as Nancy had on Ronnie. So what if it looked a little silly? It must have made pleasant contrast to the marriage he'd had before.

She knew it was time to forgive. It was even time to admit that her mother had used her editing job and her literary friends to put down her father's intelligence and culture. Juliet began to see how her mother had co-opted her in a conspiracy against him. Certainly Sheldon was entirely capable in the practical world. His wine engineering, his palate, his skill in labor management—all these had made him one of the most successful vintners in

Napa, in the world for that matter. What did it matter that he wasn't an intellectual.

Now he clearly wanted to comfort her—as did Shirley. How could she reject him when he was so eager to share his wine-making knowledge, to help her on her path, to make it up to her? What had he done but make the all-too-human effort to have some love and compassion in his life? How could she hold on to her resentment after the way her own life had turned out?

Would her mother have approved of Hank? Juliet suddenly realized that she would not. She never would have made it past his politics. And thank God she hadn't seen his bookshelves. Juliet saw that she had chosen a man her father would like—and had liked—rather than one her mother would have approved of. She cringed to think of how it could have gone if her mother had been alive now. Likely, she would have felt relief that Juliet had escaped such a Philistine. And would she herself have come to feel some of that disrespect toward Hank? Did she feel it all along? Had she loved him enough?

How many days had it been before the requests for money had started coming in from alleged friends of Hank's, alleged friends of her own? How had these people even found out where she was? They told such pitiful stories. How could she justify saying no when she had so much? It became difficult to be polite when one more can't-miss investment scheme or just-until-the-property-closes loan turned out to be the real topic of the sympathy call. How many more friends she had now! She gave, and hated herself for the poverty of spirit with which she did.

Eventually, she felt too much guilt for upending the Quinta da Agostinho household, and retreated to the Ashe Mansion. There Mr. Peters dealt with her calls, and everything else. He turned out to be a godsend.

The house had belonged to Hank's paternal grandparents, then to parents who had died in a plane crash in Aruba. Unlike the Palm Springs villa, the house looked as though someone had cared, even if the caring had involved collecting conventional French, Chinese, and English antiques, and jumbling them together to no coherent purpose. Mr. Peters excluded, the staff made her uncomfortable, never allowing something she moved to remain in its new place. She hid out in the sitting room attached to one of the master suites—one that had no view of the water—and read books from morning to night, though she often discovered she had worried herself through many pages of unremembered text.

Juliet had been having trouble sleeping since Hank's death. She saw the clock reading 3:48 or 4:10 morning after morning, and went from one uncomfortable position to another for hours after. Every week or so it caught up with her; she would sleep like the drugged for a day. Of course, she was drugged, and couldn't face life without antidepressants.

Though her father called frequently, she never seemed to have the energy to talk. She had even lost interest in the winery. Weeks passed. Sheldon, Ann and Mike came several times for Sunday dinners at which they had to carry the conversation as Juliet sat poking at Ms. Edward's beautiful meal. But one day she got up, took the BMW from the garage and drove to Napa, leaving the distressed chauffeur behind. She found her father supervising the repair of a corking machine, and began to talk as though she couldn't unburden herself fast enough.

"Daddy, I can't sleep. I can't think. I'm scared I'll never recover."

"You've had a terrible trauma, Julie. I'm surprised you're doing as well as you are."

"I'm not doing well. How am I going to deal with—I was going to say Hank's life, but that's rather poor wording. I don't think that life can ever be mine. There're these houses, the plane, the boats, staff, gardens, security, my driver, maintenance, spa fees! I've had to learn to read spread sheets! Or rather, I look at them. I hate it all. Mr. Peters is great. He's totally competent *and* he gets $115,000 a year! I probably should be doubling it. I'll never get my head around this stuff. And what am I going to do with my houses? I don't even know anyone in Palm Beach. I'm going to put it on the market. Do you know it has 35,000 square feet? Mr. Peters can keep himself busy laying off staff. And then there's the house in Big Sur. Mr. Peters had to get down there last week with a crew to move out everything in case that fire changed direction. And apparently there's some lawsuit involving the neighbor. I told you that hurricane toppled a tree onto the pool house in Las Ventas and the security company went out of business and Mr. Peters had to find a new one. We were all right but some guards were stripping houses."

"That doesn't seem like the sort of thing that should be stressing you."

"You're right. But it does."

"Julie, just don't think about it all. You don't have to make any decisions about any of it until you're ready."

"They think I'm . . . I don't know what they think. And I thought I had a staff of five at the mansion. Listen to me: *The Mansion.* But the other day, I found out it was seven! I'd never met two of them. And those are just the ones that live there, not the contractors. I think there may be rooms I haven't even been in. It's the most appallingly decorated *museum* I've ever seen. I've decided to use a bedroom that was Hank's mother's, and one of the maids acted like she thought it was sacrilege. I started to wonder if she's a spy for Louise. I stumbled on her outside my room and she started like she was guilty. So, I wanted to change some of the furniture in the room. The stuff was so dark and I liked the bedroom suite in one of the other rooms. It's white, painted with poppies. And I told this maid— Ida—and I told her again. She made excuses for a week and I knew she was doing it because she hates me and doesn't think I belong there. And I found myself thinking she was right and maybe I'd move out, but then I realized I was supposed to get Mr. Peters to handle it and of course he did and I felt like such an idiot. But then he let her go so I guess I wasn't imagining a certain surliness. There's this hierarchy in the house. It's like Manderley! Oh well, maybe I'll figure it out."

"What's Manderley?"

"Oh, it's the name of the house in this book, *Rebecca*. The housekeeper tortures the new wife with how perfect the dead one was and the wife is a mouse of a thing who doesn't even rate a name in the book." Sheldon listened and winced. But after a couple more hours of similar venting, Juliet drove back feeling slightly better.

Juliet's support group also included George and Alex, both of whom called nearly every week. George had taken on the project of helping Juliet sell Hank's boats. Alex made her laugh, listened patiently as she tried to make sense of the life she had inherited, and told her hopeful stories of his projects in New Orleans. He had become a confidant.

Juliet was still in bed when the phone rang. "Good morning, Mrs. Ashe," Mr. Peters sang. "Mr. Lemoine is on two."

"I'm not calling too early?" Alex asked when she

answered.

"No, no. How are you? How's things?"

"Nothing new. It's been raining for three days. What are you doing?"

"Well, Dad presented me with an application from UC Davis enology program yesterday."

"Enology? That's wine, right? That's excellent! Have you filled it out?"

"I wonder if I can even concentrate in school. I feel as though I've lost fifty IQ points."

"You've got fifty to spare."

Juliet harrumphed. "I haven't even read a whole book since—"

"You'll have no trouble, Juliet. I know how much you already know."

"You sound like Dad."

"So? It's agreed? You'll apply?"

"You don't think it looks bad, Alex? It hasn't been very long."

"I don't think going to school is considered disrespectful. When's the deadline for the fall?"

"It's like immediately. Though Dad says I could apply for delayed entry."

"I say go for it. Hank was all for you getting your degree, wasn't he?"

"Yeah, that was the plan, but now I have all these responsibilities."

"Come on. I know you have a good team in place. You can do whatever you want. I think you should do it. This isn't good, the way you're living."

"I have a terror of just giving in to the money and never doing another thing as long as I live."

"No, no. That'll never be you. You're going to do good things."

"Thanks for saying that, Alex."

Juliet applied and was accepted. She worried that her father had pulled strings—he knew everyone in the department—but he assured her she had gotten in on her own merit. He admitted that Lou Minetti had called him and asked if she was his daughter, but it had been after the letters had gone out. Promise? Promise.

She and her father grew closer. Now that she'd be going to school in a few months, Juliet was more and more eager to walk the fields with him, to discuss equipment, to taste and evaluate vintages in the cellars. He listened patiently as she rambled about her financial empire, deciding to do this one minute, and that the next. Every day there was some new problem. Hank's boats for example. It appeared he'd had five, not just the ones she had seen—the ketch in Florida and the racing Columbia that had scared her silly when the wind leaned it so far over the sails threatened to fill with water. There was even one that had been in dry dock for years. Hank had considered it too much of a collector's item to part with even though he'd never gotten around to the repairs. No more boats for her, no more ocean. All were on the market. George had found a buyer for the ketch, and for the four remaining, slip fees, repairs, painting, the consideration of offers, guards . . . all continued.

The airplane needed pilots, crew, a maintenance lease, a cleaning and stocking lease, and hangar rental. Christ. She had sent Mr. Peters to La Ventas in it, otherwise it had been sitting since she came back from Thailand. Surely she could get by on leasing. Surely she could get by on commercial! There was an office building in downtown Los Angeles—luxury space, $1200 per square foot. The management company (don't forget *their* lease.) felt it

85

needed new wiring. The management company seemed not to have many tenants to manage, but that wasn't their fault. It was the wiring. She was told she couldn't put it on the market now because it wouldn't go for what Hank had paid.

Though the hassles went on ad nauseam, that was not to suggest that most of Hank's investments weren't doing beautifully, wonderfully, stupendously. Pharmaceuticals, corn syrup, oil sands, baby-seal killing clubs . . . . The last an ugly joke of course, but it was true that Hank had not been above investing in companies that made money on the backs of the poor and the ozone layer. It was the blindness of his lifetime of privilege, Juliet thought; she would have brought him around. Now, she had the burden of bringing the portfolio around.

She fantasized about selling it all and putting the money under the mattress. Of course, the money would have to *be* the mattress—or mattresses, more like. She thought of the appliquéd quilt her grandmother had made depicting "The Princess and the Pea" for her childhood bed. No good night's sleep for her now with obligation as the constant irritant, poking at her to be wise and prudent. Such a mountain of money took on a life of its own, a life the financial team assured her they knew how to nurture.

Alex understood much better than her father what it was like to be weighted with wealth. She began to ask his advice, to get his suggestions on how to approach the Nibels on various issues, and how to get them to accept investments he had recommended. Naturally, she met with resistance, but as time passed, as she felt buoyed by Alex's confidence in her, as she anticipated returning to school and again being Juliet rather than Mrs. Ashe, she began to stand straighter. Now and again she'd get up the nerve to hold her ground.

Before school began, Mr. Peters found her a condominium in nearby Sacramento. One bedroom. No staff. Simple furnishings. Her rings were put aside. Mr. Peters bought her a downscale wardrobe and a little Toyota. She planned to tell no one about her marriage and her money.

Juliet couldn't fathom why Hank had left her the Ashe Mansion with all its family memorabilia: if he had wanted to spite his sisters, he had been very successful. Paige's had not been the only effort to revisit the bequest. Juliet suspected that Fred had not bothered her with the half of the family's machinations. And how could she not be sympathetic to their feelings? She sometimes thought it had been wrong of Hank to put her in such a position, and she would gladly have handed the house over, if going against his wishes hadn't been too much to face. She kept the entire staff on too, waiting for time to make the way clear. In the meantime, Mr. Peters moved with her to Sacramento and took an apartment nearby. He did her grocery shopping, dealt with the condo management, got the Toyota's emission sticker. It was like having a wife. Juliet sighed and accepted the help, which seemed to come with genuine kindly interest.

"Hello there, Miss Juliet." Alex had an accent that always made her smile—a special New Orleans upper-class intonation along with all those Southernisms: moonlight through the magnolias, bourbon on the veranda.

"Oh Alex! I'm so glad you called. I've had a miserable day."

"What happened?"

"Fred came over here to Sacramento. I told you we were having a meeting. I thought I was getting my head around Hank's business affairs, and now it seems Fred neglected to tell me that Hank was audited before we were married. The accountants have been dealing with it for something like ten months. I thought really rich people didn't get audited! It's knocked me off balance. I just wonder what else Fred isn't saying. I'm going to have to tell him that I can't stand these surprises. I have to know it all."

"Sounds like you're distrusting him."

"No, no. I suppose I wouldn't know if he was robbing me blind, but I don't believe it. He just wants to protect me."

"I sure hope you're right."

"I spend *hours* on this stuff, Alex, and I know I'm smart—well, I thought I was smart—but you can't believe the number of pies Hank had a finger in. Hedging! I apparently have my very own boiler room longing and shorting imaginary somethings. And I don't believe in any of it. I'm a land kind of girl, a vineyard kind of girl. My financial advisors are telling me the hedging is making me a fortune, and getting out would be a big mistake. They clearly think I'm a big mistake too. And where do I get the time now that I'm in school?"

"I wish you'd let me help, Juliet. My family has a wonderful team—I told you they're ready to take you on."

"I appreciate it, Alex, but I don't think I can do without Fred. He's my consigliere."

"You aren't suggesting there's illegal stuff."

"Not that I've discovered. But if I ever need anyone to sleep with the fishes, Fred's my man."

"Who do you have in mind?"

"Oh, the Nibels, I guess."

Alex remembered Fred from Thailand, overheated and overweight. He hadn't looked formidable, but maybe he should take the warning. "And how's school?"

"Aiee, I'm working my bleep off with this organic

chemistry."

"Here's a proposal for a bit of a break. I have to come out to California. May I come visit you?"

"Wow. When are you coming? It would be great to see you again."

"I'll be there next weekend. I have meetings in LA during the week, and then I thought I'd fly up to Sacramento to say hello."

CHAPTER FOUR

After the warm chats, after the first visit to Sacramento, and the visits that followed—chaste palling around Napa, Point Reyes, the Embarcadero—Alex had begun to seem as indispensable to Juliet as he had hoped he would. And he had become her lover.

At Davis—studying viticulture (the cultivation of grapes) and enology (wine and wine-making)—she was known by her maiden name, Juliet Pierce. Alex was the perfect companion for an heiress in hiding. Louise had spoken the truth; the only man she could trust not to exploit her was one with enough money not to want hers.

Alex was really wonderful. He hadn't gotten his graduation sorted out and couldn't yet apply to law school, but he was tireless with his philanthropic projects. Juliet visited him in New Orleans at Christmas. Alex drove her around to point out a dozen of his renovation projects; unfortunately, it was during the school year, so she couldn't see the kids in their apprenticeships He had a grand old house in the Garden District, just visible to the outsider behind iron fences, palmetto, and live oak. It was packed floor to fifteen-foot ceiling with antiques—old family pieces, his grandparents' and great-grandparents' collection. An equally grand house nearby belonged to his parents, who had been out of town. Unfortunately, George and his wife, Mimi, were gone, too. It was wonderful to see that New Orleans had not lost its Garden District in the storm, though it had lost some tourism—the result being they could get a table at Commander's Palace or Galatoire's on a whim. However, Alex preferred to visit her in California, and she found no time to return to New Orleans after that one visit.

And Alex was so satisfyingly responsive to her advice about books. No, he wasn't well-read, but he clearly had a mind that hungered for it. He bought everything she mentioned and produced thoughtful comments. He never showed up without a recommended book under his arm.

Though the condo gave them all the privacy they wanted, Alex's presence at the Ashe Mansion was problematic. She couldn't dream of having him stay there, with Hank's staff still jealous of their dead employer's prerogatives. Now, over a year after his death, the time was coming closer to write the glowing letters of recommendation, give out the enormous severances, and send them all away. She was nearly ready. How sweet to sleep, not to be depressed, to be loved. And, best of all, to love.

"I'm thinking about you. I'm *really* thinking about you, honey bun," Alex said seductively.

"Hmm, me too." Juliet squirmed happily. No more than a hint of Alex's erotic prowess was required to arouse her.

"I'm thinking I'm going to have you over that chaise longue in the living room. I think we'll have to proceed there as soon as your driver gets me in from the airport. It would be best if you aren't wearing any panties, don't you think?"

"Yes," Juliet said in a voice constricted by desire, "Yes, that would be best."

"You're wet just thinking about it, aren't you?"

"Yes."

"And that's the way I want you to stay until tomorrow."

Juliet was spending the week in San Francisco for the quarterly Nibel meeting; Alex would be flying in the next day. The scene in the living room was out of the question, with the staff still idling away their sinecure, but she and Alex would be driving up, first to Napa and then to Sacramento, and something very like it would undoubtedly take place at her condo. A minor but respectworthy vineyard, Clos August, had come on the market. Sheldon thought it would be a good buy, and Juliet wanted to head up as soon as possible to see if she agreed. If she did, it would be her first major purchase. Perhaps the Nibels wouldn't give her too much trouble. Anyway, she couldn't care less what they said, though it would be nice if someday they thought her shrewd.

She was looking forward to an idyllic weekend. It would be impossible to drive by *all* those wineries without a sip. They would go to the reserve tasting rooms with their paneling and antique furniture and paintings of race horses. She would be recognized. They would drink the pride of the winery, on the house. She would be tingling with sexual anticipation. Juliet was almost gay again, with someone to trust in the world of mistrust Hank had left her, someone to laugh with, someone who made her thrill with youth and desire. Lord knows, she'd held Alex off as best she could—eleven months—but Hank's memory grew faint. Alex's mouth would form a firm line as he bent over her. It made her weak.

Would they marry? Naturally, Juliet thought of little else. She evaluated and scrutinized every gesture that could illuminate his character. He was strong and manly. He adored her and made her feel adorable. She forgave her breasts, which were too large for designer clothing, because he loved them; she forgave the little jut of her belly because he doted on it.

She grew more and more certain that Alex was serious about their relationship. He seemed right for partnership, though in the past he had made mistakes and been foolish and wasted money. But the sincerity of his repentance, his efforts to make amends, and the acumen that had allowed him to more than recoup, made him more appealing than if he had stayed on a responsible path all along. And he couldn't pass a stroller without peering inside.

Not that they'd talked of marriage yet. Not that she was willing to talk. In the old days there had been rules for how long to wear black and what sort of events it was appropriate to attend when one was widowed, and now there was only one's unsteady and unreliable conscience to consult. And if grief lessened prematurely, which Juliet feared it had, didn't you have to wait longer still to hide that unseemly fact?

Though Juliet was posing him no problems, Alex was not entirely easy with the way his courtship was going. True, he now had her in bed, and oh, what a delicious bit she was, well worth the long, long delay. But keeping up his façade of wealth put way too many balls in the air. If he were to get her to marry him, he would have to introduce her to his parents. He had long ago met Juliet's father who had been easily won over by his hastily acquired interest in all things wine, but his parents would not be so easy. Elopement was the only way.

Alex had wildly misrepresented to Juliet the degree of disappointment he had been to his family. His self-deprecating confessions had minimized the amount of money he had blown, and had skipped entirely over the debt he still carried, the check kiting incident, and the ugly divorce in which his parents had taken their daughter-in-law's side. They hadn't yet forgiven him; there was no way they would back up the posture of wealth so essential to Juliet's faith in him. Was his storyline going to have to move them to Shanghai, or kill them off? Juliet would just fly to China, or expect to support him at the funeral. Better avoid a ruse too far. Yes, his only hope was elopement, though he was considering ways to get her to contribute to debt retirement even before the wedding. Her gift to his housing foundation had been very helpful, but hadn't exactly put him on sound financial footing.

Aimée, his girlfriend in New Orleans, hadn't been a problem either. She was satisfied that Alex finally had some good business prospects, even though they took him away from New Orleans every few weeks. In between, he was entirely attentive. Alex was a charming and decorative escort, a wonderful lover. She had very mixed feelings about marriage, having already failed twice, and while it had looked last year that Alex was nudging her toward a third try, now it didn't come up and she didn't mind. They were having as much fun as ever. Truthfully, she didn't really care enough to puzzle over the change. She could afford Alex—and had to. Depending on him to pay for fancy meals and getaways would seriously cramp her style. Aimée was content with her decorator business, her solid investments, and her house in the Garden District—one of New Orleans' finest—which she had extorted in her first divorce, in return for the promise not to out her ex-husband.

Juliet, Alex, and the agent walked through the vineyard for over an hour. It was a bit hilly, which would mean different parts would be ready for harvest at different times, complicating the process. She would have to spend time monitoring sugar content as the grapes ripened, but that was more a happy prospect than a drawback. Sheldon, and Davis, had impressed upon her that a vintner must live with his, or her, vines. They were lyre-trellised, very healthy. After the tour, they sat under an oak on the edge of the field and uncorked a three-year-old bottle of wine from the vineyard. The cabernet vines had only been five years old when the wine was made, but Juliet was impressed. Before they left, she told the agent her offer.

At dinner Alex listened attentively while Juliet analyzed the market in California and in Mexico, which was supplying a surprising portion of her wine money. The grapes from the thousand of hectares in which Hank had invested filled fleets of refrigerated semis that delivered to U.S. winemakers each fall. They were suitable for smoothing a disappointing harvest, stretching production of intermediate quality wines, and filling the bargain bottles that had helped the U.S. nudge out France as the largest consumer of wine in the world.

"What do you say, Alex? Want to go down and look at my Mexican vineyards? Most of them are in the north near Hermosillo, which isn't exactly vacationland, but some are over near Querétaro and San Miguel de Allende. People say those places are lovely. We could stay in old haciendas. There's time before next semester if we go right away."

"I can't think of anything better." Alex pulled out his BlackBerry. He had any number of obligations: board meetings, important presentations and dinners, but *what luck*, he was free for the time she proposed. Juliet said she'd have Mr. Peters make the arrangements. They could go in her plane, fly directly to Querétaro, rent a car, and go off on their own. Alex was returning to New Orleans on Wednesday; she could fly over and pick him up there on Friday. Alex looked at Juliet's shining eyes. Grapes and haciendas. Nothing was likely to put her into a better mood.

In Mexico, a large Toyota SUV awaited them at the airport, and they headed south toward Ezequiel Montes through wild and beautiful country. Where there was no cultivation, giant cactus—prickly-pear decorated with red fruits at the edges of the paddles—reached six or seven feet high. Fleshy, spike-tipped agaves grew equally large and showed in sharp grey-green contrast against the dark mountains beyond. Palisades of stone broke through the mountains' smooth curves. The occasional slumped landslide revealed soil roasted deep umber or rust-red, and as though nature had become bored after using every hue of green and brown, it had clustered masses of electric-pink cosmos along the road, over an entire rectangle of fallow field, or behind a row of dark cypress.

It took some hunting, repeated requests for directions with electronic translator in hand, the constant intrusion of the Portuguese Juliet had picked up at the Teixeira estates, and heavy reliance on hands helpfully waved in vague directions to track down her manager, Víctor Arce. He had learned his trade in California

97

vineyards and spoke quite passable English. His eyes had gotten big as Juliet introduced herself. Their correspondence had been brief, informing him that Hank had died, that the project was going forward, but not preparing him for the pretty, young woman who stood before him.

Alex looked on impressed as Juliet consulted, advised, and accepted local wisdom. Señor Arce led her and Alex to fields where they found vines as beautifully tended as could be wished. She asked him to prepare soil and water samples that she could take back for analysis, and told him she'd likely want to purchase more land, plant more grapes. Would he look out for good land for expansion? He had his eye on fields already. The time passed quickly. Señor Arce and Juliet had hit it off, and Alex contentedly tallied up the money she was prepared to blow on this Mexican whim. His estimates of her wealth were obviously not inflated. Jump in the Falcon 100, head off to buy up large parts of Mexico . . . . This was a dream come true.

Were there sights nearby, charming villages that they could tour while the samples were collected? Haciendas made into hotels? Señor Arce named several villages and showed their locations on the map. The area proved to be liberally scattered with colonial pueblos, each with an old church, a plaza surrounded with shady arcades, and picturesque houses with private courtyards and roses in profusion.

Lots of houses were being refurbished in these villages. Who was moving in? Rich people from Mexico City? *Gringos*? They saw posters for cultural events even in tiny towns. Clearly some people of sophistication were around. It was all very intriguing. Did Alex think he'd ever like to spend time here? He took his cue from her obvious interest. Indeed he would.

San José Xoloitzcuintle—the ancient Anáhuac

98

name now conjoined with a conquering saint—was approached by a perfectly terrible road. They climbed into dark mountains on a dirt track no more than a bulldozer's pass around their sides. Where the road concaved between ridges, the rains had brought down fans of earth, some swamping more than half the roadway. Teams of workers with pickups and wheelbarrows were busy cleaning up. In one particularly bad place they were building a stone retaining wall. San José was reportedly a nearly pristine colonial pueblo; one could guess why it had remained that way.

The SUV finally mounted the *cumbre*—the pass. They looked out over a breathtaking vista of rocky, green mountains. The pueblo centered near the lowest point of a great bowl. It looked like a hidden Shangri-La.

As they descended, they passed scattered buildings, a humble neighborhood, grand houses. Where the buildings were plastered, they had been painted gold or deep red or rusty orange; where unplastered, the adobe of their walls and stone of their parapets were visible. Apparently every house had a dedicated gardener. Finally they came to the plaza and the jewel box of a church with a dome of orange and blue tile, a single sharp spire on top of a belfry, and a façade entirely covered with bright ceramics. It was the most charming village they had seen.

A columned porch with grand arches proceeded around the three sides of the square not occupied by the church. They parked near a restaurant—La Mina Real. Tables with intensely colored cloths left only a small central aisle for passage through the arcade, however, there was no impediment to stepping at any moment into the street since there was so little traffic. They took a table and were greeted and given a menu by a young woman who spoke to them in Italian-accented English. The fare was pasta and pizza, salad and tiramisu. The pasta was advertised as handmade.

"Wow. I think we've hit the jackpot here," Alex said. "This looks like a rather sophisticated menu. I think I'll have the carbonara."

"I might try the arrabiata."

The waitress returned and placed a basket of homemade bread on the table. Juliet ordered *vino tinto*—red wine. Alex asked about the beer selection and chose Negra Modelo. The waitress called their orders, in Italian, back into the interior rooms and was answered by a distant *"Bene."* Juliet wondered where on earth she was. Italians?

"This town is adorable." Juliet smiled to the young woman. "Is there a nice place to stay for the night?"

"We have two very good guesthouses. There's Mesón Dante—"

"Dante! More Italians? You are Italian, right?"

The young woman laughed. "Yes, we're five Italians in this town. My name is Elena, my husband is Silvio, and the guesthouse is owned by Michele and Fabrizia. Her brother Raul lives here too. He is a painter."

"How did you find this place?" Juliet asked.

"Just very good fortune. But there are other *estranjeros* here—*gringos*, Canadians. Mexicans like to have second homes here too."

"Where is the guesthouse?" Juliet asked.

Elena began to give directions, but was interrupted by the church bells ringing the time. She waited until they had been informed by three loud double bongs that it was the three-quarter hour. The guesthouse was across the plaza, down one block, around the corner. She went to fetch their salads.

"If you decide to stay here tonight," Elena said as she put their plates on the table, "you must hear Enrique

Carbajal play his cello. He is giving a recital in the church."

"A cello recital? Fabulous!" exclaimed Juliet.

She and Alex lauded the perfection of the food, gazed over the pretty plaza, moved on to coffee and tiramisu, giggled happily. What a sweet vacation. And the Mesón Dante proved to be another delight. It was built around a patio, with part of it extending up two stories. A broad set of stairs rose to the second floor where their room—Luna de Miel, Honeymoon—looked down on the courtyard with its tiered fountain. The room was painted dusty rose, furnished with a mirrored wardrobe, a carved bed covered with smooth sheets and a duvet, and decorated with antiques: a toy horse-cart driven by bride and groom porcelain dolls, early photos of stiff newlyweds in elaborate frames, a washstand with flowered china, and cross-stitched mottos. Juliet had a momentary superstitious aversion to the name of the room but suppressed it.

Alex dug in his suitcase for some of the marijuana. (Ever so nice to have the VIP freedom from inspection Juliet and her plane brought.) He had lost no time getting his black market doctor's certification to shop California's dispensaries, and was working his way through the exotic offerings. This was some Jack Flash that he'd heard was especially good for sex—hopefully not quick sex—and busied himself rolling a joint while Juliet worked out the meaning of a motto painted above the bed.

"*Amor con amor se paga.* Let's see: Love with love pays itself. Um . . . Love is repaid with love."

Alex pulled her against him, and in a surprisingly sweet voice and dead on key, sang into her hair, "And in the end the love you take is e-e-e-qual to the luh-uh-uh-uh-ove you make."

"That was beautiful. I didn't know you could sing like that."

"The original was sung in harmony—Paul and John I suppose. Want to harmonize, sweetheart?" Alex gestured with the joint.

"Let's go out and see the sights first," Juliet smiled.

"As long as there's not too many of them out there. The sights in this room are certain to be the most interesting."

Fabrizia had a couple of tables set up at one side of the patio, and when Alex and Juliet came down from their room, they all sat together as she served them juice and advised on the town's sights. They should see the church (They heard again about the concert and that Enrique was not only a wonderful musician but the town doctor.), the Presidencia with its deep portal, the unusual architecture of the Asociacíon Ganadero—the Cattlemen's Cooperative—and the old hacienda on the edge of town.

Alex and Juliet held hands as they strolled down the hill from the plaza, bumping playfully into each other. Alex stole the occasional kiss and whispered sexy things into Juliet's ear while she batted him gently and exclaimed over the lovely houses and the warm colors. She practiced her *"buenas tardes"* (only said *"boa tarde"* once) and was rewarded with smiles and greetings in return. Ahead was a little river, a cemented ford, and a foot bridge. Beyond it was the hacienda.

It was red like the red of Knossus, a dark, rich red, stained at the base of the walls with a complementary mossy green where rain had splashed. The variegation of the color suggested that pigments had been mixed with the plaster. Columns and surrounds on the windows and doors were stone; the windows were protected with ornate iron bars. It was grand, beautiful, and falling into ruin. There was a *"Se Vende"* sign on the column on one side of the gateway. "For Sale."

"Uh, oh," Alex said. "Here we go."

"Don't worry. I don't need a fallen-down hacienda," Juliet laughed. They crossed a prickly yard to study the collapsed wall and roof near the recessed entrance. The roof that remained had a definite swayback. "Just a little exploring. What do you say?"

"Looks condemned to me."

"That's what I like about Mexico. Live at your own risk," Juliet said as she peered into the interior gloom visible beyond the porch.

"This makes me think of plantation houses along the River Road around New Orleans, except that they're always white. Peach at most. Our family has cousins who still have a cottage up near Belle Rose. Mother was going to have inherited one of the best, but it burned down years ago. We probably wouldn't have two pennies to rub together if we'd been tryin' to keep it going all these years."

"I imagine those houses in the Garden District are a challenge too."

"Strictly a labor of love, darlin', a labor of love. And now we have the Vietnamese termites to worry about. New Orleans limps from crisis to crisis. But this is made of adobe, looks like, and that will last if the roof is intact."

"I wouldn't say the roof looks exactly intact," Juliet sighed.

"There you are."

The church bells began to ring again: two bongs for each of the four quarters followed by a sweeter count of One, Two. They paused and listened. "Nice," said Juliet.

"I hope they don't do that all night. We're pretty close to the church."

"Come on. It's romantic!" Juliet nudged Alex as they climbed the stairs.

"Hmm. Maybe I'll wake up on the hour and discover I have to have you again. Would you like that?"

"I might," Juliet said with a happy smile. They had entered a series of large rooms. First, one that they thought was a living room until they found an even bigger one with a grand fireplace. Next a smallish kitchen, other rooms of not-readily-apparent use, a retro-fitted, abysmally ugly bathroom that looked as though it belonged in a rural filling station. Outside was a walled garden with roses on their last legs. An enormous barn was attached to the house at one end, and at the other, another wing hid behind a locked door.

Alex said, "It sure is big."

"God, yes. This must have been something." They went back out to the porch in front. Juliet looked into the room with the fallen roof that opened off it to one side.

"What is this big thing?" she asked as she took some tentative steps among the broken tiles and adobes toward a large, wooden, box-shaped object. "You know what? I think it's an altar. This must have been a private chapel. That's rather fabulous."

Alex came close behind Juliet and wrapped his arms around her. He kissed her neck and pushed his hips and a growing erection against her. Juliet brought his hands to her breasts. "Is it time to go back?" she whispered.

"Unless you fancy being ravished in a chapel," Alex murmured. "A bit of a black mass on the altar? Would that be kinky enough to drive you wild?" He turned her around and squeezed her buttocks, lifted her up to her toes, and stooped to kiss her hungrily. Juliet returned the kiss without reservation. Her darling, sexy Alex.

After the afternoon idyll in Luna de Miel, Alex made his move.

"Juliet, I'm going to put my life in your hands."

"You are?"

"Marry me."

He lay against the pillows, naked and beautiful, cradling Juliet's head against his chest. She twisted to look up at him. "Oh, Alex," she said, smiling a dazed and happy smile.

"I love and adore you, Juliet."

"I love you, too. I do, and part of me wants to say yes, but . . ."

"What part doesn't, cherie?" Alex said with a look of distress.

"I have a little pang that says it's too soon."

"Don't have a pang, precious. I don't like to think of you with a pang. Juliet, I want a life with you so much. I never met anyone who cares as much as you about the things that matter. Think of what it would be like to live that life together."

"I do think of it. You are such a gift to me. But Alex, how could we put our lives together with you so bound up with New Orleans and me with my vineyards?"

"I've been thinking that we could divide our time, or I could just go back once a month for a few days—something like that—and otherwise work from California. What I do there is real important to me, but when I put it up against you . . . well, you're my everything."

His everything. She hadn't known she could be this happy. They kissed, and her reservations faded nearly away. But at last she drew back.

"I don't want to let you out of my sight, but I couldn't think of marrying for a while. Please understand I have to wait. You know I do."

"I know how you've honored Hank. No one could think—"

"Oh, sweetheart. People *could* think, believe me. But mostly, I have to be sure *I* don't think it's too soon. Be patient?"

"You don't have legal issues do you?"

"What do you mean?"

"I mean they won't take your money away if you remarry, will they? I couldn't bear to do that to you."

"No, there's no problem with that. I guess it's something we'd have to talk about though." Juliet turned her head so that Alex couldn't see her face. He took the opportunity to glance at his reflection in the wardrobe mirror. His penis was hidden between his legs; he arranged it upright on his abdomen and lifted his hips slightly.

Juliet had never wanted to contemplate her responsibilities regarding the money and remarriage. Was it now her turn to think about prenupts? No. She would never go there. How could she have the sort of marriage she wanted if she began it thinking like that? Though of course, Hank had.

Juliet turned her head back, put her chin on his chest and looked up into Alex's eyes. "When we marry, I want an agreement we both sign: Everything I have is yours."

Alex pushed a bit of hair off her forehead. "You are my perfect treasure."

A most attractive man walked out of the vestry, stood before the altar, and smiled at the twenty-five or so people in the pews. Juliet and Alex sat toward the back, close, holding hands. The man spoke for a while in Spanish and then changed to English. He thanked them for coming to hear his good friend Enrique Carbajal who was too seldom prevailed upon to entertain his neighbors. The man's English was only slightly accented, both colloquial and erudite. He used the word *coruscating* and made a reference to Yo-Yo Ma.

"I had no idea that there were people like this in Mexico," Juliet whispered to Alex, "and it makes me feel like a snob to realize it." She watched the handsome announcer slip into a pew beside a woman whose black hair was decorated with red flowers. He leaned toward her to whisper something. Juliet moved closer to Alex, wanting to feel equally attractively escorted.

To warm applause, an older, slightly disheveled man carrying a cello appeared. He wore a sagging tweed jacket and a tie-less shirt. He bowed, smiled, said something that didn't carry, which made the people in the front rows laugh, and announced that he wished to play Bach's Suite No. 2 in D minor in six movements. He sat in the chair in front of the altar, fussed with its angle, bent to listen to the tuning, smiled and nodded again at the audience, and finally sent the first notes into the dim expanse. Around the lower portion of the dome, larger-than-life figures of saints or popes or bishops peered down and cocked their heads, their eyes glazed in rapture.

"Where *are* we!" Juliet whispered to Alex when the Prelude was over. As the Allemande began, she closed her eyes.

Alex also drifted away, back to the marriage proposal in Luna de Miel. It had been just about perfect, he congratulated himself, with Juliet in the afterglow of one of her ready orgasms, full of love and earnestness. It would be beyond wonderful to have a life with this exquisite creature. He had even made it through the all-important question without upsetting her. If she were to forfeit the money upon remarriage, living in sin would have to be the way to go. He'd have been ready to convince her that having the wherewithal for good works overrode all other

107

considerations. Everything I have is yours! He'd died and gone to heaven. He heard hardly a note of the austere music.

The following morning, Alex paid for the room—not so bad with her providing the plane and renting the car—and they reluctantly left San José Xoloitzcuintle. They met with Víctor Arce, picked up the samples, returned to Querétaro, and spent another night. While the Falcon flew first to New Orleans to drop off Alex, they whispered together.

"Why do we have to have Karen on board? I want to mile-high you right now. Can we send her up with the pilots?"

"Stop it, Alex," Juliet giggled. "We're behaving badly enough already. This was Hank's crew, you know." Juliet nodded to Karen to take away her plate. "When can you come to California again?"

"You know I want to, honey bun, but I can't get away any time soon. Damn! I was enjoying putting all this stuff away for a while, but it's all waitin' for me. I'm in a pickle—just temporary—but pickle-ish enough right now."

"What's wrong?"

"Augh, it's so embarrassing. I wasn't paying sufficient attention and I've pushed my liquidity to the edge. It's those office buildings I've been buying. I know the city will come back better than ever, but I got carried away trying to pour in money to make that happen. I know I'm going to make out like a bandit in the end but . . . seems a guy who was investing with me turned out to be a lot less than reliable. Anyway, he doesn't have the money and I've got a month to come up with a little over six million, which I just can't pry loose right now. A shame to lose my down payment. I have to scramble to sell something and that won't be easy 'cause about the only person buying is me! I can't give up my housing foundation—I just can't—but I just might have to put it on hold, and I'm pretty bummed."

"Wow. How long have you known about this?"

"That my investor was going to disappear on me? I signed the contract two months ago, payable within ninety days. His money was in the wire transfer and again in the wire transfer, and then he went quiet on me."

"Let me help you out, Alex. It would be my pleasure. You can pay me back whenever. I can't stand to think of your projects suffering."

"Juliet, that's just not right. I couldn't take the money from you. But, how about this? I'll send you all the specs on the building, contracts and such, and if you think it's a good investment, we could both win."

"Put them in the mail. We'll get this taken care of."

"Hi, Fred," Juliet said into her cell phone as she drove toward Napa some days later.

"Juliet, I received these papers about the Millot Building in New Orleans? I'm not sure what your under-standing is with Alex, but this contract doesn't actually—"

"No, Fred, it'll be okay. This is a personal friend thing. I've already talked to the Nibels about selling some tar sand stock."

"What did they say?"

"What do you think? 'Mrs. Ashe, that's up to sixty-eight. It's definitely going higher. You really shouldn't sell that now.'"

"Juliet, I don't know—"

"Is there a problem?"

"I'm not entirely sure about the contract. I just want you to be careful."

"I'm being careful, okay? This needs to move quickly. Trust me, Fred. Send it on over."

"And I still haven't received the tax information you need to deduct your donation to Rebuild New Orleans."

"I'll remind Alex."

Fred just won't see what a deeply fine person Alex is, Juliet thought when they'd finished talking. Invest in oil sand petroleum extraction when you could be helping those criminally neglected people in New Orleans? Heat the atmosphere with that super-dirty oil, feed the hurricanes with warm water, and grow bigger and bigger storms to devastate the Gulf Coast? Enough was enough.

"Juliet, my sweet darlin', you've saved me to fight another day," Alex said during a call a week later.

"*De nada.* That means 'It's nothing.' Working on my Spanish, you see. Got to do better the next time I go see those Mexican vineyards. Really, I'm so glad to help."

"There's some other help I need, baby. It's been two weeks and I'm having serious Juliet-withdrawal. My memory's going. I have only the blurriest recollection of your body and now I'm wondering if I was just too carried away when I thought it was completely perfect. I'm going to have to evaluate it all over again."

"Well, maybe this time you could take notes," Juliet laughed deep in her throat. Was there ever a man who could give more delight?

"Do I detect a certain flipness? I might have to set you straight, Miss Juliet."

"Ooooh, yes."

Aimée had heard enough. She turned and tiptoed off the porch of Alex's apartment. That fucking weasel. Who was he talking to?

Alex never heard her go. He reclined on the sofa, his back to the French windows near which Aimée had stood, giving Juliet the best telephone sex she'd ever had, and from him the last, as it turned out.

The call reached Juliet in San Francisco where she and Mr. Peters had gone for a Nibel conference.

"Ashe residence."

"May I speak to, uh, Ms. Ashe?"

"May I say who's calling?" Mr. Peters asked.

"Aimée Mills."

"And what is this concerning?"

"This is private business."

"Just a moment."

"Hello?" Juliet said.

"Hello. This is Aimée Mills. I'm calling about Alex Lemoine. Do you know Alex?"

Something seemed to sink in Juliet's body. "Yes, I do. What is it?"

"I'm calling because I saw your telephone number on Alex's bill."

"What is this about?"

"Well, I saw all these calls to California—I know he goes out there all the time—and the other day I overheard Alex talking, uh, perhaps to you. Could it have been you?"

"It could have been."

"It was . . . intimate. Could that have been you?"

Long pause. "Yes."

"The way the conversation went I thought you ought to know that Alex is having a relationship with me too. I didn't know about you, and I thought maybe you didn't know about me."

"No, I didn't know about you," Juliet said in a small voice as a feeling of embarrassment and shame swelled

111

until it threatened to choke her.

"I thought he'd been going off on business trips, but I guess he's been visiting you?"

"He has visited me." Oh, God. The marriage proposal, the money.

"And not doing any business?"

"I . . . I'm not certain."

"You know, you couldn't believe the detail he gave me about his exciting new prospect. He isn't going to manage a string of eco-resorts—"

"Tell me, is Alex investing in office buildings and running a foundation to rebuild houses?" Juliet felt as though she already knew the answer. When Aimée laughed a bitter laugh, she was sure.

"Not likely. Alex is entirely insolvent as far as I can see and I've observed him for about three years."

"Does he live in a mansion in the Garden District?"

"No! *I* do. Did Alex tell you about the house?"

Juliet closed her eyes. "I stayed there with him."

"When! Not *Christmas!*"

"I'm afraid so." Juliet heard something bang in the background.

"Christ. When he housesat. He's a fucking piece of work." Aimée had thought she didn't care but hadn't pictured this.

"Is he friends with Sean Penn?" Juliet asked wearily.

"Sean Penn! He forgot to introduce *me!*"

"I wish you'd called a little sooner. I think I've been a perfect fool."

"Sorry. I *am* sorry, but join the club."

Juliet took to her room to try to think up an innocent explanation for Aimée's revelations. Alex would be coming the following day and she rehearsed the confrontation: "Who is Aimée? Alex, do you have someone else you're seeing? A woman called me yesterday . . ." She had a sinking feeling that he'd have her offering him abject apologies in no time. Look how convincing he'd been about Sean Penn.

But maybe there was a chance it was true. Juliet Googled Sean Penn and Katrina and found images of him in a pitiful little boat with rescuers and rescued, none of whom were Alex. Next she went to Alex's foundation webpage. It still was without any links or other signs of activity, including any note of the generous contribution she had made. Googling Rebuild New Orleans yielded only the webpage link—no newspaper articles, TV spots, grateful families moving into refurbished houses, nothing. Anyone could make up a webpage, she thought bleakly. More Googling found a Lemoine Mansion in Moreauville, Louisiana, wherever that was, but none in the Garden District. The only Lemoines in New Orleans lived on Delachaise and Marengo, not Prytania, where, sure enough, an Aimée Mills was listed. Couldn't even one of the things he'd told her check out? In one of the bravest acts of her life, she called Fred and confessed to him that she was now suspicious of the building purchase.

Fred cursed himself for ignoring his prophetic soul. How close he'd come to having Alex investigated. He'd wanted to respect Juliet's privacy; he'd never make that mistake again.

"It's my fault, Juliet. I should have insisted. That's my job. I'm afraid with the check made to him personally and the contract only agreeing to repay your investment out of his 'interest' . . . . If it turns out that he doesn't have any, there won't be much we can do."

"You mean I don't have any ownership in that building?"

"I'm afraid not. But don't be too hard on yourself if you've been swindled. There are people who are born to lie and decent people like you are born to trust. It can happen to anyone."

"Fred, maybe it's not that bad, but I'll certainly never keep you out of the loop again. Alex is coming to see me tomorrow. What should I do?"

"Do you want me to see him? I could tell him I need some more information. Feel him out?"

"What if he's honest? He'll be so offended."

"I won't make any accusations unless they're warranted."

"Yes, yes, of course. Please talk to him. I can't face it. There are some other issues, too. He should be here at the house a little after three. Can you come then?"

Alex called that evening. Mr. Peters told him the story Juliet had requested, that she was out, but was expecting him the next day. She was on her bed in a fetal position when he tapped on the door to ask if she would like some tea. She nodded.

"I can't stand to see you like this, Mrs. Ashe. Has something happened with Mr. Lemoine?"

She heaved herself up and leaned on the pillows, accepted her tea, and sighed a colossal sigh. "Sean, if you don't call me Juliet I'm going to fire you. The woman who phoned yesterday with her private information? It appears she's Alex's girlfriend. And she had a plausible contradiction to about everything he's ever told me."

"Maybe there's an expla—"

"Don't bother. There's an explanation all right and you know what it is. He just got a pile of money out of me."

"That happened to me, you know."

"What? Somebody took you for your money?"

"Yeah. My boyfriend before Rafe. I'd socked away about three hundred thousand and we were going to go into business together. A household manager training institute—Peters Everly Academy. We had a great business plan. We were going to not only train but provide continuing support for butlers and managers. The best florists, stationery, linens, caterers, vetted staff, that kind of thing. It's a long story but it ended up with him, and my stash, gone. I really loved him too. Took me a while to get over it, I'll tell you."

"That's a sad story."

"Live and learn."

"Alex had asked me to marry him."

"He did? What did you say?"

"I almost said yes. I would have said yes soon probably."

"I'm sure he does love you . . . Juliet."

"Juliet. Thanks, Sean. But what about that woman?"

"You don't think she might have set him up 'cause she got jilted for you?"

"It appears she isn't jilted yet. And I checked out various things he told me online and none of it seems to be supported. The house he said was his is listed under her name in the phone book."

Sean sighed. "Sounds bad I guess."

"I am not equipped for this. I am *so* not equipped." Juliet put down her cup, leaned her head back against the pillows, and let the tears roll down her cheeks.

"Come on. Let's sing a round of 'I Will Survive.'"

Juliet snorted, laughed. "You aren't going to let me feel sorry for myself, are you."

"You just don't have the right instincts. You're way too nice. You should be looking for ways to get revenge!"

"It's too late to stop the check. He got six million out of me."

"Ouch. But, forgive me, it's kind of a drop in the Ashe bucket."

"Yeah. It's only when you put it together with the other-woman thing that slashing my wrists starts seeming like a good idea."

"Are you serious?"

"Not really."

"Are you sure?"

"I promise."

"I think you'd better talk to somebody, Juliet. Besides me."

Juliet's chauffeur brought Alex from the airport, and Fred met him when he came in from the garage.

"Hello, Fred. Where's Juliet?"

"She's just upstairs. Do you have a moment to go over your office building partnership with me? I've got a few questions."

"Uh, sure. What's the problem?"

"Let's go up to the library. I left all my papers there."

Juliet stood at the top of the stairs listening to the murmur of voices from the library, sick to her stomach. She kept thinking of that early movie version of Henry James' *Washington Square*. What was it called? Who was the heroine? Bette Davis? Olivia de Havilland? Some unspeakable beauty playing plain Catherine Sloper, standing unmoving, resolute at the top of the stairs, while the man who believed he would elope with her, and her fortune, pounded on the door below. Juliet and her mother had noted how the movie had perverted the book's storyline.

Down there in the library Fred was playing Catherine's domineering father. And Alex? The fortune hunter, she feared. Fred would be asking Alex to explain the contract, asking him for better security for Juliet's interest, proposing alternatives for dealing with the situation if it turned out to be unsatisfactory—the return of the money, restitution of any that had been disposed of, legal action. Fred had warned her it could be hopeless, but there was a chance that Alex had good intentions. Wasn't there?

She was startled by quick footsteps. Alex walked quickly across the Persian carpet, opened the cut-glass front door, and left. The door closed behind him with a discrete click. No! He wasn't even going to speak to her? What had Fred said? She should never have gotten him involved. Juliet ran down the stairs and found Fred gathering up his papers in the library.

"Why didn't Alex talk to me? Why did he go?" she cried accusingly.

"Embarrassed, I'd say. He didn't have much of an explanation, I'm afraid. Let's get Mr. Peters to bring us a drink, and we can go over the situation."

Juliet sat heavily on Hank's leather Chesterfield sofa. No attempt to see her—what could it be but proof of perfidy? Why had she bothered with foolish hope? The name of the movie sprang into her head: "The Heiress." Did she have to be a goddamed cliché?

Juliet returned to the Masters program in the fall, once again battling depression. She retreated from the other students, her attention on nothing but study—chemistry, mathematics, biochemistry, microbiology, plant biology, pathology, soil science and meteorology. She did field work in her new vineyard, nourishing the promise she had sensed

117

there. She studied hard and did well, but left with a network of cooperative colleagues rather than close friends. It seemed none of them had learned about her money.

After Alex, her sleeping problems came back with a vengeance. Now, when she awoke at three or four, it was too often because of the shark. It swam toward her out of a darkness that a moment before had not even been water; it appeared in the pool at Las Ventas in Palm Beach; it was dead somewhere waiting for her identification, and she had to spend an endless, tedious, and anxious night trying to find it. She had escaped it in Thailand only to die by the thousand cuts of these nightmares. She had her medication increased. Sean felt the need to remind her more than once about a therapist he knew—Marilyn Hansen, with her practice devoted to the very rich.

"What does being rich have to do with my shark nightmares, Sean?" she asked. "Don't you think they're about Hank's death, not the money or Alex?"

"Well, they didn't start until that thing with Alex, did they. I just think you need to talk to somebody, and here's what I've seen in my job: People of means can be treated with great callousness by psychologists and psychiatrists, not to mention friends and colleagues, when they get in trouble. It's a schadenfreude sort of thing. At some level they can be glad you're suffering because it relieves the jealousy."

"So, is she rich herself?"

"I don't know, but she's probably getting there with the fees she charges. But she's good, I hear."

"Like how much does she get?"

"I think about $700 a session."

"Like the Nibels' billable hours."

"She'd have to charge more than that for the money to scare you, Juliet. Just try her. I think she could be helpful."

"What are *your* billable hours worth do you suppose, Sean?"

"Oh, girlfriend, you know I'm here for you 24/7. That probably works out to minimum wage. Let's see. Let's round it off . . . $100,000 divided by 50 weeks equals—"

"I thought it was 24/7? *Now*, you have a two week vacation?"

"Juliet, did I once say you were too nice? Forget it."

"Maybe I should get my calculator."

"*This* is why they told us no first names when I got my Certified Household Manager training."

"Did we blow it?"

"Of course not. Just joking."

"But you aren't using your training, are you. I can "regret" an invitation all by myself now. I'll never give a fancy party. I'll never use more than a couple of rooms. I've sold almost everything, and sent scores of people to fend for themselves on the job market. The boats are gone, the plane is gone, Las Ventas and Big Sur are gone. Just this house and my condo. I've shriveled Hank's life to almost nothing. Just don't remind me of how much more money the Niebels have to work with now."

"I don't think you'll need me much longer, it's true."

"But I couldn't have made it this far without you, Sean."

"Life has dealt you some bad hands."

"Hank, yes. But I asked for the last one. Strictly bad judgment. Did you suspect Alex?"

"No. But I wasn't that crazy about him, I guess. He sure is handsome, though. Give him long hair and he'd look like Fabio. Lucky for me he doesn't swing my way. I'd probably have overlooked my doubts and fallen for him too."

Dr. Hansen was a beautiful woman in her fifties who always wore a necklace of multi-colored South Sea pearls even bigger than Louise's. She fed Juliet tissues, warmth, and understanding.

"Do *you* feel you have no right to be unhappy, Juliet?" she asked when Juliet told her what Sean had said about schadenfreude.

"Exactly. Anyone would say, 'Look at all your money. Look at all the people who have nothing!' That's it. I'm unhappy and I'm ashamed of myself for being unhappy. It's so disgusting to be like this when I could have anything I want."

"What do you want?"

Juliet squeezed her eyes shut. "I want to stop being depressed. I want to trust people. I want to be a normal person. I *used* to trust people."

"Not everyone is like Alex."

"Enough are like Alex! That's not paranoia; that's the truth! And if they're trustworthy, they die. My mother, Hank."

"You've had some terrible losses, not the least the loss of your innocence, with Alex."

"And where do I go from there? I *dread* my future! I should never have married Hank. I don't want this life! Even if he'd lived, I could never have gotten over the doubts about why I married him. I have Rich Survivor Guilt—RSG; I'm going to try to get it in, what do you call it, the *Diagnostic*—?"

"*The Diagnostic and Statistical Manual of Mental Disorders.*"

"Right. And then I take up with Alex."

"Juliet, doesn't it seem that someone who had behaved selfishly wouldn't be likely to doubt themselves so strongly?"

"I could be doing this to trick myself. I mean, I could be telling myself, 'See, you're so scrupulous. You don't need to deal with any guilt.'"

"Why isn't it working?"

"I don't know."

In another session, Juliet told Dr. Hanson, "I dreamt about the shark again."

"What happened in the dream?"

"I went to a water park. I *knew* I shouldn't be in a water park because there are sharks there. It was designed so you could only go one way through these rooms and passages, and there was a tank with a huge underwater viewing port. A shark came up to the glass and looked at me and I *knew* it was the one. It jolted me awake. I couldn't go back to sleep."

"That shark may be symbolic, or it may be that you have Post-Traumatic Stress Disorder from a very traumatic encounter with a very real shark. It can last a long time, or appear long after the fact. Sometimes Cognitive Behavioral Therapy can help. Perhaps we should focus on the event. If you learn how to deal with those memories, you'll have techniques to cope with the intrusive feelings of guilt."

"You think you could get that shark out of my head?"

"Why don't we try?"

In subsequent visits, Dr. Hansen had Juliet relive the shark attack over, and over, until she could contemplate it with little more emotion than sadness. The beast did retreat from her dreams, but unfortunately, they did not become sweet.

Juliet would dream that she had an imminent business meeting involving a tricky negotiation for which she needed to master reams of information. Not only was she not ready, she had forgotten she even owned the company, or that she had been told she was supposed to buy the stock—while at the same time she knew she *did* know or *had* been told. It would seem the whole night was spent in anxiety, shame, and fear.

"The thing is, Dr. Hansen," Juliet said as she tried to figure out the meaning of the dreams, "the thing is that I have no need whatsoever to know anything about my investments, or to know anything about anything. What does it matter if I earn my Masters? I can hire the finest vintner. I *already* hire the finest vintner—my father! What does it matter if I forget some crucial business detail? I'm paying something like seven and a half million a year for my financial team. If you can buy the best, what's the meaning of striving to be good enough yourself? What do you even do with your days?"

"You feel your life is meaningless, but you have resources many wealthy people do not. You grew up without money. You learned about the satisfaction of work before the money came into your life, and you have a fine basis for making a meaningful life now."

"I may forget it all! I'm terrified of getting lost. I let Sean do everything! But it seems silly to remember to get toilet paper and pick up the clothes from the cleaner. If you aren't doing that, though, you'd better be doing something important that only you can do, and what on earth might that be?"

"We can always find someone somewhere that does any particular thing better. You don't have to be the best to be worthwhile. But we need to find ways for you to think of the money as means rather than end—a dead end."

"You mean philanthropy."

"Philanthropy is a solution many wealthy people choose, yes."

"I *love* the idea of philanthropy. Hank and I talked of it, though I didn't get to see if he was serious. He wanted to make more money first—so there would be more to use that way, he said. Really, Hank seemed to find investing and sailing enough. He seemed like a contented man. Of course his divorce had been hard, but if there was ever a simple, untortured soul, I think it was him. Maybe he hid his self-doubts from me, but I don't think so."

"But, for you, things will not be so easy."

"No. But I do want to find a partner and have children. If I had someone to love maybe all this would be clear, but of course we know the pitfalls on that quest."

There were a few more downsizing achievements: Ms. Edwards—the chef—was encouraged to, and did, find another position, and the Ashe Mansion staff departed at last with their generous severances. The house was still maintained perfectly, of course, but with contract services. In Sacramento, Sean often cooked for Juliet and his husband, Rafe—he was as good as Ms. Edwards—and sometimes the three watched TV or attended an event together. To her fellow students, Sean was letter perfect in the role of friend.

The portfolio shrank in corn syrup and increased in solar cells. The return was less and she didn't care. She sold the hedge fund to another hedge fund. Still, it was but a nibble around the edges. Every time she downsized, more money flowed into the investment pot.

The Mexican vineyards continued to be very profitable. The wines in the bargain bins—those $7-, $6-,

$5-, even $1.98-wines that were drunk around the world these days—not a few were made from, or blended with, grapes grown on those vast fields with that cheap Mexican labor. Not that the pay wasn't decent by Mexican standards, Juliet hastened to reassure herself (and made a note to increase it), but cheap nevertheless. She was studying how to make fine wine; it was ironic that she was becoming enriched with wine that was little more than an alcoholic beverage.

Juliet didn't manage another trip to Mexico until after she had received her Masters. She arranged a tour for the second half of the summer she graduated. The harvest was earlier in Mexico; she could see the grapes at their perfection, and get home to supervise her own harvest at Clos August. She kissed her father and Shirley goodbye and headed for the border in a new SUV. Now nearly twenty-six, she hadn't done anything by herself in years. She was going without Sean, pilot, driver, attendants, reservations, with only her own thoughts—poor company as they were. It was some kind of statement. She hoped it might mean the worst was behind her.

PART THREE

LUIS VILLARRUBIA ZARAGOZA

CHAPTER FIVE

Juliet crossed the border at Calexico/Mexicali and took the nearly empty roads to Santa Ana and on down toward Hermosillo. Flat and featureless, covered with thorny scrub, the unpromising land extended toward the Sierra Nevada looming in the east. But at the anticipated mile marker, vineyards in lush profusion appeared on the left side of the road. After she turned off into the lanes between the fields, she found sun-baked workers tending vines hung with grapes like cabochons of citrine and garnet, but none of the men were close enough to be questioned about the whereabouts of her manager, Octavio Reyes. At last she came upon a group layering cuttings in sand to make new starts. With some repetition and gesturing, she determined that Señor Reyes was over two fields and down one, at the office.

He was as taken aback at her youth and beauty as Víctor Arce had been. Though they had spoken several times over the phone—his English was also quite good—

he hadn't pictured an owner like the one who sat across from him discussing pests, trucking regulations under NAFTA, yields, and labor relations. Juliet had already asked for soil and well-water samples from these vineyards to take back for analysis; Señor Reyes had her labeled containers ready—all the vineyards, all ten wells. It was a very agreeable meeting. Juliet promised to return when the grapes were ripe, packed her samples and continued south.

There had been a time when she had been nervous about doing business in a country known for machismo, but that was forgotten. From dealings with Mexican farm hands in the U.S., and with her manager at Ezequiel Montes, she had realized that, if Mexico worked on the principle of machismo, the word had been poorly translated into English. Octavio Reyes had actually said as they parted, "At your feet, señora." Wow.

Now, to reach the other vineyards near Querétaro, she had to cross the great mountain chain known on both sides of the border as the Sierra Nevada. As the range entered Mexico, passes became rare. She could have crossed between Hermosillo and Chihuahua, but took the next opportunity nearly two days south, between Mazatlán and Durango. The route was called El Espinazo del Diablo—The Devil's Backbone—and it turned out to be one of the driving challenges of all time. For three hours one hairpin followed another on a meager two-lane road. What did those signs translate? Beware Trucks Invading Your Lane? And here they came one after another, semis not even *trying* to keep to their side of the road on the turns. There were scores of opportunities to be forced over thousand-foot drops with no bothersome guardrails to crash through.

Climbing up the cliffs that lined the inside lane, a profusion of unknown foliage passed by her peripheral vision. Here on the edge of the tropics, plants were more baroque than anything seen in the temperate zones. An occasional and welcome turnout provided the chance to view mountain ranges as far as the eye could see in unpolluted air.

She climbed from sea level on the Pacific side and exited into the high central plateau at around six thousand feet. Excellent roads brought her to Durango, Zacatecas, Aguascalientes, and on into the historic Cradle of the Revolution—Guanajuato, Dolores Hidalgo, San Miguel de Allende. Along the way was Mexico at its most intensely charming: hotels in the homes of sixteenth-century grandees, slyly irreverent folk art, color intensified to the limits of the spectrum. And sitting alone at the dinner table, attempting to exchange pleasantries with the waiter, having drinks with temporary friends at the hotel, visiting historical sites, bargaining for a cluster of magenta and orange corn-husk gladiolas—whatever she did—no one knew who she was or had any way to find out. No one knew about Hank, no one knew about Alex. It was akin to the feeling of anonymity she enjoyed when she visited New York City. She would never run into anyone she knew, leaving her free to be whatever she wanted, even her innermost self. As she stretched to fill her neglected corners and cul de sacs, she could feel in the process how cramped, how huddled, how hidden her existence had been since . . . when? Since Hank had died? Since Louise had introduced her to the burden he had left for her? Since Alex had made her a heartbroken fool? Since whenever it was, this felt like living again. And she slept night after night, all the way through.

How could she resist? She took the road again to San José. She had thought of it so often in the last year, especially the lovely night in the church and the hacienda with the ruined chapel. This time the plaza was decorated

129

with red, green, and white drapes and swags, spilling from gold medallions embossed with the Mexican eagle, snake, and cactus. The celebration of Independence—September 16th—was the following day. She took the same table in the restaurant on the plaza. The same young woman took an order for *vino tinto* and cocked her head at the sight of Juliet.

"I was here a year or so ago. I remember you. I had great arrabiata," Juliet said.

"How very nice that you came back." And it was nice, more than nice. She didn't picture Alex there with her; the bustle and color seemed to wipe his memory away. An older couple—clearly not Mexican—and a striking woman who could be, came around the corner and took a nearby table. The couple smiled and said hello.

"You're here for a visit?" the older woman asked.

"Yes. I was here once before. Do you live here?"

"We do!" She spoke with infectious cheer. "Did you eat here?"

"Yeah. I had the arrabiata."

"Lasagna's my all-time favorite," the man said.

"Currently I'm having the linguini alfredo every chance I get," added the plump woman. She had grey-streaked hair and wore a pretty, embroidered blouse. "By the way, I'm Judy; this is my husband, Joe; and this is our friend, Zoë."

Juliet introduced herself: Juliet Pierce. "This town is *precioso*," she said.

"Yes, it is," Zoë agreed. "Where do you live?"

"I live in San Francisco, but I'm suddenly thinking I might like to have a place in this area. I'm interested in growing grapes." Juliet listened to herself say this with hardly any amazement. Elena appeared at the table with a glass of red wine. "Oh, yes. I'll take the linguini alfredo."

"We have a guesthouse around the corner, if you're

looking for a place to stay," Judy offered.

"Hi, amigos," Elena said to the group of three, her accent lovely, lilting. "How are we today?" Kisses were exchanged, orders placed.

"There are vineyards around here. Have you seen them?" Zoë asked Juliet. She was an extraordinarily beautiful woman with long, straight black hair, exotic features, and a dress with magenta and red embroidery. Was she the woman from the concert?

"Yes, I've been checking them out. It looks like they're doing well. Do you know of any houses or land for sale here in San José?"

"We call it Itzcui," the man, Joe, said, pronouncing it *Eets-quee*. "Xolo*itzcui*ntle is the name of a hairless dog the Aztecs kept. They're still around. There's one in town."

Judy broke in. "There isn't much land. People don't sell very often here, but Elena—that's Elena serving us— usually knows about real estate. You should talk to her."

"Have you heard about anything, Zoë?" Joe asked.

"Let's see. I heard Enrique has a small field he wants to sell."

Enrique.

So Juliet asked Elena about real estate as she consumed her perfect linguini alfredo. "What do you think you want?" Elena asked. "A house in town, land where you could build?"

"I guess a house with land where I could plant grapes would be ideal. Is there anything like that?"

Thus, Juliet found herself standing again before the grand wreck of the hacienda—La Paloma, The Dove—and knowing that she had wanted this all along. She let Elena introduce it to her as though it were previously unseen. There was the generous porch, more like an outdoor room, with arch-topped columns. To the right was a door to what had indeed been a chapel. It appeared that even more of the roof and wall had fallen. Straight ahead was the door to the interior.

The house was grand and still. Had it been cleaned up a bit? Elena showed her the entry room, about sixteen by twenty, the *sala,* considerably larger with an enormous carved-stone fireplace, the shabby kitchen and another room, perhaps for dining. Toward the front of the house, a door opened to a large bedroom—and its awful bath—that likely shared its right wall with the chapel. It had three high windows looking out toward the town and offering a lovely view of the dome and belfry of the church. The floors were terra cotta tile with old cracks worn smooth. The dining room, kitchen, living room, and entry hall each opened to a wide porch. Red columns supported high arches; philodendron with leaves the size of turkey platters climbed up them.

"Look at this," Elena said, going out through a door in a wall at the end of the porch. On the other side were the huge double doors into the attached barn. It too seemed to have lost more of the roof, but still had great hooks and pulleys hanging from the beams that remained. The earth floor was piled with debris. The house seemed intended for something between mansion and working farm.

Elena led Juliet through the house and across the entry room to another door leading to a north wing. "In this area there's space for maybe three more bedrooms or a big studio. Of course it needs lots of work." There were piles of rubble and wood, another decrepit bathroom.

"It's practically a public-works project," laughed Juliet."

"Pardon?"

"I mean, I agree. Lots of work. What about the

132

land?"

"The hacienda and the land up behind it include a little over five *hectáreas*."

"And there's over two acres to the hectárea, right?"

"Yes, I think so."

They walked through the walled garden with its tangle of un-pruned roses and a twisted tree Juliet didn't recognize. At the back, large double doors opened to a steep, roughly terraced slope planted with corn, tier upon tier. Juliet could imagine the vines. It would look like Tuscany.

"There is more land than just this part you can see," Elena said, pointing up the slope. There is a valley and another ridge. I haven't seen it."

"How much does it cost?" Juliet asked.

"Three million pesos. That's about two hundred eighty thousand, U.S."

"I think I'll take it." Juliet laughed at her own audacity, and Elena joined her in surprise and delight at the prospect of the commission. *She'd take it.* How insane was this. But why not? Maybe this was just a place to stay while she developed her vineyards. Maybe more. I don't care, she thought. I'll figure it out later.

Joe and Judy's B&B was reached through an entry passage about halfway down a street of contiguous colonial facades. One went from the sidewalk to the shady arcade and courtyard through a space wide and high enough to have once admitted horses and carriages. Joe and Judy lived in the part of the house that faced the street. On either side there were rooms for guests. The kitchen and utility rooms were in the rear.

Above the solid double doors that closed Juliet's windowless room, a glass transom admitted light. A second set of doors with glass and sheer curtains for privacy made the room bright when the heavy doors were open. The usual Mexican crescendo of color clashed happily on pillows, bedspread, and wall décor, and a remote ceiling was supported by heavy beams set slightly out of parallel and painted alternately red and blue-green. Since the house had clearly been built when indoor plumbing was not even a gleam in a householder's eye, the bathroom made the room's shape into an L.

Juliet busied herself with mental hacienda-renovation as she lay in bed. She had been awakened before dawn by a barrage of church bells and a volley of rockets—celebrating Independencia—but had quickly fallen back into dreamless sleep. If the bells had tolled the hours, she had missed it. Now awake again, she plotted the order of the improvements. First the wall of the chapel, which threatened to come entirely down, then roof inspection and repair. Next an upgrade of the bathroom in the south wing and replacement of broken doors and shutters. Then she could camp out there, when she was in Itzcui, as construction gradually continued.

Hearing talk and laughter, she got up, dressed, and emerged from her room. Joe and Judy sat at an ornate iron table on the sunny side of the courtyard.

"Good morning!" Judy called. "Sit with us, Juliet. Coffee?"

"Wonderful," Juliet said. The maid poked her head from the kitchen, wished Juliet good morning, and disappeared again. A moment later they heard *"Hola"* at the front door and Zoë came in to take the remaining chair.

"*¡Rosa¡ Otro cafecito. Zoë esta!*" Joe called.

Zoë was dressed in jeans and a huipil—a lavishly embroidered blouse. Today Juliet could see she was probably in her late thirties or early forties. Her black hair was braided with ribbons, looped up behind, and as shiny as hair in a shampoo commercial. Something about the planes of her face looked oriental. She had flashing, intelligent eyes and graceful hands.

"Heaven help you. Elena says you're getting La Paloma," she said to Juliet.

"So you think heaven will be needed?" Juliet smiled.

"You're going to need either that, or all the money in the world."

"Well, it certainly won't be the latter." Juliet avoided Zoë's eyes.

"Oh, don't get me wrong, I'd have it if I could. It really *is* beautiful—that chapel, those lovely arches. My house needed lots of restoration too. The roof on one side had collapsed and the kitchen had to be entirely redone. I managed to keep the old cooking surface with its openings in front for feeding in the wood. Very picturesque. Entirely useless. I'll show you soon. I've also have some photos of your house that are quite good."

"Zoë's a photographer," Judy said. "Very, *very* good. Famous too."

Zoë did not bother with any modest demurral. "Do you speak Spanish?"

"Poorly. I speak Portuguese and it interferes."

"Too bad. My Spanish has gotten fairly good and I find it's essential. So, are you single?"

"My husband died." Juliet had decided the night before that she would admit to being a widow. Respect, protection . . . something like that.

"Oh, my goodness! I'm so sorry," Judy cried. "And you're so young!"

"That's terrible!" Joe exclaimed.

Zoë managed to keep her sympathy under control. "*My* husband died a few months ago—my ex-husband that

135

is. We'd been divorced for quite a while. He got MS after we split up. Thank goodness he had his sister to take care of him. I'm no good at anything like that. Not that I could have dropped everything. I recently lost my little dog, too. She was a shih tzu and the dearest thing. Wasn't she?"

"Yes, yes she was." Judy shook her head in sympathy, but was still looking shocked by Juilet's announcement. She had lived through, and been called on to re-live, every detail of the dog's demise.

"She died in my arms just as the vet came to put her to sleep. I had dreaded calling the vet. They say they don't have the right drugs here. They actually give the animal a shot in the heart and I heard they can leap up and convulse. But she was so old and was suffering so much I didn't feel I had a choice. Well, she died peacefully. I don't think she was in pain when she went.

"So. I came to invite you all to come over this evening. People want to meet you." Zoë nodded at Juliet as the coffees arrived along with a basket of pastries and a plate with pats of butter.

"Thanks, I'd love it," Juliet smiled. She rather liked that Zoë had her own agenda. Grief could still occasionally ambush her if she received too much sympathy in a weak moment.

Zoë drank her coffee hastily. "I have workers these days. Got to get back before they get too creative. About seven? Pepe will be there with his tacos. She was on her feet. "You can bring your vodka if you want," she said to Joe.

"Where do you get wine here?" Juliet asked.

"Ah, well. We usually stock up when we go to town, but Elena and Silvio have some Concha y Toro and such for sale. You, however," she said to Juliet, "are to bring nothing. There will be wine if that's what you like."

"*Buen dia!*" she called as she disappeared out the door.

"You always know you've been visited when she comes by," Joe laughed his big laugh.

"How many foreigners live here?" Juliet asked, feeling unreasonably happy.

"Let's see," Judy said, twisting her mouth sideways. "There's us and Zoë. Randall and Peter, the gay guys; Patty and Ron—they're in their seventies and Ron doesn't go out much. Then there's the Italians: Silvio and Elena, with the restaurant, and Michele and Fabrizia who also have a B&B; Fabrizia's brother, Raul. It makes us feel right at home having Italians around. We used to live in Italy. There's more people who have a place here but just come sometimes. That's all that's here now. Did I forget anybody, Joe?"

"Annette."

"Oh, sure, Annette. She's Canadian and she's also lost her husband." Judy made a sad face. "She has a spectacular renovation project going. You're going to want to consult with her. She's found old iron work, and an antique dealer in Querétaro who has the most wonderful pieces."

"Do you socialize with the Mexicans?" Juliet asked.

"Sure, we have some interesting Mexicans here. Luis. His English is perfect. He's a writer from Mexico City. And Enrique, our doctor. He's wonderful. Passionate about plants, and opera, and the cello. Socorro, who you met last night. She has a million friends—musicians, artists—and entertains all the time. She lives on the plaza. Probably everybody I mentioned will be at Zoë's tonight. Zoë's Spanish is very good, and Joe's is too, but most of our socializing is done in English. At least the part I understand!" Judy barked out a laugh, if anything, bigger than Joe's. "Lots of these Mexicans are totally bilingual—puts us to shame. If you learn some Spanish, they'll love you for it. You're going to need to talk to your workers, too. They won't be speaking any English."

"God, I hope I can learn. I've studied some, but the only person's Spanish I can understand is mine."

"Ha! I know just what you mean," Judy guffawed.

The night before, the three of them had eaten, played multiple games of dominos—Mexican Train—and drunk any number of vodka tonics. Judy and Joe made frequent refreshers and found everything that was said so delightfully funny that soon Juliet had joined them, gasping with laughter and holding her sides. Joe had a leonine head, if lions can have manes that recede over the top and halfway down the back and sides, a smile that spread wide, and a laugh that accompanied a sideways shake of the head, as though the profundity of the world's foibles had overcome him. He had a story a minute. He had worked for the Foreign Service in Italy where preposterous things apparently took place daily.

Around ten, Joe had cocked his head at the sound of the band from the plaza. "Time to go," he said pushing back his chair.

"What is it?" Juliet asked.

"The *Grito* is coming up. Can't miss it."

"What's the Grito?"

"What would you say? 'The Yell?' 'The Cry? The Shout?' Anyway, some fiery oratory at the start of the War of Independence from Spain, delivered in the town of Dolores near San Miguel," Joe explained. "Hidalgo did it, and now the town is called Dolores Hidalgo, and every year it gets repeated all over Mexico."

The three found what must have been the rest of the pueblo already crowded into the plaza. Tuba, trombones, and trumpets were blaring; clarinets were scrambling to catch up—ignoring the nicety of staying in tune. The musicians clustered near the bandstand, which had been usurped by the queens and princesses of the occasion. Half the crowned and gowned were dewy young beauties; half were from the senior center.

"Oh, that is too much," Juliet laughed. "Look at those darling old ladies!"

"They're the queen and princesses of the Third Age," Judy said. "I'm hoping I get a chance some day. When I get old enough!" She laughed at the notion that she wasn't old enough already.

An elegant woman in front of them turned around and greeted Joe and Judy. Judy made the introductions. "Socorro, you must meet Juliet Pierce. She's going to buy La Paloma. Juliet, this is Socorro Barrera."

"A pleasure," Socorro said, shaking Juliet's hand. She began to speak but was interrupted by Joe.

"Okay, here we go," he said. "There's the *presidente*." A man mounted the steps to the gazebo, and the crowd fell silent. From the far side of the plaza an honor guard with flag approached in military step. Cornering smartly, they stomped to attention in front of the bandstand, and passed the flag to the presidente.

"MEXICANOS! VIVAN LOS HEROES DE LA PATRIA!" he cried.

"VIVAN!" the crowd screamed.

"VIVA NUESTRA INDEPENDENCIA!"

"VIVA!" The square erupted.

"VIVA MEXICO!"

"VIVA!" Juliet shouted with the best.

"VIVA MEXICO!"

"VIVA!"

"VIVA SAN JOSE XOLOITZCUINTLE!"

"VIVA!!"

When the presidente waved the flag wildly over the cheering populace, Juliet felt her eyes fill with tears. Who could not love this place. The band struck up the National Anthem and everybody had a good loud sing with references to *guerra*—war—being about as far as Juliet could understand. She joined in the salute, arm and hand rigid across the heart. Then came the church bells and rockets, the cheers and whistles—a total blowout.

"This seems more meaningful than the way we celebrate the Fourth with the 1812 Overture. Where did we get that? The lifting of Napoleon's siege of Moscow?" Juliet commented to Joe and Judy as they walked home. The bells were still ringing.

"I guess it's the bangs and bongs. Nostalgia for canon and big, loud church bells," said Joe. "We've got no lack here. Church bells, that is. This is a fine place to live. You arrived on a good day, Juliet."

The following morning, after Zoë had issued her invitation and left the breakfast table, and Juliet was finishing her second cup of coffee and a big plate of *huevos rancheros*, the same band started up again. Those clarinets were unmistakable.

"Oh, that'll be the parade," Judy said. "Let's go watch."

The street was full of parents and little costumed children hurrying toward the plaza. The girls were in bright peasant costume—long, colored skirts, white blouses, and striped *rebozos* holding baby dolls against their backs. Their dark hair was braided with ribbon, and the braids joined in a loop, as Zoë's had been. The tiny boys wore white pajamas, sombreros, and crossed cartridge belts over chests, against which rested crudely carved wooden rifles.

The band played while pickup trucks with Mexican flags flying from antennae jockeyed to organize themselves in a line. Horses carrying stolid-looking farmers waited patiently to one side.

"Those boys are dressed like Pancho Villa and the girls are Adelita, one of the female fighters," Judy said. "I guess this will be the tenth Día de la Independencia parade we've seen. What do you think, Joe?"

"I think you've gotten your fiestas mixed up, old girl. Pancho Villa and Adelita were in the revolution. We celebrate that in February."

"But the kids dress the same way, don't they?"

"True. But remember at that parade some of them dress like the *ricos* who are being overthrown, in cutaway coats and top hats and frilly dresses and parasols."

Judy had a laugh at herself. "What would I do without you? But anyway, it must be ten years now, don't you think?"

While Joe and Judy counted up their years of parade watching, Juliet noticed a strikingly handsome man on the other side of the plaza. Aristocratic. Erect in his posture. He was shaking hands with a group of men who were standing about, clearly going through the elaborate politeness rituals required in Mexico, no matter how often one met, no matter how urgent a communication to be delivered: *Good day. How are you? How is your family? Pardon, the church is on fire.* He had to be the announcer from the cello player's concert.

"There, Juliet, that's Luis. Isn't he gorgeous?" Judy said as she saw the locus of Juliet's attention.

"He certainly is," Juliet agreed.

Zoë ran up with a camera. "I need 'Juliet: The Beginning.'" She took four rapid shots, danced around Juliet to get a better background, and took four more. It

141

was impossible not to smile when Zoë came on the scene. Then she swung toward the little children and sat right down on the ground, challenging the tiny freedom fighters to posture fiercely in front of her, and making the girls giggle.

She turned back to Juliet, Joe, and Judy. "How could I forget it was a holiday? Of course the workers didn't come. I'm sorry I'm not going to be able to show off finished tiling in the guest bath."

"It seems there's no way I can get anything done on my purchase either," Juliet said.

"No, no way. When I was buying my house, the nightmares of bureaucracy I sank into! I'll tell you all about it someday. Half of the house had actually never been separated from the *ejido*, the old collective farm—there was a family dispute—"

"Mexico has collective farms? Like in Russia?" Juliet asked.

"Close enough. There was a constitution that broke up the haciendas and gave the land—Oh! There's Luis. I have to invite him for tonight. See you."

Luis had strolled off from the edge of the plaza. Zoë ran after him, threading her way through costumed children. He stopped and kissed her cheek, and they walked on together in animated conversation. Looks like they're together, Juliet thought. What a gorgeous couple. She remembered the ejido.

"Will my hacienda have ejido problems, do you think?"

"I don't know," Joe said. "Better ask Elena about it this evening."

"To tell you the truth," Judy grinned, "I get tired of waiting for these things to start."

Joe laughed. "They'll mill around for an hour or so

142

with nobody the least bit antsy and not one child needing to go to the bathroom. Then they'll march four blocks to the park, present the colors, and sing the anthem. Then everybody will go home."

"Don't forget the rockets," Judy said. "Did you hear them this morning?" she asked Juliet.

"Yeah, and now that you remind me, I blessedly *did* forget the rockets."

"Just wait. There will be plenty more where those came from."

In the end, the three hung out on the street with everybody else and waited the hour, periodically flinching when rockets went off. Annette, the Canadian with the gorgeous house and antique-dealer connections, presented herself and waited with them. She was a handsome middle-aged woman, thrilled to hear that La Paloma was going to be taken in hand.

"You have to let me come over and put my two cents in, Juliet. Oh, I think Beto is finishing up a job. He did some really good work for me when I was doing the heavy construction. Do you want me to introduce you?" Juliet did.

So the day passed with dazzling color, loud music, darling children, and many warm greetings. Itzcui felt as though it could be home.

The church bells proclaimed that it was seven exactly while Joe, Judy, and Juliet were strolling the three blocks to Zoë's house. It was built on the usual colonial plan: a square of rooms opening to a porch, all surrounding a courtyard. The deep porch was strung with colored lights; clusters of sofas, chairs and tables were arranged here and there. One table held tequila and wine bottles, glasses and ice. Nuts and cheeses filled fanciful bowls and plates. A mobile taco stand had been rolled into the courtyard and the perfume of caramelized onions wafted from it. Laughter and rapid-fire Italian competed with English chatter as Zoë waved from across the space and came to greet them, breathtaking in a shimmering full-length dress with multicolored flowers on lace-edged tiers.

"Wow, that dress is dazzling," Juliet said.

"From Chiapas. A town called Chiapas del Corso. It looks like Frida Kahlo's closet down there. Come meet our Italians."

"You told me no one would dress up," Juliet whispered to Judy as they followed Zoë across the courtyard.

Judy laughed. "Zoë dresses for all of us."

Juliet already knew Silvio and Elena of course. Michele and Fabrizia remembered her too—she hoped they didn't resent her switching B&Bs—and Fabrizia's brother Raul gave her a smoldering greeting. My God. There was a pretty man. Dark curly hair, an upper lip that turned nearly back on itself, a face sculpted, smooth and rosy. He seemed to know he had a Tom Cruise sort of smile, and he turned it on her. But then they were all beautiful, the Italians, and full of laughter and whispered in-jokes, and all spoke English when required.

Socorro arrived. She told Juliet how wonderful it was that she was getting La Paloma, and seemed to mean it. "You make me think of my daughter," she said. "Come to me if you need any help." She was in her sixties, slim and beautiful in her beige silk dress and heavy gold jewelry. She brought a pretty niece and a bizarre dog with her. Juliet was enchanted.

Randall and Peter—the gay guys who Juliet had also met at the parade—burst in, followed by handsome Luis, and Enrique, the warmly remembered cello player. Annette

144

greeted Juliet and introduced Patty and Ron, the older couple who Judy had said didn't socialize much.

All clustered around the taco stand where its owner, Pepe, served up barbecue, roast pork, and tongue on little tortillas with cilantro, salsa, shredded cabbage, and the perfect onions. The guests poured themselves shots, sipped wine, and enjoyed themselves in three languages.

Randall and Peter toured Juliet around the arcade to look at Zoë's photographs. They were very high contrast, the blacks and whites hitting all the zones. The subjects were Mexicans—young and old, rich and poor.

"A lot of these are new," Randall said. "Zoë's just back from Chiapas. I think these are some of the best I've seen her do."

"We bought a print of this one," Peter added as they stood before a study of a little girl in her first communion dress. She was illuminated by an intense ray of light that had found her in a dark doorway.

"Oh, it's wonderful," Juliet exclaimed.

"My God, yes it is," said Peter, clasping his hands. Peter's hair was blond with more than a little gray. His eyes had a slightly surprised look and his chin was conspicuously taut. A clearly expensive linen shirt encased his soft middle. Randall was shorter, with dark hair and a neat goatee. He wore white loafers that looked to have been made from debutants' kid gloves.

"Where does she show her work?" Juliet asked.

"Oh, all over. Mexico City, New York, Paris. She's *very* successful. Zoë! Can we show Juliet the house?"

"Of, course. Not the studio."

"I wouldn't dream of it, darling."

More photographs hung in the living room, bedrooms, kitchen. There was a cluster of pictures of La Paloma in a guest room. "I hope this will all be a romantic

145

memory someday," Juliet said as she studied an image of sunlight lancing through the ruined roof. "I'd better buy one of these. Or maybe this one. Maybe one of each."

"What are you going to do with the place?" Randall asked.

"Repair it, then experiment with grape varieties. That's what I want to do. Grow grapes. Make wine."

"Oh! That's too perfect. We'll all be over to help you taste. Have you made wine?"

"I grew up with it. My father is a famous vintner in Napa Valley. Have you heard of Quinta da Agostinho? Yes? That's his work. I just got a degree from the University of California so I'm ready to try my hand. I think there are good grapes being grown in the area."

"*Pues,* Miss Juliet, we're going to enjoy watching you!"

Outside under the colored lights, a vigorous discussion was going on: "I think it's some kind of plot. Swine flu was a way to get attention off the drug dealers so the U.S. could protect Calderón," Patty said emphatically.

"But, Patty," Socorro said, "if the idea was the return of the tourists because they forgot the violence, making up swine flu was a foolish plan." She took a drag from her cigarette and a sip of her wine. She smiled, not unkindly.

"I don't think swine flu is real. Don't you know how many people die from ordinary flu every year?" Patty seemed to be both an assertive and disorganized thinker.

Annette gently diverted her. "Poor Mexico. If it's not one thing, it's another. I'm so mad at my family back in Canada. They call me every few days to see if I've been kidnapped."

"I didn't know they were that scared there too! I always think people are more sensible in Canada," Patty said.

Peter threw up the hand that wasn't cupping his wine glass and groaned. "My mother carries on the same way! It's a terrible problem because I need to get her down here so I can look out for her—she's eighty-seven!—and she's sure she'd be murdered in her bed."

Randall was deep in conversation with Enrique who hung his head slightly and looked at Randall over his glasses. She listened in.

"Jes, and then I was in Russia," Enrique said, his accent turning all his "Ys" into "Js."

"You've been to Russia?"

"Jes, and the food was so good."

"The food in Russia? Surely you jest. What, cabbage soup? Borscht?"

"Jes, the caviar of the sturgeon."

"Oh, you had caviar!"

"Jes, caviar."

"Enrique, you care so much about endangered species, how could you eat caviar?" Randall teased.

"Jes, the caviar. It was *good*." He rolled his eyes for emphasis; his understanding of English had apparently failed somewhat. "Jou know? I feed from the past and when I remember, it nourishes me."

Randall glanced at Juliet and raised his eyebrows as though to say, "Remarkable, huh?"

Enrique turned toward her. "Juliet! I must say how good it is that jou will be joining us here. I have heard that La Paloma will be jours. Jou know, I am family with the old owners. No, not own it, I do not own it. No. But we are all family here. I like very much to talk to people at times who are not knowing my family. Ha!"

"I agree. I love a fresh start."

"You must forgive me if I doubt that one so young

147

needs that. But, we will try to help."

"Do you know the history of the hacienda?"

"It was built by the Domínguez family where I am related by my mother. I think perhaps in the eighteen hundred, late eighteen hundred. They were part of the famous and ancient family of that name in Querétaro. At sometime during the revolution it went to the Sánchez family. Perhaps they killed the Domínguez."

"Goodness!"

"Jes, there was many violent things then. The old people of the pueblo remember La Paloma in *mil novocientos*, 1940. A *hacienda de ganado*—cows."

"Was the pueblo called San José Xoloitzcuintle when the hacienda was built?" Juliet pronounced the X like an H, as Joe had.

"Jes, but we say Xolo." He pronounced it *Sholo*. "There is a *códice Azteca*, an Aztec book, that tells the names of the pueblos that must send things to Moctezuma—"

"Tribute?"

"*Sí*, tribute. One of the villages is Xoloitzcuintle. That is the name of a dog. The *Aztecas* fed them corn and ate them, or kept them for *mascotas*."

Randall, who was listening, leaned in. "*Mascota* means pet."

"Thank jou, Randall. And when jou die, jou need a xoloitzcuintle to find Mictlán, the place for the dead. That is why the old ones put the clay dogs with the dead."

"That is so interesting, Enrique. I bought a copy of those dancing dogs."

"I think so they were found in Colima. Where is Socorro's Xolo? There he is." The strange dog was standing near the taco stand watching Pepe intently. It had a large head and stocky body and was nearly hairless except for a ridge along its backbone. Its skin was dark grey. It wasn't very attractive.

"That's a xoloitzcuintle?"

"Jes. Socorro calls it Xolo like Frida Kahlo called her dog."

"I heard you play your cello last year. It was wonderful."

"Jou were here before? I am *so* glad we made jou come back!" Enrique smiled so warmly that Juliet melted and almost teared.

At that moment Judy, with vodka-tonic enthusiasm, dashed up and pulled her away. "Luis says he hasn't met you!"

As they reached the opposite side of the courtyard, Luis rose from his seat beside Zoë and extended his hand.

"Juliet, our new *hacendada*," he said with a little bow. "Luis Zaragoza, at your service. You will find that I am your neighbor. Your closest neighbor. I rent the little red house near your gate." Luis had dark eyes and shiny black hair, worn a little long. His lips curved in a warm smile.

"That's lovely, well, for me. I may ask you for too much help. You write don't you?" Juliet asked.

"Come. Sit here," Luis said, pulling up another chair. "I am a writer, yes. You will find me sitting in front of my computer looking as though I am doing nothing but staring at the wall, and since that will likely be the case, you must not hesitate to ask me anything. It will be my pleasure to tell you my opinion."

Zoë laughed. "You, Luis, are more discreet with your opinion than anyone I know."

"The problem is that I have many fewer opinions than most, especially you."

"I will take that as a compliment to my active mind, and not take offense at your uncharacteristic jab."

"Interesting opinions, of course. I apologize," he

assured her, as a slight frown appeared on Zoë's brow. He turned back to Juliet. "So, I have been told that you wish to grow grapes; that you will revive the great tradition of the Franciscans who came to Mexico from Spain. Our priest will be hoping that you will donate wine for the mass and that the requirement that not a drop be left in the chalice will be his pleasure."

"I'm afraid he will have to wait some years to find out, but I thank you for the suggestion that I could give wine to the church. Let's see, one bottle per Sunday? Is that enough? That's about . . . between four and five cases a year."

"Perhaps the wine would ingratiate you with the parishioners too. I might consider going to church myself." Luis smiled at her. She smiled back.

"What sort of books do you write?"

"I write very obscure books. People call them 'experimental' when they are being kind. Just now I am writing about a priest—you will be wondering if I talk about anything besides the church—a priest who becomes convinced that the devil is living in a storeroom behind the vestry. His sermons become very strange, as he is addressing them not to the people but to the devil. It is mostly a book of his sermons."

"Could I read your books?" Juliet asked.

"Do you read highly idiosyncratic Spanish?"

"Hardly. Perhaps the day will come."

"I very much hope so."

"I can't read his books either," Zoë said. "I don't know where he gets his words. They aren't in *my* dictionary. I was ashamed to give up, but I did, and I actually read Spanish quite well!"

"The problem is as I have told you, my dear Zoë, I make up those words out of bits that suggest other words.

There is a poem in *Alice in Wonderland*, or rather *Through the Looking Glass*—the Jabberwocky poem—that uses this technique. You might be happy to know I was completely lost when I studied that poem in a course I took." He had directed his attention back to Juliet. "By the way, I know of a secret, hidden place in your new house. Will you let me show it to you?"

"Of course!"

"Come to my house tomorrow, if you are free, and tap me on the shoulder to wake me up at my computer. We will walk over to your hacienda."

"I'm afraid it isn't mine yet."

"We will hope that everything goes smoothly."

"I can bring Juliet over and show her your house," Zoë interjected. "Oh, I forgot that I have to go to San Miguel tomorrow. Maybe you can wait until I get back."

"That is very kind, Zoë, but I'm sure my little red hovel is easy to find. Have you noticed it, Juliet?"

"Yes, I have. I wondered if it had been part of the hacienda since it's the same color."

"Perhaps it was. I don't know its history."

"But tell me—your computer? I realize I haven't even asked if I can get broadband here." Juliet said anxiously.

"Yes, thank God," Zoë sighed, "but only since January. *That* was a wait. They were promising us for—how long? Two years? I was actually considering leaving, it was so difficult to deal with my shows and supplies and publicity. You had to go to the internet café and wait while the kids looked at music videos."

"Yes, we were forgetting how to *Googlear* around here," Luis laughed. "Now we are going to forget how to make conversation."

In the night, Juliet was awakened by a deluge of rain hammering above her and a waterfall not far from her door. It was still raining when she woke again in the gray morning. She, Joe, and Judy ate breakfast under the arcade, as Rosa ran around two sides of it with their coffee and eggs and juice. But when Juliet judged that it was time to go to see Luis, the rain conveniently softened into heavy mist. The street outside Joe and Judy's house faded in the near distance to cloudy obscurity. The pueblo seemed very still.

The little red house was built in a rustic style with a porch across the front. As it emerged from the mist, Juliet could see that one of the three sets of double shutters was thrown open.

"Luis?" she called as she stepped onto the porch.

"I am here," he said from the open room. He met her in the doorway and kissed her on both cheeks. "Did you get wet? Do you need a warm drink?"

"No. It's not really raining." Juliet left Judy's umbrella outside the door, and with Luis's insistence, preceded him into the house. He was dressed much as he had been the night before in a white, collarless shirt of heavy-weave cotton, fastened at the wrists and neck with loops and buttons, and tucked into well-cut khakis.

"My little refuge from the world." He gestured around the simple room. Shutters on the two windows were thrown back. No glass, no screens. A long table in the center of the room served as a desk. It was the sort of old, handmade piece covered with picturesque gouges that sold for thousands in California. There was enough space in one corner for chairs, tables, and lamps. A *ropero*—a cupboard for clothing, open and filled with books—was the only other furnishing. One of Zoë's prints hung on the wall.

Juliet went straight to the books. "Are yours here?"

"Yes, there are mine."

152

She removed a book whose jacket showed Mexican peasants tending a corn field. Luis Zaragoza.

"What does the title mean?"

"A *dicho*—a saying—about money. That which comes easily, goes easily—something like that."

"Easy come, easy go."

"Yes, exactly."

"You are interested in money?"

"In what effect it may have on people's lives, yes."

"What does the book say about that?"

"It says that reversal of fortune, in either direction, is ephemeral in its effects. That doesn't sound very profound, does it. I believe people who win the lottery show as much. I hope my characters bring an interesting twist, but as is my wont, it is in the language that I put most of my . . . investment." Juliet stared at him intently.

"You look at me strangely. What have I said?"

"No, no. Excuse me. You made me think, that's all. Do these farmers have a reversal of fortune?"

"They do. A gringo who is escaping the law in the U.S. buys what they consider to be their land. The story is about the conflict between the ideas, and money, that come from the north, and the values of the indigenous people. It is in a way the story of Mexico, though I do not pretend to have written anything of profound importance on the subject."

"How many books have you written?"

"Six that are published."

"Does this one say it won a prize?"

"Just a small one."

Luis's self-deprecating humor was very appealing and mostly made up for his curious, formal manner of speaking. Was it a result of some quirk in his education, or did it represent an unusually controlled and cautious

153

character? At any rate, judging from the books stacked in piles on the widely spaced shelves, his breadth of reading interest was impressive.

Suddenly the house was whipped with another downpour. Juliet flinched. "My God, that's loud."

"We'll have to shout. We say it's the old ones talking to us."

"That's rather poetic."

"Yes, we have a tendency to be carried away with our romanticism."

Juliet laughed as she ran her finger along the book spines. "And you read in English too. *As I Lay Dying.* Salman Rushdie. Nicholson Baker! Extraordinary."

"Do you know those books?"

"Of course. Cormac McCarthy—*All the Pretty Horses.* I love all these. Well, except for the Faulkner. I have to confess I don't enjoy him as much as I'm sure I should. And I find Rushdie too . . . you know, I'm very tired of magical realism. Oh, dear—the devil. I have shot my mouth off."

"Not everything that happens in my books is possible, but perhaps it is more like allegory. Is allegory acceptable?"

"I have to say yes, don't I?" Juliet laughed nervously. She looked back to the collection. "*La muerte de Artemio Cruz.* I've read that in English. I thought it was wonderful."

"Yes, it is one of my favorites. I am going to be very obnoxious and say that it is better in the Spanish."

"I deserved that."

"What? After what you said about magical realism? I am quite delighted with your ability to know what you do and do not like. I have not heard anyone put Rushdie in that category, and of course, it is perfect. I also feel that

154

Cien años de soledad—One Hundred Years of Solitude—seemed like both the first and last word."

"And you have many by Octavio Paz. *El laberinto de la soledad—Entre la piedra y la flor* ..." Juliet read the titles slowly and carefully.

"Your pronunciation is not at all bad. Those are works that do say profound things about the cultures of the north and south of the Americas."

"*Sor Juana Inés de la Cruz.* That's the nun on the two-hundred peso note, right?"

"Do you know about her? A prodigious intellect, a defender of women's education. One of our most important Mexican thinkers and writers. Those are her poems."

Juliet could feel the heat of Luis's body. His voice was warm and deep, and it spoke of the world she loved best, that of literature and ideas. She hoped desperately that she had not sounded stupid. He smiled at her, turned away from the books, and gestured to the next room.

"And here is my kitchen. My *muchacha* has left me some *birria* for lunch. Would you like to share it with me?" Luis pushed the kitchen shutters half-open. The room brightened slightly.

"If *birria* isn't made from insects or something."

"No, no, it is a nice meat soup made from goats. Served hot. It will warm us."

Juliet glanced into the third room while Luis heated the meal.

"That is my bedroom and there is a bath if you wish to freshen up," he said.

The room was simple. There was a blue and white woven bedspread on the double bed, a leather chair, a large cabinet, more books piled on a side table, a window that framed a view of the hacienda beyond a curtain of falling

155

water. The door of the rustic wooden wardrobe was slightly open. Inside, Juliet could see the sleeves of three shirts like the one Luis was wearing; she moved the door slightly and saw several more. His uniform, apparently.

While they ate at the kitchen table, Juliet asked, "How did you come to live here? Judy told me you were from Mexico City."

"I wanted a quiet place to write. Some place not so expensive. Some place beautiful. And you? You seem to be of an age to be in the thick of life. Why are you thinking of living here? If you don't mind my being so curious."

"It appears that I do things first and ask why later. *Sometimes* it has worked for me. I hope this isn't too crazy, jumping into La Paloma, but I'm sure I can grow grapes here—if it doesn't rain like this every day."

"No, this is unusual. I think your grapes will have lots of sun. Listen, it's stopping."

Luis was too polite to ask about her husband, though Zoë had told him what she had heard, and he had surmised that might have something to do with Juliet liking the idea of exile. He stood and gathered the plates and glasses. "Shall we go over to the hacienda?"

They emerged from Luis's house to a vista that made Juliet gasp. The clouds that had settled in the valley bowl were being chased up the mountainsides by an assertive sun. Individual trees and rocky outcrops were starkly silhouetted against the pale mist one moment, and barely noticeable the next, as new features were singled out higher up. The hacienda was brilliantly illuminated and gorgeous with its emphatic color. The curtain of mist behind it lifted until only the trailing edge of a cloud was snagged on the mountain peak above.

"Is it really possible for me to have such a place," Juliet said in wonder.

She and Luis crossed the footbridge and the lane that ran along the far side of the swollen stream, and passed under the hacienda's impressive gate. A driveway petered quickly into patchy grasses and wildflowers. They climbed the steps and turned toward the chapel.

Inside, rain had left some puddles, but the area behind the altar was dry. There, Luis showed Juliet an iron ring recessed in the floor, barely visible among the broken adobes, pieces of tile, and bits of wood. He used the edge of a board to remove the rubble enough to see the perimeter of a hatch with the ring at one end. Together they hauled the door up and back on its hinges. Musty air rose from a dark space.

"I haven't been down there, though I did bring a flashlight over once. It appears there's a stair that has rotted away. See those bits of wood? I'm afraid I didn't see any treasure."

"Let's hide it so no one gets in there before we can do some exploring," Juliet said excitedly. "Do you think we could drag the altar over it? I'm sure you didn't look well enough. There has to be Spanish gold down there," she laughed. "What a great adventure this house is going to be."

"I'm afraid the space is not likely a secret to the village. *I* found it, *verdad?* This hacienda has been empty for a long time. The owner lives in the United States I think."

"That's what Elena says. I hope my lawyer will find everything in order and the sale can go through. Zoë told me about her problems with the ejido and that made me nervous, but Elena assures me that isn't an issue here. I am already so in love with this place I don't know what I'd do if I couldn't have it."

"I am sure all will be well. I think so. Let's shove this altar back a bit as you wish." It moved with more ease than expected and the door was easily hidden.

"Now I must get back, Luis. Thank you for lunch and showing me this."

"My pleasure, Juliet."

Juliet reclaimed the umbrella and walked up the hill toward the town center. What a lovely man, she thought. Such manners! Such *foreign* manners. Was it possible to really know people whose speech was so courtly and careful? She remembered how impressed she had been with his introduction of Enrique in the church. He clearly was educated and very attractive, but apparently taken by the formidable Zoë. That was almost a relief; Luis was too handsome, too intelligent. Still, how wonderful that there would be someone near who could, and seemed willing to, translate the culture for her. She had the sense that it was out of the question to ask about his life directly, which made her feel her secrets were secure as well. The ridiculously low price she was paying for the hacienda, even considering its semi-ruined condition, would not arouse suspicion as to the size of her resources. She could easily have sold an ordinary house in the U.S. and had that much money. Her vineyards near Ezequiel Montes? She just wouldn't talk about them. If overseeing them meant that she left town frequently . . . well, she'd think of some excuse.

Luis did indeed look at the wall when he returned to his study, but he was thinking of Juliet rather than considering sermons. What a lovely young woman. An exquisite shape, fine skin, and that American enthusiasm for life. She was what they called a "California girl" with sun-bleached hair and guileless blue eyes. Guileless, but deep even so. Not filtered. Educated and well-read, though she looked as though she should be playing volleyball on the beach. Not that she looked silly or stupid. No, no!

Still, her conversation was a surprise. Too bad a non-native speaker would likely never be able to appreciate his writing. He suddenly wanted to know if his work in translation could interest her. He smiled at the possibility that he would be dismissed like Rushdie.

He thought back to his college years in the U.S. where he had learned about Americans—Eastern aristocrats, mid-westerners, and those California types. His four years in the country had given him time to assess the good and the bad. It had opened his eyes to the varieties of the world and made him realize how circumscribed the life that he was expected to live in Mexico was. It had made him rebel. Juliet stirred something in him, reminding him of that freedom he had found so appealing.

Home for Luis was a mansion set in a large walled park in the Polanco district of Mexico City. The estate was the largest private property remaining in a neighborhood that was more and more filled with luxury hotels, boutiques, and the finest restaurants in the capital. If asked, Luis would allow that his father had a store in the city, but the truth was that his father was the owner of the Ferre del Mundo empire—World Hardware. There were eighty-three stores in Mexico City alone, over a thousand in the country, and stores in Guatemala and Costa Rica as well. There was even one in tiny Itzcui—thanks to Luis—remarkably well-stocked for such modest need and much appreciated by the inhabitants.

Miguel Ángel Villarrubia Reyes—Luis's father—had immigrated to Mexico with his parents when they found themselves on the losing side in the Spanish civil war, and President Lázaro Cárdenas had offered refuge. Luis's grandfather had escaped with just enough money to open the first store. The hardware enterprise had already expanded impressively when Miguel Ángel took it over upon his father's death and proved a genius at the gathering of riches.

When Luis was young, it had been assumed that he would be next, but things had taken a different turn. It was his sister, Sofía, who had shown a passion for business, while Luis was reluctant to take his head out of the literary clouds. He had studied English literature and philosophy at Yale; Sofía had done an MBA at Harvard and now worked at her father's right hand. Miguel Ángel had acquiesced gracefully to this surprising twist of family fortune. He was immensely proud of his son, believing that Luis's success in the arts—fame, in fact—raised the family's status to the level the material accumulation deserved. He acquiesced too in Luis's use of his mother's name as nom de plume. *Their* world knew who wrote the books and won the awards, though he couldn't but hope that someday the rest of the world would know that Luis Zaragoza was Luis *Villarrubia* Zaragoza.

Social position loomed as an issue with the elder Villarrubias. In Spain they had been an old and prominent family, but in Mexico they'd had to start over. Miguel Ángel's father, a lawyer before his emigration, proved flexible enough to try his hand at retail, though with some shame. And then fortuity had made him rich and the wealth had opened the ears of Mexico's aristocracy to previous Villarrubia glory in Spain. Now, no family was better situated.

Luis's father had become an art collector with heavy emphasis on gloomy Spanish portraiture. A Velázquez was his principal possession. It was a small portrait of a nun— *Inés de Las Clarisas*—unsigned but well-authenticated. One of his others was by Herrera, the teacher of Velázquez. These somber psychological studies in browns and grays, so perceptive the eye could hardly leave them, contrasted with his collection of brilliant Moorish tile. The most important piece was an ancient tile-topped stone table in the center of the colossal entry hall. Squares of tiles were framed for the house or mounted in the garden. An offering of a pattern he hadn't yet acquired drove him wild; several groupings originally in the Alhambra were in his sights.

No family in Mexico would be anything but thrilled at an alliance, and one of the best had been delighted to have a son marry Sofía. She loved Alejandro very much but it was accepted that he could devote as much time as he wished to polo while she attended to Ferre del Mundo. Someday soon she would have to stop, briefly, and have a child.

But who would Luis marry? His mother had her worries. Her son moved charmingly enough through society but wouldn't settle on any of the girls of his class, and now he had given up the parties, the dinners, the amusements entirely and moved to San José Xoloitzcuintle. Though she wasn't neglected—he never let as much as six weeks go by without a visit—she complained she hardly saw him except when he attended an award dinner or sat on a panel discussion of contemporary Spanish literature in the capital. She had her hopes that he would come back and raise children near her. She always had a suitable choice for a wife seated next to him when his home visits created the occasion for a dinner party. He would kiss his mother and tease her for her transparency.

Even though Sofía would inherit the running of the empire, ownership would be shared, and even now, his father insisted Luis take as much from the business as Sofía did. Luis spent three thousand pesos a month on his little house—under three hundred dollars—and barely touched the rest. He took great care that no one in Itzqui knew who

161

he was.

Despite his resistance to his mother's matchmaking, Luis was lonely. Now at thirty-five he knew he did want a wife, did want those children his mother never failed to mention. He thought of Victoria Contreras who he had taken to the symphony at the Palacio de Bellas Artes when he had last been in Mexico City. Victoria was tall and very slim. She parted her black hair in the middle and pulled it to her nape, showing off the elegant shape of her head. Her hands were pale and expressive, her skin flawless. Luis felt he could look at her forever, but not that he could listen to her. They'd had an affair for a time; she had broken it off because of an engagement that had subsequently ended as well. Her family was no less anxious than Luis's about the issue of marriage. Her brother played polo with Sofía's husband, and she had gushed during the interval over an upcoming tournament at Costa Careyes on the Pacific coast. *Everyone* was going. Fox had a home there. Deepak Chopra as well. She was staying with María Elena and Tigre. Did he know Costa Careyes? Oh, wasn't it beautiful? But didn't he play polo anymore? What a pity!

"But Victoria, I might fall and injure my typing finger."

"Do you write your books with one finger? I never learned to type either. My father tried to get me to help with his law practice correspondence, but he said I was too slow. I was glad. It was so boring. He thinks I don't have enough to do but I don't see anything wrong."

Luis had been raised among the polo brats of Mexico City and couldn't remember when he hadn't known Victoria, but he thought he would go out of his mind if he had to live that life, or indulge a wife who did. But what *did* he want? When he was writing, which he nearly always was, he didn't question whether he was leading a meaningful life.

What sort of woman would give him that space, and lead a contented life herself? He needed a woman like Sofía—his clever, enthusiastic, engaged sister. A woman who, also like Sofía, would find his money irrelevant. Of course he hid who he was. Any person in Mexico would be stupefied by the prospect of befriending the Ferre del Mundo family, never mind marrying into it.

What would his mother think if he brought home a woman like Juliet? Not that he could without giving himself away . . . but what would she think? Was she so distressed by his anti-social life that even a Juliet would look like a savior? Was she desperate enough to accept a gringa, likely of no family? Perhaps she was. Luis shook his head with a short laugh. How had his mind gotten all the way to marriage?

Perhaps it was because Juliet was a widow. He was traditional enough to be titillated by that condition—a woman sexually experienced but blameless, freshly chaste, deprived and alone, needing a man. And he was liberal enough to laugh at himself for such old fashioned ideas of women's sexuality.

Her purposefulness was intriguing. A winemaker—excellent profession. Randall had told him she had an advanced degree. He found himself resolved to pursue the possibilities, though Zoë was not likely to be pleased.

Another woman with purpose: Zoë. An exciting artist, clever and bold—Luis liked that she'd speak her mind and that what she had to say was so original. Beautiful, obviously, though rather too self-involved. She was four years older—that was nothing—and had been amicably divorced from a man who, she reported, had tired of her energy and globe trotting, as she had tired of his preference for the sedentary. It had occurred to Luis that his indolence might have been the first signs of the disease

163

that ultimately killed him, though Zoë had dismissed the idea. She was not one for much self-examination, or for guilt. Nevertheless the sexual temptation had been strong and the invitation clear. Luis had hesitated, but Zoë's lure had been too much for him.

And yet she had proved strangely uninteresting as a sexual partner, as though her animated conversation, exotic clothes, and artistic skill were the limit of her passionate connection with the world. He knew she regarded him as highly desirable and herself as a suitable match for a famous author, as the only inhabitant of Itzcui who could match his intellect and charisma. They had been lovers for two years, but Luis's visits to her candle-lit bedroom were becoming more widely spaced. He suspected she was sleeping with Raul, and he was ready for it to be over.

So now Juliet would come into their little community. She was buying in with some resources left by this departed husband, or perhaps by her family. How much? It was of no interest to him. Her delight at the hidden room, her admitted impulsive character, her soft femininity—these did interest Luis. He strolled out onto the porch and looked over at the hacienda. He would soon have a neighbor he wanted very much to know better.

CHAPTER SIX

Juliet's purchase of the hacienda took place in what was, for Mexico, record time. She did however miss the harvest near Hermosillo, and was in danger of missing California's too, when at last she headed north. Gradually, on the long trip back, the idea of some time in Mexico began to evolve toward a greater commitment. Her plans entertained her as she drove. She remodeled and furnished her rooms, planted her terraces, imagined the morning walk to the *tienda* or to the restaurant for a cafecito, with the colorful village around her. She wouldn't be lonely. All those people she'd met were unusual and interesting, and few enough to relish a newcomer.

Luis had translated a document related to the sale for her; they had sat across from each other at a dinner party where Zoë left no space in the conversation for them to speak; and an appointment with a notary had made it impossible to accept his invitation to see a waterfall. Then Luis had left on a trip. That had perhaps been just as well.

She would have to break the news to her father that

she was going to be spending some time very far away. There would be much emphasis on the ease of the flights back and forth. Perhaps with boats and homes and staff disposed of, she would retain the indulgence of chartering planes. He would see—she had many pictures of the pueblo and La Paloma—and he would love it, though her mother would have loved it more. Juliet decided to bring her there in spirit by transporting her library to the hacienda.

Her mother's collection of books had filled shelves in the living room, her bedroom, and down a hall. She had believed that should a child have a moment of boredom, a fine library must be at hand, and that tactic had made a reader of Juliet. She had gone through the children's classics and moved on to those of the adult world. When a Nobel in Literature was awarded, the work of Mafouz, Saramago or Coetzee, Garcia Marquez, Grass or Naipaul was placed there beside Solzhenitsyn, Sartre, Mann and Undset, and beside the un-Nobeled Byatts, McPhee, Durrell, James, Proulx, Pagels, and Seth, to name a few. Juliet and her mother had had their own world of reference, of allusion, of name-that-literary-fact games. Her mother had died with much satisfaction in Juliet.

But after her mother was gone and Shirley had come, the library was seen as décor that narrowed the hall and collected dust. Juliet had removed the entire collection to San Francisco where it now sat in boxes in the basement. Now she intended to make a home for it, have the books packed for shipping and prepare shelves for them at La Paloma.

On the drive back, she also made the decision to merge her vineyard, Clos August, with Quinta da Agosthino. Her father would be surprised, since she had insisted so on keeping them separate. There would be things to be put in storage and things to sort and pack. The soil and water samples had to go immediately to UC Davis for analysis, and the Sacramento condo had to go on the market. The quarterly conference with the Nibels was coming up. She'd be putting the final nail in the coffin of her suitability by announcing she'd be spending time in Mexico. She'd be lucky to be out in two months, even with Sean to manage the transition. Would it be the time to give him up when she was through?

At some point that fall, as she put the plans she'd made on the drive in place, and with the loose ends resisting her efforts to tie them down, Juliet realized she'd need to stay for the December quarterly. She had huddled with Fred, decided to let go her chief financial advisor, and promote his assistant—with whom she'd developed a good relationship—in his place. Her reports would now have to reach her in Mexico. Getting phone, fax, and computer would be an immediate need. She had made arrangements to divest entirely in pharmaceuticals and to go deeper into alternative energy. She hired Bill, a quirky genius from Willits, to evaluate environmental projects. The Falcon was sold; the pilots went with it to the new owner. The Nibels were informed that the March quarterly would be held in Mexico City, and Sean was given three months notice, severance that would enable him to reconsider Peters Academy, and the assurance that the door of La Paloma was always open to him and Rafe.

Juliet was filled with enthusiasm as she finally made her departure in a new long-bed pickup, piled high. The truck held many boxes labeled "books." Some actually contained a part of her library, some her favorite Quinta da Agostinho cabernet sauvignon, 1999. She hoped to get the wine over the border without discovery since she had no import permit. Strange that she exported by the *tonelada,* but

167

could lose her fine wines for want of a permit if they were discovered. In addition she was carrying computers, file cabinets, her grandmother's carved rosewood chair, family photos, catalogues, three large oriental rugs, and four ruby-red glass vases made in Puebla—the only Mexican objects in the Pacific Heights collection—now going home.

She met with Señor Reyes at the northern vineyards to inspect the acid injection devices that would prevent mineral-rich well water from crusting over the drippers. She crossed the mountains and sped down the toll roads toward her new home. Spanish language CDs played in the truck. She talked out loud to them and made herself carry on conversations in hotels and Pemex stations. Sometimes she received blank stares in return, sometimes a waterfall of Spanish—which was just as bad—but now and again she understood a few words in time to make a response. She worked on door-openers such as *muy amable* and *mucho gusto*, useful for acknowledging the great kindness and pleasure in which encounters were always steeped. Juliet thought of Luis's polite phrases. He may have spoken in English, but translated Mexican sensibility.

She pulled into Itzcui about eleven one night. When Joe finally opened to her knock, it was with hugs and kisses. In her room she fell into a deep slumber and only came to awareness briefly as the town found another six a.m. occasion to ring bells and set off rockets. This time it was to honor the Virgin of Guadalupe.

After breakfast, Juliet's first visit was to Annette to deliver a ceramic bowl she'd bought as a thank-you gift. They had talked frequently by phone and Annette had been very helpful in obtaining approval for Juliet's telephone installation, and in lining up a crew to work at La Paloma. She would have Beto, Juan Diego, Guadalupe, and Marcelino—two masons, two helpers—for the work.

Annette said Guadalupe, or Chango as he was nicknamed, was a slightly goofy teenager and might or might not work out, but the rest were experienced and solid, if you could overlook a few too many Monday morning "colds" that Juan Diego was subject to. It would be best to dock his pay, she advised, if it happened too often. Annette called Beto to arrange a meeting at the hacienda for eleven. Juliet said Joe had volunteered to translate.

"That should be *some* help," Annette said, "though his Spanish leaves lots to be desired."

"Judy said his Spanish was good."

"I'm not sure she could tell. Joe tends to say *strada* for *calle*," Annette laughed.

"Well, his Spanish has to be better than mine," Juliet sighed. "I lie awake at night trying to think how to say raise high the roof beam, carpenters."

"You can rely on Beto to know the local building techniques, and if something isn't the way you want it, just have them do it over. They'll knock it down and have it back up the same day. They'll never bat an eye. Though, why should they? You're paying!"

Juliet laughed. "By the way, my deed says the hacienda is part of the patrimony of Mexico. I understand I can't make changes that aren't compatible with the style. How do I know what's allowable and what isn't? Is someone going to check?"

"The town authorities might check just out of curiosity, eh? I don't think they'll give you any trouble unless it starts looking like the Pompidou Center."

"I've been thinking that, since the wall of the chapel has to be put back up, I'd like to have an oval window high up—what they call an ox-eye window. I've seen them in books. But of course it would be on the front of the house and would really change the appearance."

"Yes, but in a very traditional way. That would be fabulous. I'd go for it."

"I think that's where I need to start—with the wall of the chapel and the roof over it and the bedroom. Keep the place from falling down even more."

"Good idea."

Back at the B&B, Juliet and Joe shared another cup of coffee, and talked about adobes, beams, roof tiles, tools, and the convenience of Ferre del Mundo. When it was nearly time to meet the workers at the hacienda, they walked over. They encountered Luis on his porch.

"Julieta, my neighbor," he called. He came down to kiss her cheeks and shake Joe's hand. "Welcome back. My muchacha has already told me that you arrived in town. Joe, how are you today? How is Judy?"

As Luis joined them for the house inspection Juliet asked his opinion of adding the oval window to the chapel wall. They gazed at the façade, eyes squinted. "I think it will be very interesting. If it sits higher than the tops of those windows, I believe it will look quite good," Luis said.

A pickup arrived and then another. Juliet met her crew. Luis made a speech about how much the young señora would be relying on their experience and knowledge. They nodded gravely and pronounced themselves to be "at her command" and "with her permission" they would inspect the chapel wall. There followed a torrent of commentary among them, with Luis interjecting this and that, and Joe deferring to him, nearly as lost as Juliet. "As Zoë said, I'm going to need divine intervention," Juliet whispered to him out of the corner of her mouth.

At last the conference wrapped up. Luis gave a report. "I have explained to them about the window. They feel this part of the wall here should be pulled down to the foundation before they build it up again. They will arrange to have eight hundred adobe bricks delivered and think they can be here by tomorrow. Now they will look for a place to dig the earth for putting between the adobes, remove the loose bricks, and start to clean the floor."

"We must talk about their pay," Juliet said.

"I believe masons are receiving 2000 pesos a week and the assistants, 1800."

"That's going to be 3800 . . . 7600 . . . wow, about $700 a week for the four."

"It is fair, don't you think?" Luis said.

"I'm ashamed it's so little."

"That's the union rate, however. So shall I make that offer?"

"Yes, of course."

The crew nodded again. "*Bien*," Beto said.

"*Señores*," Juliet began. She had rehearsed a little speech that, translated, went: "I wish that you have patience as I speak your language. Please speak very slowly and say when I do not make yourself clear. Perhaps Luis will help when do not understand. I know that your work is very good. Thank you."

"No, no thanks to you, señora. At your command!" Luis translated as Beto and the rest bowed and smiled. The work had begun.

"Luis, you must not let my work interfere with your writing. I think you are being too *amable*."

"I will stand back whenever you wish, Julieta, but I am happy to be of assistance. It is very thrilling for me to see La Paloma begin to fly."

"I'm heading back," Joe said. "I think you are in good hands." Juliet kissed him and Luis hoped that he would go well. They watched him cross the yard.

"I should have driven him over," Juliet said. "It

171

doesn't look to me as though the circulation in his legs is very good."

"No, I think his health is not good," Luis agreed. He called to Joe and asked if he wanted a ride, but Joe waved him off with thanks. He needed the exercise, he said. They watched him head slowly up the hill toward the plaza.

"My pickup will have to be unloaded," Juliet said, "and I don't know where I can store my things."

"Does this door lock?" Luis indicated the door to the wing on the left. "It looks as though the lock's been broken. Perhaps we could install a new one. Why don't we walk over to Ferre del Mundo for a lock, and then have some lunch at La Mina Real?" Juliet tried to damp her delight as she accepted the invitation.

Lunch on the plaza was no place for a private conversation, had one been wanted. Luis was on his feet every few moments, greeting, introducing. Juliet had "the great pleasure" to see Enrique, to meet the man who would some day be connecting her to the sewage system, and the woman who would set up her electricity account. Randall came by and approved the ox-eye window, and Judy passed with vegetables from the *tienda*.

"Did you finish your sermons, Luis?" Juliet asked in a quiet moment.

"Nearly. I have been working a very long time; I'm a slow writer. I think this may be my best book. However, I have been staring, not at the wall, but out of the door to see when you would return. I was beginning to wonder if you would."

Juliet laughed at his flattery. "It was very complicated to get away. My father is not at all happy that I'm doing this. I had to put some things in storage and buy the pickup. I thought about staying through Christmas but my dad has remarried and doesn't really need me. My mother passed away a few years ago." Juliet paused. "You may have heard that my husband also died."

"I am very sorry to hear of your losses, Julieta. How long ago did your husband . . . ?"

"It's just over three years now."

"Did he have an illness?"

"No, it was an accident."

"Ah, it was sudden. That is especially hard. I'm sorry. How do you have the courage to come to a foreign country?"

"I think it will help me get on with my life. I've taken my degree in winemaking and this place looks good for trying out what I've learned. I don't want to go to work for a vineyard in the U.S. What about you, Luis?"

"What would you like to know?" He smiled.

"Well, let's see. When did you start writing?"

"I published my first story when I was twelve."

"My! And where did you learn to speak English so well?"

"I had the chance to go to school in the U.S."

"Where did you go?"

"I went to Yale."

"Yale! Very fancy!"

Luis tried to minimize the incongruity of the elite school with his humble façade. "I was fortunate to have a scholarship. I think they liked that I was publishing already. I loved my time there. It did everything a university is supposed to do for you. I learned and I thought and I smoked marijuana."

Juliet laughed. "And your poor parents got their boy back ruined."

"Fortunately, I have a sister who is everything they could want, especially since she is married—though she doesn't yet have children. But my parents are proud of me even if I'm not married. Ah, Zoë! *¿Qué tal?* What are you doing today?" Luis stood as Zoë appeared at the table.

"I'm on my way to the bakery. What are you two doing? You look thick as thieves."

"We are only as thick as builders, whatever that may mean. Beto and the crew are at work already at La Paloma. Juliet and I are buying a lock for her door," Luis said.

"It looks like you're eating."

"Just a quick bite."

"Sit with us, Zoë." Juliet pushed a chair back, wishing to erase the impression that she and Luis were thick as thieves. "Have an espresso with us."

"All right. Luis, I found my copy of the Saramago. I'll give it to you if you drop around."

"I will come soon, Zoë. I must read it."

"Which is it?" Juliet asked.

"*The History of the Siege of Lisbon* by José Saramago. I am in love with his books, but I have not read that one. Some people compare my books to his, which makes me feel very flattered. I don't read Portuguese well and Zoë has an English translation."

"I've read it," Juliet said. "I know a little Portuguese too—though I also read the book in English.

"Really!" Luis's face brightened. Zoë's didn't. "How do you know Portuguese?"

"I worked for a year in a vineyard in Portugal. The truth is that I don't know how to say much more than winery-related things. Lucky for me the word for grape is the same in Portuguese and Spanish. I saw the movie they made from Saramago's *Blindness* when I was in California. Have you seen it?" Juliet asked.

"Ah, movies are our great lack here." Luis shook his head sadly.

"A movie. That could hardly catch Saramago's

language, could it," Zoë interjected with a touch of scorn that failed to have its intended effect. Luis continued to watch Juliet.

"No, the language couldn't come through," Juliet said to her, "but that book actually had a plot. Anyway, I liked it. But *The History of the Siege of Lisbon* is my favorite. They'll never make a movie of that."

"Look, Zoë, we will have another person in town to talk with about books! We have to keep ourselves stimulated, Julieta. It's a constant struggle. Do you know that Saramago never attended university? He claims that accounts for his special language. It makes me worry that I studied too much."

"He must be talking about his punctuation. I can't remember. I think he only uses commas. No quotation marks for dialogue or 'he said, she said' either. Do you write that sort of thing?" Juliet asked.

"Saramago's punctuation is too idiosyncratic for me to copy it, though I might wish I'd thought of it first. I do allow interminable paragraphs. But I am known, if at all, for my made-up words."

"If your language is too difficult for us to read in Spanish, when will you give us translations?" Juliet asked.

"I do sometimes think of translating the books, but there is a certain anti-English movement in the Spanish-speaking countries; translations will force me out of the club I fear. Still, it would be fun for me to try to find English equivalents for my new words. I already think about it, and occasionally something occurs to me, but I'm not sure if I could be successful. I really am a Spanish-language snob, as well."

"An agreeable snob," Juliet said, sounding more flirtatious than she had intended.

"Don't insult him," Zoë said. "He likes his

snobbery served cold. It's just hard to tell with that incessant politeness."

"Ah, Zoë." Luis gave a tight smile. "You know me too well."

Zoë looked at Luis with a cocked eyebrow, started to speak, but apparently thought better of it. She beamed a smile of somewhat inappropriate radiance and put her hand briefly on his arm.

"Okay, too long to wait for an espresso. I'm off for my bread before they run out. Goodbye, Juliet. See you later, Luis." She performed another of her abrupt exits.

Juliet watched Zoë cross the plaza, her rose skirt swinging under a red and green poncho. She looked down at her own jeans and scooped-neck tee. Luis wasn't watching Zoë go; he was peering inside the restaurant for Elena. Still, maybe she should kick it up a bit.

It was a few days later when Zoë saw Luis on the plaza and called for him to wait. "Please come over and eat with me tonight," she said when he'd turned back and they'd met by the fountain.

He kissed her cheek. "How lovely you are looking today. I would love to come."

"I have some new prints to show you and it's been too long since we talked."

"I agree." Luis thought of the Saramago book, but didn't mention it; the discussion at the restaurant had been awkward. "Shall I bring wine?"

Luis arrived at seven and found the house, and Zoë, dressed for the occasion. Candles were on every surface. Zoë had one side of her hair tied up with gardenias; the other fell as a silky rope over her shoulder. She served oyster bisque, salad, and a delicate custard.

"I've never had a more elegant dinner," Luis said as he peered through his wine at a garnet-colored candle flame.

"There isn't really anyone else here that one wants to put out pearls for," she said seriously.

"You are sounding a little dissatisfied, Zoë. Surely Socorro and Randall and Peter are nothing like swine. And our Italians have fine palates, even if a little heavy on the preference for pastas." He wanted to mention Raul whose senses were likely being well-stimulated but was too polite, and indifferent.

"You are being obtuse, Luis. You know your eye for beauty is special. You've been too preoccupied to visit with me. We haven't spent any time together since well before I went to Chiapas."

"I'm in a final push on my book, my poor, lonely girl. Something like the way you don't speak to a soul when you are putting a show together."

"Ah, but that is *my* choice. I am never dissatisfied with my own choices, and now I am not doing any printing."

"Well, I don't know how these magnificent new pieces managed to be on paper then."

"I finished my work on the images. Don't quibble with me, Luis. You are evasive."

"Indeed I am not. I would never dare that with you. I know I would be found out."

Zoë sighed. He had retreated behind his screen. She had seen it before. "When do you think the book will be done?"

"I'm still on the final sermon. The priest will have convinced himself that the devil's camp is correct, but I'm struggling with just how far he will go. Sometimes I feel I've reached the limit of my intellect. It is not a feeling that

177

leaves me feeling very social."

"Oh, so your mind has become too feeble for our banter."

"I believe you have figured it out, though I still protest that you could not be neglected because the world cannot resist you."

"*You* are resisting me, Luis."

Luis looked at the shiny black hair flowing over her shoulder. He remembered a time he had wrapped that hair around his hand as he made love to her, simulating an intensity that was in truth absent. The gesture—primitive man taking a woman by the hair—which had not progressed past the gentlest tug, seemed to say it all about their relationship. Zoë's remarkable beauty, talent, and boldness existed only out of bed. Was sex any more to her than the opportunity to show off her still-taut body, to claim ownership, to loosen her hair and drape it, as though wild abandon was afoot? Or did he fail to excite her? Perhaps Raul had an entirely different experience.

"My dear, what do they say? All good things must come to their end?"

"End! Luis! Why on earth should we burn our bridges? One never knows when the moonlight may strike at a perfect angle." She cocked her head and gave him a sharp look. "You *are* going after Juliet, aren't you. I *knew* it! Are you already sleeping with her?" Her look did not quite convey the casualness she was striving for.

"Zoë, I protest. She and I hardly know each other. Don't you find Juliet a little too sad for such casual play?"

"That is not an assessment I've been paying close enough attention to make. And you think what we had was casual play?"

"Certainly play, the loveliest imaginable, and you the most exotic orchid of a woman I ever hope to know."

178

Luis reached for Zoë's hand and brought it to his lips. "And we will always be close friends."

"But you don't want Juliet to think we are a couple."

"Ah, Zoë. You have never wanted to slow yourself down to match my pedestrian progress, but don't think that I haven't loved catching you in your occasional languorous moments."

The thrust and parry continued, but Luis went home in the end with Zoë only slightly mollified by his efforts to avoid an unpleasant break, given that he wanted a break nevertheless. Itzcui was too small for this, he thought with annoyance. Who would have thought that a Juliet would show up.

Before the crew had their break for Christmas, they had repaired the wall, built the oval window, and replaced the roof beams and tiles over the chapel. They were well into cleaning the floors of the interior and patching the walls. Juan Diego was building a new door to replace one joining the living room to the porch so that the house could be securely closed. A woman named Margarita had been hired to clean and cook, though as yet only cleaning was required, and one Pedro had come and asked for a job as *mozo*—gardener and general handyman. He lived in a village a few miles away and was only slightly known to the rest of the crew. The north wing was still untouched; the barn was a distant project.

Juliet flew her father and Shirley down for part of the Christmas holiday. They stayed in Joe and Judy's B&B with her, fitting right in with the drinking and laughing and Mexican Train. Juliet realized that Judy and Shirley were two of a kind with their easy and infectious laughter. They were each plump and comfortable, unpretentious and

179

generous. To love the one and disdain the other was clearly absurd. Juliet discovered that she could be affectionate to Shirley and felt much better for it.

Sheldon found everything delightful. La Paloma was magnificent. The pueblo was charming. Enrique was impressively knowledgeable about grape varieties, and Socorro was enchanting. He and Shirley carefully followed the rule not to talk about Juliet's life. They did not meet Luis who was in Mexico City with his family.

On the first afternoon, Juliet and Sheldon climbed up the hill behind the house where corn had been growing when she'd first seen the hacienda. The earth was loose where the plants had been uprooted. The farmer had harvested his ears and hauled away the stalks for his cows.

"I'm thinking that this slope will take six terraces with three rows on each terrace. But I can't decide if I should get a large tiller to cultivate them or have it done by hand."

"I take it you're doing this as a landscaping feature. You won't get much wine from here."

"Oh, I think I can get a ton of grapes, or nearly. And it will look so pretty up behind the hacienda. I can't resist. My boutique vineyard."

"You may as well have it tended by hand. Plant some roses at the end of the rows."

"Yeah! I love it!"

"You're not the same person, baby."

"It's good for me here, Dad."

"Who could be unhappy with such fine volcanic soil."

"Ha! Just give me first rate drainage and I'll flourish. I don't think I'm going to have to add anything but potassium."

"Are you still thinking to start with pinot noir?"

Sheldon said as he looked up the slope to the tops of the mountains just visible beyond it. "This really is a lovely place, isn't it."

"I'm so glad you like it, Dad. But I think you were right about not committing to one variety, and pinot can be so picky. I'll plant some cabernet and shiraz, too. Oh, and I am going to do the aleatico. I can't resist that rose-water finish."

"There's not much market for dessert wines you know."

"*I'll* drink it then," Juliet said, laughing. "Napoleon called it his consolation during his exile on Elba, and it will be mine here."

"Do you feel exiled?"

"No, no. Just joking. And my other grapes keep me too busy for much introspection anyway. Let's go see them tomorrow."

Her father had never been told about the Alex debacle; as far as he knew, the romance had just petered out. Juliet had made a good show of normality around him since. She had been running toward Mexico, rather than away from her life in California she had assured him, and it was almost entirely true.

Juliet drove Sheldon and Shirley the forty-five minutes to her winery, Las Fincas. Now the vines were resting, but she had much progress to show her father. The manager, Señor Arce, was at the building site beside the highway when they drove up. A Ferre del Mundo semi parked behind the construction, was being unburdened of rebar, bags of cement, wires of all sizes and sorts, and cement block.

"*There's* a delivery, Julie!" Sheldon said "Very impressive."

181

"Daddy, you wouldn't believe my account with that hardware store. If they ever have a problem, it won't be because I don't give them enough business. They're very responsive. Out here the next day, never fail. It's easy to do business with the merchants in Mexico; maybe not so easy to deal with the bureaucracy."

"But don't they have Home Base here now? Why don't you use them?"

"You know, I really prefer to buy Mexican. I mean I'm here now, and I think Ferre del Mundo does an excellent job. I don't know. Home Base stirs up that guilt in me. I know Hank sold a long time ago, but that's where the money came from. I don't feel right about undermining local business."

"You make Ferre del Mundo sound like a Mom and Pop. Isn't the owner right up there with Carlos Slim?"

"I hadn't heard that. I guess I won't worry too much about them failing, but they *have* earned my business."

Juliet's Spanish was now adequate to introduce her father and Shirley to Señor Arce and the workers, praise their efforts, and ask simple questions. The project was in the early stages. Someday, she explained, there would be high, beamed ceilings, aged-wood doors, a pergola, a restaurant with an open, tiled kitchen, and storage for many bottles of wine located below ground. She was jumping the gun—the first vintage wouldn't be drinkable for two years. In the meantime, she had formed a partnership with other local wineries. They would market each other's products and were exploring joint advertising for the area.

In a shed near the building site, Juliet had a portfolio of artwork she was considering for the campaign. One series combined images of manly wine drinkers and horses, beside catchphrases of pride, patrimony, and dignity. *Caballero*—horseman, rooted in medieval knighthood—was the word for gentleman in Spanish. Other samples showed couples in fine restaurants with glasses of wine in hand, and others featured businessmen toasting presumably lucrative deals. Travelers on the main highway would see these images on billboards. Someday she'd advertise in lifestyle magazines too. The plan was to make this place, the Valle de Zamorano, a famous location for Mexican wines, and Las Fincas synonymous with the finest. She would open as soon as possible, offering tastings and leisurely, gourmet meals to people on the wine tours that she was also organizing. Initially, she would sell her neighbors' wine—bringing them up with her would be to her advantage as the region became famous—and would introduce her own wines as soon as she could.

Mexico had a long way to go to become a wine-appreciating country, though a growing middle class was more and more intent on having the good things of life. They were ripe to be hooked with inexpensive, competent wines. Juliet told her father that she could bring in her wine at twenty-five cents a liter, six tons an acre, and sell it to compete with the Chilean and Argentinean wines flooding the country. When she could cultivate grapes that would make artesanal wines, she would charge accordingly. Her circle in Itzcui had her convinced that there was a growing sophisticated clientele. Sheldon didn't involve himself much with the business end of Quinta da Agostinho, but from what he'd absorbed, he thought Juliet's plans were good ones.

Behind the future tasting room and restaurant, the road passed a ten-hectárea field where leafless vines were being pruned by a company of men and women. Juliet, Sheldon, and Shirley stopped and wandered among them. Father and daughter largely approved their technique, occasionally taking the pruning shears and suggesting small changes. Señor Arce was doing a fine job of training and supervising. He had spent ten years in California, moving up from pruning, picking, and tilling to managing crews. After his English had gotten good enough, he had achieved positions that required familiarity with the science of grape-growing. She intended to earn his loyalty and make him a good life by building a house for him here on the property.

The processing buildings behind the field, and beside an even larger one, were hidden by a wall of caliche with colossal wooden doors. Everything would be state-of-the-art here: stainless tanks, huge oak barrels for finishing, bottling, corking, and labeling machines—all cleanable with high-power hoses. The equipment was rapidly being assembled; Señor Arce had a customs broker who did little more than usher Juliet's shipments into the country, though the colossal tanks were being manufactured near Tequila. The vines in the surrounding fields were, some of them, ten years old—reaching their peak. Juliet didn't plan to sell another harvest. There were only a few months to get everything ready. The work at La Paloma was desultory by comparison.

It was a healing visit. Sheldon and Juliet spent a happy time talking soil additives, irrigation systems, and sources for equipment as they sat in Juliet's room long after a surfeit of vodka tonics had sent Shirley to bed. The conversations continued on the porch that looked toward the hillside above La Paloma, while the work on the house made pleasant clatter behind them. The time was too short in the end, and Juliet saw them to the plane with regret.

After Easter, Juliet began to be impatient to move into the hacienda. At some point before her purchase, one end of the bedroom had been partitioned and divided into a closet and a bathroom. The bath had a shower that drained into the middle of the floor, and a toilet paper holder positioned so that the paper always got wet, but the room was large enough to be retrofitted with a tub and an enclosed shower that would keep the rest dry. She had bought the Victorian-styled fixtures that Ferre del Mundo carried, alongside the modern ones, and had gone to Dolores Hidalgo for *talavera* tile in one of the patterns that had been used since the sixteenth century. After lead-based colors became illegal, more intense and garish tones had replaced the lovely terra cottas and soft greens. Juliet avoided the problem by choosing cream with blue flowers. Juan Diego had been assigned the task of tiling the re-plastered walls.

Other details were coming together. Bookshelves covered all the walls of the dining room and the spaces between the shutters in the living room. More shelves for cookbooks were installed in the kitchen where those beautiful old tiles you couldn't get anymore glowed all the way up the walls. Here and there, the tiles were cracked and applied without strict adherence to plumb and level, but that made her treasure them even more. She had, however, drawn the line at the vintage stove and refrigerator, and had replaced them and installed a dishwasher. The refrigerator was hidden away in a new pantry that took up the corner nearest the kitchen of the still-generous dining room.

The bedroom was so large that Juliet had the end toward the barn, including one of the three windows, partitioned off to be used for an office. Phone line and internet modem had been installed leaving no excuse for her avoidance of the churnings of the Ashe empire.

After Juan Diego finished the bath, he plastered the bedroom and office with a pinkish-orange clay from the hills. The color looked spectacular with the Kermanshah

185

carpet. Juliet put her grandmother's chair in the corner and went shopping for a bed. Annette had given her the address of her favorite antique dealer in Querétaro; Juliet drove over one day in March, with Luis to help her shop.

The old part of the city was nearly unchanged from colonial times. The residents had needed fine furniture for centuries, and some of it had made its way to the shop of Señor Aguilar.

"A bed. Yes," he said smiling at the handsome couple. "I have one very beautiful—very fine. Look at this! Mesquite, eighteenth century, no later than the first decade of the nineteenth. Pre-revolutionary. Old, but of a size to take a queen-sized mattress. That is rare. The older beds are usually very small." The immense headboard was decorated with acanthus leaves, lattice, and angels. The bed stood high on great claw feet, its wood glowing with well-cared-for age.

"Oh, my," sighed Juliet. "How much?"

Luis and Señor Aguilar murmured together for a time. Luis raised his eyebrows. Señor Aguilar gestured toward his chest and nodded his head.

"It's going to be 80,000 pesos—about $7,000 or a bit more," Luis said, having no idea how Juliet would respond to this.

"Okay . . ." Juliet wanted both the bed and not to be seen throwing money about. The bed won. "I think I'll take it. It's beautiful and I can *just* afford it. I wasn't going to spend so much, but I love it. I'm hopeless."

"I think it's a good price. Querétaro is a very traditional Mexican town, no tourists to speak of. I think this is a local price for a very fine piece," Luis said.

"But how will I pay for it? I only brought 30,000 pesos. They don't take credit cards, do they?"

"No, credit cards aren't trusted much here. We

could go to a branch of your bank and wire the rest of the money to him," Luis suggested, "but he wouldn't get it until tomorrow at the earliest. I doubt we can take it back today."

Señor Aguilar had understood most of the English. With their permission, could he ask where the bed was to reside? Ah, San José Xoloitzcuintle. How precious! If the money was to be wired, he would be more than happy to deliver it. Did they know the lovely Señora Annette? Please to give her his salutations.

With routing number exchanged for location of delivery, the two parties exclaimed over how kind the other was, how great had been the pleasure, and how the pleasure had been exclusively their own. Señor Aguilar would be at their command in perpetuity. Under such a load of amiability, Juliet and Luis barely made it to a nearby sidewalk café where they ordered glasses of wine and salads with goat cheese and grapefruit slices.

"It's truly obscene how I can enjoy spending too much money," Juliet sighed.

"Yes, you have taken on an entirely obscene glow."

"I dread you saying that is as much money as one of your books brings."

"Oh, ho, ho! If *only* one brought so much!"

"Okay, I'm ashamed," Juliet laughed, "and I'll be more ashamed when I've run through all my money."

"If you become destitute, I'll let you live in my house, but you may have to share my bed." Luis minimized his comment by appearing to concentrate on spearing a section of grapefruit.

Juliet barged ahead without thinking. "Forget *your* bed. Wherever I go, *my* glorious bed goes." Her giddy laugh broke off suddenly. "No, no, no, I am joking, Luis. That's enough. We are getting carried away."

"Please let me be carried away, Julieta," he said leaning toward her and fixing her with eyes that had an unmistakably seductive intensity. "I am entranced by you."

Juliet felt a stab of apprehension, fell silent, and looked away. What if it was that glorious, and expensive, bed that had inspired the declaration?

"Ah. I see I have not had the effect on you that I hoped." Luis sighed. "Please excuse me. That was too much. I have . . . . Let's change the subject, enjoy our day."

Juliet still didn't look at Luis; her day had clouded over. The money. Zoë. Luis was getting too close and she was enjoying it too much.

"But no, I must ask you if I have misunderstood. I thought we were especially enjoying each other's company," Luis said.

"No. Yes! Of course we . . . I enjoy your company, but . . . ."

"Perhaps you are not ready to move on," he said after waiting for Juliet to finish her sentence. "Then we will be good friends? Perhaps we should go buy something else and make you happy again? Wait, I'll be right back." Luis jumped up from the table and disappeared around the corner.

What on earth to think of Luis? Caution and attraction fought for the upper hand. Was he a new Alex, or infinitely better? She remembered his voice, low and soft, and she felt a surge of arousal. He wanted her. And she was allowing him to believe that her heart was dead. But what about Zoë? Were they all supposed to be very adult and sophisticated about their sex lives? She looked toward the corner where he had turned and caught him coming back. Under his arm was a three-foot-high porcelain greyhound that she had noticed in Señor Aguilar's shop.

"Here," he said, placing the dog beside the table so that it cast its aristocratic eye in her direction, "My offering. I hope you aren't allergic to dogs."

"Oh, how beautiful. It's really finely done, isn't it? I didn't mention it, but it caught my eye. These dogs are so *baronial*. I'll put it beside my grand fireplace and La Paloma will be nearly back to its former glory. Thank you!"

"In return, Julieta, will you listen to one more thing? There are many doors through which a man and a woman may pass. I do not know how many are open for us, but I would like to say to you that I do not now see any that I want to keep closed."

Juliet blushed, glanced very quickly at his earnest face, and then away, entirely at a loss for what to say. Luis got to his feet, put a handful of notes on the check and his hand on the back of her chair, encouraging her to stand.

"Have you ever seen such clean streets?" he asked, as though nothing had transpired. "A small army of sweepers comes out at dawn every day. Let's walk over and see the Casa de la Marquesa before we go. Sixteenth century, Moorish architecture . . . ."

Spring was sweet in the Itzcui valley. The roses at La Paloma, which had been pruned in February, were again in full bloom. Juliet kept her bedroom shutters flung wide all night. She had Pablo transplant some of the courtyard's gardenias beneath her window so that their scent might fill the bedroom someday. The cold mists of Northern California . . . could she ever live there again after this sweet climate?

The Nibels, along with several of their wives, appeared in Mexico City for the quarterly meeting. The change of pace, the margaritas by the pool, the sightseeing, and the new director seemed to improve the tone, and decisions were reached with none of the previous dissension. Maybe they were getting used to her. Maybe they had given up.

The meeting occurred at the same time as Sean's departure. He had prepared schedules of payments, reports of inventory, and lists of suppliers. It was an accounting so detailed there were even two pages of instructions for washing the bed linens. The bills would be handled in Fred's office. The only remaining business was to fix the date of Sean and Rafe's first visit.

Dr Hansen had agreed to continue her treatment by telephone if she was needed, but after two sessions in a row involved nothing more than friendly chats about Mexican pleasures and foibles, they agreed to terminate.

The hacienda felt like her first real home. She had only to articulate a wish, however inarticulately, and her *muchachos* would make it happen. The appalling second bath, in what would be the guest wing, gradually transformed. A half-bath was installed in the public part of the house across from the pantry. The two small rooms on opposite sides created a hall, still quite wide, between kitchen and dining room.

With the delivery of the bed, her room was ready. For a while the file cabinet stood in for a bedside table but Juliet soon found a pair of small chests that freed it for the office. Juliet now did her shopping on private trips, or with Annette. She didn't blink at the purchase of items that suited the hacienda's scale. Luis certainly never asked prices, though she saw his eyebrows rise when a low cabinet ten feet long appeared in the entry, one that looked—and perhaps was—a couple of centuries old, and again when an equally antique dish cupboard found a place in the kitchen.

Since the day they bought the bed, Luis had taken

great care with Juliet, making space for their friendship to deepen while her reserve, he hoped, dissipated. They saw each other nearly daily and often shared meals. Sometimes they sat late on opposite ends of the sofa, the fire burning, the porcelain greyhound looking down its nose at them. Luis and Juliet trying to find ways to tell who they were—without telling who they were.

"Have you heard of the Happy Planet Index, Luis?"

"No, what's that? Are you going to tell me it says that Mexico is a sad, death-obsessed place?"

"On the contrary. At least it has the same sadness, or happiness, as the U.S. Pretty happy in the scheme of things, almost as good as Canada, miles better than Russia, or Niger."

"Great. Niger."

"Sorry, low blow. But listen. The index also measures how much of the world's resources are used to achieve this level of happiness."

"So are you going to tell me that we're happy picking fruit from the trees and you're happy going for drives in your Hummers?"

"Ha! Something like that."

"Good for Mexico. What country looks the best?"

"Maybe Costa Rica."

"That's not surprising. It's a very well-run place. Does it have to do with climate? The tropics?"

"No, not really. Indonesia and Vietnam and such aren't impressively happy. Norway and Finland and Sweden are."

"I thought Finns were sad."

"I don't know. Maybe there's sad and then there's *sad*." Juliet laughed. "But, you know, I watch my neighbors here. They have so much time to chat and gossip, so many fiestas. It looks happy."

"They have so much time to chat because they aren't reading. Do you think Mexicans are lazy?"

"How could I think that? Shame on you, Luis. Actually, looks to me like the old story: The peasants work like dogs and the ricos have three margarita lunches."

"And you want them to drink fine wine instead."

"Of course. It's much healthier. Pour me some more of that fine wine there, *por favor*. But Luis, I've been thinking about something you said when we first met."

"What was that?"

"You said one of your books was about peasants and a gringo who buys land."

"Ah, but there is no problem with a *gringa* who buys land."

"Do be serious. What do you really think about an American buying La Paloma?"

"Luis sat up and scratched his head thoughtfully. "It's a tale too often told to stop the telling now. The friction of the fourteenth against the twenty-first century wouldn't go away if the gringos were forbidden to cross the border. We Mexicans carry both inside us, or we pose as carrying both."

"Margarita told me to tie a red string around the avocado tree so the avocados wouldn't fall off before they were ready. Seems like that idea could have come straight from Aztec horticulture."

"You're right. For some, fourteenth-century ideas are no pose and twenty-first century notions are the bizarre ones."

"Are we just talking about education and class?"

"No, not entirely. There is a notion we call *espíritu de cuerpo*. It's hard to translate. Cuerpo means body; espíritu de cuerpo suggests having a body generous enough to hold all family, all community, all culture, all history. Some say gringos do not have espíritu de cuerpo, and we do. We don't understand how you can leave your families and come here, and we forget that millions of us can think of nothing but getting to the other side—though from painful necessity in many cases."

Juliet was taken aback. This was something she'd have to consider. Had she left her family?

"It must be difficult, even with espíritu de cuerpo, to hold on to Mexicanness with the U.S. so overbearing in so many ways."

"You've heard the saying: Poor Mexico. So far from God, so close to the United States. I will think, Julieta, about this question and see if I can explain it better. But you shouldn't feel that you are unwelcome here, or resented. I don't hear any of that. Perhaps we want so much to share your land that we are careful not to resent you sharing ours."

"I hope you're telling me truth." Juliet sipped her wine, took a chocolate from the box on the coffee table, and held the box toward Luis. "Do you want another truffle before you go?"

"Before I go. Another night I'm being thrown out."

Juliet showered in her beautifully renovated bathroom where the water was hot, the towels thick, and the toilet paper dry, and crawled into bed. Luis was nearby. Soon he would come back and be warm and funny, respectful and familiar. He would pour the wine. He would know where everything was. He would be clean and calm, familiar and exotic, intimate and lovable, and he would look at her with desire. He would be dressed in one of his peasant shirts—from Michoacán he had told her—that he somehow made look both elegant and bohemian. Did Luis

193

know how beautiful he was? His torso was broad and strong with none of the weight around the middle Mexican men often carried, though someday he might add that gravitas, Juliet suspected. He had a solid look, like a man one could rely on, a man from a culture that taught him what a man should be: proud, respectful, loving to family. Espíritu de cuerpo, perhaps. He made her think of Pierre in *War and Peace,* and she smiled to imagine that she herself could end up plump as Natasha beside a substantial husband. She was falling in love.

Somehow confident of their destination, confident that at least someday Zoë would be no impediment, that they would move closer and closer until finally the only thing between them would be her secret, Juliet imagined what would happen if she revealed it. She was almost more afraid that he would refuse to accept a position of having less than that he would value the money more than her. How could she reassure him? Would his pride rebel? Would the money endlessly stand in the way, good only for buying lonely beds?

From that bed she watched the moon prepare to impale itself on the cross on top of the church's spire. On the far side of the murmuring stream the small square of Luis's bedroom window shone. How long could she risk letting him believe she was still grieving, without his losing interest? It was embarrassing to feign a noble motive for chastity she had no wish to maintain—quite the opposite. And yet how could she tell him of her fears and her past foolishness? This culture with its poetry and tenderness . . . At your feet, señora. At your feet of clay, señora? Would he really want someone so *American,* someone who blurted out prosaic thoughts, and worse, who might well be thought to have married a husband nearly thirty years older for his Croesus wealth? Could she bear to cheat him by withholding the truth; could she bear to risk losing him by telling it?

The formal way he expressed himself could perhaps not be dismissed as no more than translated Spanish. She thought it might speak to something fundamental in his character, some deep seriousness beneath his wordplay and humor. He gave her the sense that having sex with him was not to be lightly entered into, because he would not take it lightly. It did feel that it could be love he was offering, if she dared to believe it.

But did she dare? She watched Luis, covertly she hoped, every time she saw him near Zoë. He didn't exactly flirt but he could too often be seen laughing at something she'd said or addressing a comment to her. More than to others? Juliet was too involved to judge. And though he was often at her own side, he seemed to make an effort not to give the impression that they were especially attached.

There was a scene she couldn't forget. One morning she had gone into town for some eggs. Zoë and Luis were coming from the direction of Zoë's house. Her hand rested on his arm and her lips whispered into his inclined ear. Juliet had quickly turned a corner. Their behavior had been so intimate that she didn't think she could meet them calmly. Certainly they had just gotten out of bed. But then Zoë could exude sexual innuendo with others too, with her overflow of exotic, dark-eyed beauty, and Luis wasn't the only man who took notice.

Step by step, Luis was becoming the most important person in Juliet's life and all the unknowns surrounding him were taking on great importance. She could not shake the fear that she'd never be able to tell what he was thinking. He spoke like someone in a play, in a historical novel. And Zoë was the match for Luis if there ever was one. Juliet felt ordinary and dull beside her and yet

. . . I am entranced by you, he had said. Luis had said he was entranced.

And if he really did care for her, perhaps it wouldn't matter that she had so much more money. He didn't appear to think about material things. That, Juliet could believe one moment, and the next revert to a fear that her hacienda, her furniture, her workers . . . all those tipped her hand, though in truth they represented such a small part of what she had. How did he even live anyway, if his books brought so little? When her thoughts reached this impasse yet again, her happiness would falter. What if Luis should be entranced? How much more would he be when he found out?

Socorro had invited everyone for an evening of music. She had discovered a young Mexican singer and guitarist—*so* talented. All her friends must hear him. The party would be the following weekend; Juliet decided she needed new clothes for the occasion. As she sat with Zoë, Joe, Judy, Randall and Peter eating tamales at a table on the street, Juliet asked Zoë if she got any of her lovely clothes closer than Chiapas.

"You might try going to San Miguel. It won't be cheap but there's the best of Mexico on offer there. It's all those years of rich Texans coming to shop."

"I haven't any style—not like you, Zoë," Juliet said, "but I might like to look a bit more festive at times. Would you like to go over and shop with me?"

"Oh, I haven't any time for that just now. Sorry." Zoë could be dismissive with such lack of awareness that no one ever seemed to take offense.

"Well, Judy, will you go with me?"

"Oh, Juliet! You want to go shopping with us, not Judy!" Randall exclaimed.

"Randall, the truth comes out! You think I have no taste!" Judy cried.

"Judy, you are the dearest thing in the world, but just look at our Juliet! She needs a makeover! Jeans, jeans and more jeans. You'd think she was out in the fields every day."

"I *am* starting to work on my hillside."

"Juliet, Socorro is going to have her friends from Guanajuato and Mexico City and San Miguel! We *have* to do something with you."

And since Randall and Peter had friends—Uli and Alfonso—in San Miguel de Allende, two days later Juliet found herself in their grand house. Uli's grandfather had been the German ambassador to Mexico and had bought the house—actually two that had been co-mingled—that had made its way up the family tree to him and his long-time partner Alfonso. It was as antique-filled as the Ashe Mansion, but with style completely absent in Hank's family home. When Juliet commented that she had a Kermanshah in her bedroom much like the one in the dining room, and Randall recounted some of her decorator coups at La Paloma, she was granted recognition. And after she presented two bottles of the Quinta da Agustinho cabernet sauvignon she had smuggled in the book boxes, Alfonso eagerly involved himself in the search for Juliet's new clothes. He was good friends with the owner of *the* most precious boutique.

But shopping would be for the following day. That evening Alfonso and Uli, who prided themselves on their cooking, were planning an extravaganza. They had disappeared into the kitchen with their two houseboys while Juliet, Randal, and Peter sat under the hundred-year-old jacaranda and sipped triple-strength margaritas. Peter was being naughty, and pleased with himself, about Raul.

197

"Pity he seems to prefer Zoë," he quipped.

"Peter loves to pretend he's on the prowl just to torture me," Randall said, rolling his eyes. "Pay no attention to him."

"It's true," Peter sighed, "I'm not the magnet I once was. Remind me to tell you about Tennessee Williams, Juliet."

"*Not* Tennessee Williams again."

"I'll let you tell about Rock Hudson, *querida*. Lucky we found each other before we fell into decrepitude."

"Do you think Raul and Zoë have a thing going?" Juliet asked, so innocent she practically batted her eyelashes. "I always thought she liked Luis."

"You can't tell what Luis is up to. Our Man of Mystery," Randall said.

"Why do you say that?"

"You don't think so? He's never seen with any family or anyone he knew before he moved to Itzcui. I believe he's quite an important Mexican writer and went to school in the U.S. and yet he seems to have no background. Perfect manners. That assumption of . . . I don't know. He gives off a vibe of privilege, something like that. Don't you think? Privilege in an impeccably tailored, handwoven shirt."

"He told me they're peasant shirts from Michoacán."

"Peasant my eye."

"I think they look rather modest, and he told me he'd come to Itzcui looking for an inexpensive place to live," Juliet reported. "He does live simply."

"Maybe he's from degenerate aristocracy. Whatever, *I* think there's a mystery about him." Randall darted out a pointed tongue to take a bit of salt from the rim of his glass.

Juliet tried to think of how to bring the subject back to Luis and Zoë. "You two are good friends with Zoë, right?"

"Oh, yes. She's quite marvelous," Peter said.

"What does she say about the mystery of Luis?"

"Oh, I think Zoë maintains a rather smug silence on that topic. Don't you think, Peter?"

"Smug? Yes, maybe. She does give the impression that she knows more than she's saying. But what about you, Miss Juliet? Are you trying to solve the Luis mystery?"

"I hadn't realized there was one."

"Hmm. Do *you* think Zoë and Luis are having an— Oh, Alfonso! Are you ready for us? We're going to spoil our dinner on these margaritas. Not that I'm complaining."

"We're ready. Come in right now. The cabernet is being poured as we speak," Alfonso called from the top of the broad stone stairway that descended to the garden.

Dinner featured a creamed soup of roasted poblano peppers with scallop medallions and a dash of truffle oil followed by turkey breast in pecan *mole*—Alfonso's invention—with potatoes and *chayote au gratin*. Desert was a tart made from the roasted heart of the blue agave used to make tequila. It had a smoky, sophisticated, caramel taste, absolutely distinctive. Peter declared himself to be *ravished* by the flavor and was generously promised the recipe. The two bottles of the Quinta da Agosthino cabernet insured that the evening was a great success.

CHAPTER SEVEN

Luis put another log on the unnecessary fire. The night was so mild they had left the door to the porch half-open and the scent of gardenias made its way into the room.

"Margarita told me today that her sister is *embarazada*. What is that about, Luis? How did Spanish get a word for pregnant that sounds like embarrassed?"

"Yes, that's one of the words that new speakers are always warned to look out for."

"Surely being pregnant isn't always an embarrassing state. Margarita's sister is properly married and all."

"No, both the words have the meaning 'burdened'—one, a burden of shame; the other, a physical burden. I believe that is the connection. In English we sometimes say 'an embarrassment of riches' meaning a 'burden of riches,' no? Not a 'shame of riches,' I think."

"Do you think riches can be a burden?" Juliet asked disingenuously.

"Well, I suppose they might," Luis replied,

seemingly as innocent as she. He changed the subject. "I'm happy to see that your Spanish is improving. You are having conversations with Margarita?"

"She is very patient with me. I beg her to correct me. She won't do that but she will fill in a word if I hesitate. If only I'd chosen Spanish in high school or college."

"There was probably a time when you wished it had been Portuguese."

"Yes, briefly."

"Don't worry. You'll get there. Shall I speak Spanish to you?"

"I should say yes but it's so nice to actually *talk*. I'd get lonely if I didn't have someone to really talk to."

Luis smiled and reached for his wine glass. "I think you have Annette and Judy." He paused. "I might go away for a while. Vanderbilt University has asked me to be a visiting professor and teach an advanced Spanish Literature course."

"In Nashville?"

"Yes."

"Oh." Juliet's heart sank.

"But I think I won't accept. I would have to cancel a writing workshop I agreed to teach in Spain, though my mother thinks that if I took the Vanderbilt position I might find an American wife—one of my students perhaps—who speaks passable Spanish."

Juliet blushed and hoped it wasn't noticed. "Would she like you to have an American wife?"

"The poor woman is grasping at straws. She remembers how happy I was when I was in school there and believes I am partial to American women. And she is concerned that I do not seem to be choosing a Mexican woman. Naturally *I* wouldn't consider an American wife a 'straw.' She could likely hold one up as well as any lifeboat."

Juliet was not at all sure what they were talking about. "So you had American girlfriends when you were in school?"

"I did have some girlfriends, yes. I found some girls who would overlook my being Mexican."

"Did you have to pretend you were a descendant of Aztec nobility? No, I mean, really, did you encounter prejudice?"

"What do you mean 'really'? Aren't *you* afraid that I will suddenly be full of *machismo*, that I will tell you your behavior is not acceptable or that you must do what I say?" Luis smiled distantly.

"No, that hadn't occurred to me. You don't *seem* very threatening. But perhaps Mexican men save that for after the wedding."

"No, indeed. Why wait. I have been meaning to order you to give me your feet so that I can massage them. I learned that American women like to have their feet massaged, but of course that would not be relevant. It would only be what *I* enjoy—as a Mexican man."

"So, Luis, if you enjoy massaging feet, why on earth hasn't some woman found a way to ensnare you?"

"Aside from my strong, sensitive fingers, don't you think I look as if I might have limited appeal as a man who writes books and sits around and thinks?"

"I think I hear some false modesty." She smiled, feeling flirty. "What kind of girl do you want?"

Luis did not say, "One like you," though he wanted to. He turned his face away and looked pensive. "I want a girl who understands and completes me." Then he returned to his playful mood. "Of course, to understand me she must guess what I am like because I am not so sure myself. Hmm. How *will* I know if she understands me if I don't understand myself? I think I have detected an impediment to my search for the perfect girl. Now give me your foot," he demanded.

Juliet kicked off her shoe and extended her foot toward him. He wrapped his fingers around her instep, pressing firmly and confidently. Their eyes met in an awareness of the intimacy of the touch.

"Oh, but now I have changed my mind and I want something else," he said. Luis slid along the sofa until he was within reach. He cupped her face in his hands and pulled her toward him, touched her lips with his and sat back. "No, that is not quite what I want either. I want to kiss you more like this."

Luis kissed Juliet until she forgot herself, made a little moan, and reached to hold his face in return. When they parted—dazed, aroused—they stared into each other's eyes. "Oh, my," Juliet whispered.

"Oh my Julieta."

In silence they each calculated frantically. Should she lead him to the bedroom? Should he pin her to the sofa? How would a proper Mexican widow act? How should a suitor impress a woman with his respectful but mad desire? They waited too long. Juliet made a tiny frown; Luis stood up and went to stand facing the fire. He pushed a wayward log with the poker, turned and looked at her. Did she look disappointed? Or had he been rejected?

"Don't run away from me, Julieta. I understand if you need time. I will say goodnight now. In fact, I could not keep my hands off of you. Sleep well." Luis left the room without looking back.

"Good night," Juliet called weakly behind him. She heard the great door shut and sat staring into the fire for a time while her thoughts tumbled. Finally she rose to bolt the doors before going to bed.

From her window she saw the light of his bedroom

between two of the cypresses that grew along the edge of the yard. Beyond was the crooked street with yellowish globes illuminating walls of red and ocher, and the dome of the church. Clouds appeared as solid as ebony where their substance resisted the moonlight and shimmered like silvery silk where they welcomed it through. Juliet's eye went again to Luis's bedroom window.

She knew she would have given in if Luis had only asked—Zoë or no. She was still aroused from their kiss. How could he not tell? Why did he hesitate? She was confused by his delicacy, his scrupulous care of her presumed sensibilities. It made her afraid of seeming too eager. How strange their relationship was. She could never tell what he was thinking or when he was serious. And why did he mention marriage? Surely if he were cavalier about his relationships, he would never bring *that* up.

The next morning Luis called to say he had to go to Mexico City for a few days. Juliet had only a few moments to wonder if he was deliberately avoiding her when the phone rang again. It was George! He and Mimi had brought the *Viridian* to Cancun and had the idea that they would "just run over" the following week. Juliet invited them eagerly.

She and Beto did a hasty assessment about what could and could not be accomplished on the guest room, following which she took off for Querétaro and Señor Aguilar's shop. He had a fine bed and matching wardrobe, a couple of chairs, and a little table that would do nicely. Juliet was by now so trusted a customer that she was permitted to transport the things immediately and wire payment later. By the time she was back in Querétaro to pick up George and Mimi at the airport, had taken them to the Costco for gourmet items not available in Itzcui, and had delivered them to the hacienda, the guest room and bath were passable.

The next morning they all walked into town to get breakfast. Mimi gushed with approval.

"Juliet, I sure thought you were crazy, but I'm going to have to say this is beautiful. I just love this town to bits. And to live in a hacienda! It's too romantic for words. And that red! You must have had in a gay decorator."

"I'm going to need *someone* special to match the color where we made repairs."

"Maybe you should just leave those adobe bricks showing on the chapel. It kinda has a good look."

"I guess I will if I can't figure out the technique. It appears that there's a layer of mud plaster, then a cream-colored plaster, and the red over that. But I don't know if it's a wash or mixed into the outer coat. I guess it has to be mostly iron oxide. I've thought about planting something that would grow up the wall and hide the edge of the patch. There are three colors of trumpet-vine that I've seen. I'm thinking of the one that is bright orange. "

"Well, I can't imagine more entertaining problems. I think George is going to have to stop frettin' over you," Mimi said.

"Look at that green butterfly, Mimi. Isn't that the prettiest thing you ever saw? But no, Juliet, you might need some more frettin'. I'm afraid you might get lonely out here."

"You know, George, it really works the opposite way. The fewer the people you have to socialize with, the more you need each other, and the closer you are. For instance, I'd be really remiss if I didn't offer you two around for people to meet. That would be a breach of the social pact. That's why we're having everybody over tomorrow. It probably won't be much of a party 'cause only about six people can sit down at once. They'll probably get tired of standing and go home. Maybe I should say 'bring a bottle and a chair.' I seem to remember going to a party like that once. Or maybe it should be 'bring a bottle and a dining table, or a desk, or a lamp.'"

"Oh, stop carryin' on about your house not being furnished, Juliet. I think the whole place is just heavenly and I couldn't be more comfortable."

"My sideboard surely would be more adorned, if I had a sideboard." Mimi and George had brought two silver candelabra that cried out for an important place to sit.

"If you're talking about the candelabra, George's family has more than you could shake a stick at. You're doing us a favor taking some off our hands. Now *you* can find somebody to clean them."

Juliet laughed. "I bet Margarita didn't know she was signing up for silver cleaning. I bet she's never *heard* of silver cleaning."

The church bells bonged the information that it was nine o'clock. "Oh, my," said Mimi. "That makes me think of growing up in New Orleans. We lived near Our Lady of Lourdes and always heard the Angelus—six, twelve, and six. Do they do the Angelus here?"

"No, but we get the time, and Sunday Mass, and the Elevation of the Host, and national holidays. The bell tolls when someone dies, too. Turns out it's impossible not to send to ask for whom the bell tolls; it's big news.

When they reached the restaurant they found Socorro and Annette at one of the tables. "These are your friends, eh?" Annette said. "Come and join us."

After introductions, Juliet told Annette about the candelabra. "You are going to be jealous when you see them. I'm surprised they let that much weight on the plane." And to Mimi and George, "Annette is our

207

Architectural Digest-type. Her home is absolutely exquisite."

"I can see Juliet's going to be on the house tour pretty soon," Annette said.

"We're from New Orleans and we love old houses, don't you know, and in our French Quarter the architecture is really more Spanish with courtyards and all, like here," George informed them.

"I think we just grow up there lovin' to look at houses," Mimi added.

"Well, won't you come over and see mine?" Annette offered. Mimi's hint had succeeded.

"And please, mine as well," Socorro added.

"Oh, Socorro's is in a category all its own. She's not playing foreigner-buys-colonial-house," Annette laughed. "She has the real thing. It was her grandparents' and most of the furnishings are original. It's that one right opposite, see it? The three story one? With the balconies?"

"There are private homes right on the plaza? The door is under that colonnade?" George asked.

"It was built as the town house for a family who had a mining hacienda in the mountains north of here. It is a dark old house but it has a lovely courtyard and some fine paintings. My parents used to come here for holidays only, but I moved here two years ago. This is a very tranquil pueblo. We are happy to have young people like Juliet here," Socorro smiled in her queenly manner.

"Now won't somebody tell me about these mines," George said. "Can you see that old hacienda?"

"No. There's hardly a trace," Socorro said.

"Juliet tells me that the mines really belonged to the king of Spain—*real*/royal—like the name of this restaurant." He looked at La Mina Real painted above the interior door.

"The mines didn't belong to the king after

Independence."

"No, I suppose not," George laughed. So where are these mines, anyway?"

No one could resist George's good humor. By the time breakfast was over and the house tours completed, half the day, more than half, had been pleasantly passed meeting and greeting, admiring the church and buying more fruit than they could possibly eat. "What *is* this thing?" he had said referencing a guayaba and, taste untasted, he was not satisfied until he was absurdly well-stocked.

"I think Margarita will have lunch for us if we head home," Juliet said. "She can make a drink with those guayabas."

"Oh, Juliet, I nearly forgot. Alex was so excited to hear you were living in Mexico. He wanted to hear everything about your life here. 'Course, we didn't know much. I'm sure he'll be glad to hear what a sweet town you live in."

"How is Alex?" Juliet said feeling a chill. She was eternally glad she had never admitted their romance to George and Mimi.

"Oh, fine. He's kind of a wheeler-dealer, don't you know," Mimi laughed. "Sweet guy, though. Haver and Harvey mention you often. You heard Pete died. Bladder cancer. So young."

They passed Luis's empty house. He hadn't returned from Mexico City. Juliet didn't mind that he would not be around for any slip-ups on George and Mimi's part. Not that they were likely to carry on about her money—it wasn't done. But she could imagine George in an alcohol-lubricated tête-à-tête with someone who seemed to care for her, such as Luis, talking about how he had known her husband; how he had been in Thailand when he was killed on the honeymoon. She should mention to George and

209

Mimi that she was putting that behind her here—oh no, she wasn't putting *them* behind her; their visit was pure pleasure, just . . . you know.

Some time after George and Mimi left and Luis returned, an entrepreneurial sort named Candelario came by to show off his little tractor and blade and to brag about his skills. He had heard Juliet was looking for someone like him, and he was hired on the spot to rework the slope behind the house. She, Luis, and Candelario climbed the hill to stake out the terraces, each broad enough to hold twenty-five to thirty vines and leave room for mechanical tilling, if she decided not to follow her father's suggestion to have the work done by hand.

While she stood at the foot of the hill watching Candelario at work, she wondered again about the property beyond. It was ridiculous not to have explored it all by now, even if it was quite a climb. Elena had described the land leveling off before it rose toward the surrounding mountain. From the elevation map, it looked as though she owned at least an acre up there. Perhaps Luis would like to go on a hike.

"That sounds like fun," Luis agreed while he sipped coffee the following morning. They sat in the new leather chairs on the porch looking over the roses, bougainvillea, gladiolas, and gardenias. The plants clearly appreciated Pablo's pruning and watering, and had reached a profusion that kept vases filled daily. Margarita was mopping the kitchen floor. The crew was banging on something in the north wing. Candelario and his tractor were up shaping the fourth terrace.

"But I'll tell you what I want to do today. Let's go look at your room under the *capilla*." How had so much time gone by without going down there either? Juliet agreed excitedly.

Marcelino was called to bring a ladder to the chapel. The rest of the crew could not resist the adventure, abandoned their tools, and crowded around. They pushed away the altar, pulled up the trap, and lowered the ladder into the room below. As Juliet and Luis descended into the cool space with a flashlight, the crew arranged themselves at the edge of the opening. Beto, in his privileged foreman's capacity, pushed his way to the ladder and climbed down with a shovel. Even he could barely stand upright between the heavy beams above and the stone floor. It was hard to tell if the walls had been hewn from the stone or were part of a natural cavern, but the latter interpretation was strengthened by the room not being square or the floor level. The boys kept up rapid, excited commentary; this was *much* better than working. Beto tapped at the floor with the shovel hoping something interesting would turn up, but it was Luis who found it.

"Wait," he said, looking carefully at a wall, "There are bricks here. See this irregular area?" Luis called for a crowbar; Marcelino ran to get it. Juan Diego and Chango climbed down, and after the crowbar arrived, stacked the bricks Luis pried loose to one side. Margarita and Pablo joined Marcelino at the edge.

The removal of the first layer of bricks only revealed a second wall, but when the first brick of the inner layer came out, the way was opened to musty emptiness. Beto shouted in and received dull reverberations of considerable size. After several more bricks were removed, the flashlight revealed a passageway no higher than the room and of irregular width. It headed in the direction of the barn. Marcelino now scrambled down the ladder to join the shoulder-to-shoulder hunched group.

The adobes were pulled out until the hole was large

211

enough for one at a time to press through, with Juliet and Luis in the lead. Margarita called out pleas for their safety to the Blessed Virgin, but the only peril seemed to be the possibility of tripping on the uneven stone floor. After a turn to the left, the passage eventually doglegged back to the right. It began to narrow and incline downward until it ended against wide wooden boards, edge-to-edge, on the far side of an opening. Luis tried to move them, but they yielded only enough to indicate that they were not attached. Eventually he managed to slide one to the side. The flashlight beam showed white sacks, like those used for grain or fertilizer, packed full and piled one on the other six high. The explorers were hit with an unmistakable smell of marijuana.

"Oh, my God. Now what?" Juliet said as the workers giggled.

Luis pushed on the column of sacks; they didn't yield an inch. The chamber must be packed full. "I say we retreat and think about this."

The board was worked to its original position. All made an about-face, and with more nervous laughter, hunched back to the room under the chapel and up.

Luis addressed the group, gestured toward Juliet, spoke some more. The men shook their heads; they nodded. The workers went down again and restacked the adobe bricks in the opening, and Luis and Juliet went off for to the porch for a conference.

"What did the boys say?" she asked.

"They all said they hadn't known, and I think it's true. They seemed genuinely surprised, don't you think? They might be putting two and two together now, wondering what their cousin has been up to."

"You told them I was in danger, didn't you?"

"No, no, you mustn't worry. I'm sure no one would

harm you, but I think it best not to challenge the growers by interfering with them. I hope they will move the marijuana out and that will be that. I wonder when they put it in? Perhaps they didn't know the hacienda had been sold. Maybe they wanted to hold it until well after harvest when the prices go up, and then you surprised them by moving in. Remember, it's not cocaine—those people are not so nice. We have some locals trying to make a little extra money, that's all. I wonder if this property has been a plantation during these years when no one was here. Perhaps it is best that you never visited that far part of the land. But if they were using it, likely they will never want to again."

"So, is this a growing region?" Juliet asked.

"I know it used to be. Enrique told me he knew an old man—he's dead now—who lived beside the airstrip. He said one day he counted forty flights carrying out marijuana. Local people got rich—more or less—bought land, built houses, and when the government started giving them trouble, they mostly gave it up. But clearly not entirely."

Luis had, however, told the crew that she was in danger, and he believed it. Now that there was so much activity at the hacienda, the growers might be getting desperate. And where was the outside entrance to the underground chamber? No one had gone in the way they had for a very long time. There was no telling the size of the space or how full it was, but it surely represented an important part of someone's hopes for the future.

Luis suggested another cup of coffee. He tried to appear nonchalant but the situation weighed on him, and he was embarrassed that such a thing had happened to Juliet in his country.

"Luis, talk to me! What are we going to do? Should

213

we go outside and try to find where the opening to that chamber is? Should we report it to the police?"

"I'm ashamed to admit, Julieta, the police are not always to be trusted. It wouldn't be my choice to tell them. I think we may wish to smooth the way for the *campesinos* to take their crop and get away. When they are gone, we could 'discover' the hiding space, fill it in or uncover it, whatever seems best."

"How are we going to help them take it away?"

"I'm hoping that one of the workers will notify them that we have stumbled on the crop. Here is a plan, Julieta: I believe that you should go away for a few days and give all the workers, say, a week off while you are gone. If anyone in the household tells the growers of our discovery, and your absence, they will realize that we intend no interference. They may be just waiting for a time when things are quiet here, when they can remove their crop with impunity."

"That sounds very wise. Extremely non-confrontational. Why don't we go up to San Miguel? Together?"

"What a nice idea. Planting all that marijuana will work out well for me."

"Very funny. Candelario should be finished terracing tomorrow. I'd need to wait until then, okay?"

"I don't know. Maybe we should be on our way as soon as we can throw some things in a suitcase."

"I can't leave that fast. I have a load of adobes coming for partitioning the other guestrooms, and I have to get the money to pay everybody for the week, plus the tractor. I need two days to get that much at the ATM."

Luis frowned. For the vast majority, Mexico was no more dangerous than other countries, including the United States, but Luis had lived in one of the two segments that did experience violent crime disproportionately—cartel members and the very rich. His sister and parents had bodyguards and took many precautions against kidnapping; they fretted that he did not. He knew he was selfish to be so casual. He was after all putting his family's happiness at risk if anything happened to him. Here, he was content that he was incognito, but that was beside the point. Luis knew that dangers did exist, especially when drugs were involved.

"No later than tomorrow afternoon then," Luis said. "I'll tell the workers that you are going and that they will have the time off from work. I believe they will understand what must happen."

Luis went to deliver the message. He found everyone but Pablo—he had not gone down with them nor had been waiting above when they emerged from the underground passage. The others hadn't seen him either. They nodded gravely about the safety of the señora and said the idea of her going and shutting down the work was good. Luis told them there would be a short workday tomorrow. The señora would be gone until the following Monday and would pay them tomorrow for the time.

That afternoon Luis asked, "May I invite myself to spend the night in your guest room, Julieta? I will be at the ready for the first sign of trouble and you will sleep more securely I hope."

"Oh, Luis. That's very kind. I think I *will* sleep better, though I'm not really afraid. Poor guys. Here they are with their marijuana trapped and not knowing how to get it out. It's really sort of funny that they need us to hold their hands to help them get it away. Maybe I should leave my key in the truck. Theirs may be broken, and they don't have the money to fix it until they sell the marijuana, which they need the truck to take away."

"Let's hope we are not dealing with anything worse than that. I wonder if Pablo knows something. Seems

215

suspicious that he disappeared while we were down there. I asked the others to tell him about you going away. I hope they see him. I want this to go smoothly."

In the evening they ate a pizza Luis brought from La Mina Real. They checked all the doors and shutters, tried to pretend they were not acutely conscious of sharing a roof, and retreated to their separate wings.

But the growers, not having gotten the message, came that night.

Around two, Juliet sat upright in panic. A dream gunshot had transformed into a waking one. It was immediately followed by a string of angry pops that were all too close. Her heart pounded. In a moment there was a knock at her bolted door.

"Let me in, Juliet," Luis called calmly. She ran to the door and lifted the iron latch so he could slip inside. He sealed the door behind him. They made their way to the bed in the darkness and sat down.

"What are we going to do?" Juliet whispered.

"It's going to be fine. You know how well we're locked inside here. Every door and window shutter is bolted; all the windows have iron bars. There's no way they could hurt us. They're too busy hurting each other, or warning us. Here get under the covers. You'll get cold."

Juliet obediently lifted the quilt to climb under. Something heavy was on top of it. "What is this? A gun!" she exclaimed as she touched cold metal.

"Never mind, we won't need it. I'll put it out of the way. The safety's on," Luis said as he put the weapon on the bedside table. He sat up against the headboard beside her. "I don't hear anything. Maybe they've worked it out. Here, let me hold you. Don't worry."

"I thought you couldn't have guns in Mexico,"

Juliet said nervously as she moved closer to Luis.

"I have a permit. It's legal."

"Why do you have one?" Juliet tried to relax against him but her muscles wouldn't release their tension.

"Oh, it's a long story. I've never used it, but I'm glad to have it now. I wonder what's happening. Too bad they didn't fall in with my brilliant plan."

From between the closed shutters, a sliver of moonlight traced a path across the floor nearly to the bed. Gradually Luis's eyes adjusted until he could make out Juliet's head resting lightly on his shoulder. There were tiny rainbows glinting in her hair's highlights. It was too much to resist. He gently took hold of her chin and brought her face up for a long kiss. Their lips parted, joined again, and again, more urgently.

"Julieta," Luis whispered with mock gravity, "perhaps it *is* true that we are in danger. Perhaps these are our last moments on this sweet earth. Shall we spend them as fond neighbors, or shall we take the gift our bodies are made for?"

"You had me persuaded that we were secure!"

"*I* am secure; you, perhaps not."

Ah, yes, thought Juliet, laughing softly. Clever, darling Luis. She threw her arms around him. "I'm trembling in fear, Luis."

"Strange, I seem to be trembling too."

He pushed the cover back and touched her breast through her gown, making her nipples harden and her breath come more quickly.

"Ah, look what a lovely thing, this perfect breast." He moved his thumb over her nipple. "You know? You have the exact body to my taste. At least I believe so. Your clothes do intrude on a final judgment. I will have to rip them away." He lowered the cover farther and slid his hand

217

down her hip, onto her thigh, and back up to graze her belly. "How soft you are here. Ah, how unacceptable this gown! I love the way you curve out here, just so."

Juliet offered her face to be kissed again and opened to his sweet mouth. Luis pressed her breast gently upward, pushing it from the top of her gown. He transferred his lips to it as Juliet let her head fall back.

Suddenly a starter motor began to churn in a hopeless sort of way. It sounded as though it was just outside the window; they froze and listened. Again and again and again it ground, metal fragmenting, battery expiring.

"See, I told you so about the truck," Juliet whispered.

"Ah, what courage. She jokes in the face of danger."

The engine caught! Coughed. Died. Starter noises began again. Luis moved his hand to her bottom and explored its curves and Juliet moaned. "Shh," he commanded, "We're listening."

Starter wheezes came at agonized intervals; his hand continued caressing her in the same wholly tantalizing way. Juliet made a pleading sound and pressed herself against him.

"Is that the engine you are encouraging or are you begging me to take you?" Luis whispered as he lifted his body to remove the covers between them.

"I'm . . . ."

"You don't have to answer. I know what you want. Feel this and see what I want." As she touched him, the engine caught, revved to a screech, revved to a banshee wail. Luis choked out a laugh. "My sentiments exactly."

"Oooh, does that hurt?"

"No, angel. I just hope those pistons don't fly

through the wall." Juliet broke into a happy laugh and kissed him with delight—and groaned as the engine died again.

Luis sighed. "Ah, my poor Mexico. I will have to redeem the honor of my country. This gown must come off. There. Ah, lie just like that." He stood beside the bed and quickly removed what clothing he had thrown on when the shooting started. Juliet could see him perfectly in the moonlight's gleam, and he was lovely.

As Luis lifted himself over her, the starter began all over again. They laughed between kisses at the preposterous juxtaposition, until Luis felt his body encounter her eager wetness and, in sudden seriousness, he abandoned restraint and pushed inside. Juliet cried; the starter churned.

"Don't start, don't start," Juliet whispered through clenched teeth as Luis matched the efforts of the mechanism.

"Don't start," she choked out, her body taught and arched. But when her plea finally turned into a breathtakingly eloquent moan, Luis took her cue and gave up the game in ecstasy.

As their consciousness returned to the bed, the room, the adventure outside Luis and Juliet realized that they, and the engine, had reached their moment of truth in unison. The truck could now be heard chugging raggedly. Holding tight to each other, they listened as the strokes evened out, and the sound began to move slowly away.

Luis gave Juliet a quick kiss, crossed the room, unbolted the shutters, and swung them open. The soon-to-set moon dazzled the room. "There they go," he said. "Come look at the size of the load."

Juliet jumped up and ran to the window, wrapping Luis in her arms as the night air licked around them. They watched the towering mound of sacks teeter as the two-ton truck moved off upriver, driving without lights in the blue moonlight. Gradually the silence returned.

"Did you recognize the truck?"

"No. I don't know it. Well. I believe we have survived. I hope they got it all." Luis smiled. He turned her in his arms, slid his hands to her hips and pulled her close, found her mouth and found it waiting. When they separated, they stared into each other's eyes.

"Do you know our famous book, *Pedro Páramo?*" he asked. "No? Pedro says to his love something like this: An enormous moon was shining over the world. I stared at you until I was nearly blind, at the moonlight pouring over your face. Soft, caressed by the moonlight, your swollen, moist lips iridescent with stars . . . ."

Juliet awakened at dawn to an empty bed, but found Luis making coffee in the kitchen when she emerged from her bedroom. The heavy doors to the garden were opened and dim light filled the rooms. He smiled a wry smile. "I think we need coffee before we go out and count the bodies."

"How can you joke!" Juliet cried, laughing in her joy at finding Luis in her life. "You are joking, right?" she said, switching to apprehension.

"Yes, don't worry. There aren't any. I've looked everywhere. Just tire tracks. And I found the entrance to your underground space. Empty underground space. Wait until you see. I've been wondering what it was originally for."

"Where does it come up?"

"Inside the barn. It was under that pile of wood in the corner. There are old stone steps going down. No wonder it all sounded so close."

"This hacienda stuff is more than I bargained for. I thought it was all thick walls and high ceilings," Juliet laughed. "The *patrimonio* is pretty involved."

"Yes, it is involved here," Luis agreed. "We often wonder why you gringos want to have anything to do with us. Though I for one am very happy that you do." Luis gave her a long, good morning kiss.

Juliet smiled as they parted. "It must be partly because we haven't a clue. Maybe we imagine it's *our* next frontier—a place where we escape our own complications and can pretend almost anything, since we can't understand what's really going on."

"I remember when I was finally really good at English and could understand the conversations of people passing on the street. It was: 'It's going to take us at least an hour to get there,' or, 'I think I might have left it in the restaurant,' or, 'We've already come three blocks, haven't we?' It was mostly inane, and I thought, 'This is what I tried so hard for?' Of course, I'm not being fair. There was the *McNeil/Lehrer News Hour* too. But still."

"McNeil's been gone for a long time."

"And so have I. I'm Mexican again. And yet . . . ."

"Yet?"

"Another long story."

"You keep saying that. Are you ready for me to ask about your story?"

"Well, not now. You'd better get dressed before your workers arrive. And hurry. You have to see what I've found."

Luis pulled Juliet by the hand through the garden gate and the ten-foot-high barn doors. They stood open as usual—and as they would until some major hinge work was done. Someday there would be tasting-room décor, a bar with sparkling glasses, bottles lined up for the tourists, and barrels filled with wine. Now, piles of rubble nearly blocked their way to the corner, where boards had been thrown aside to reveal a stone stairway leading into a dim and empty chamber.

Luis helped Juliet down to a room roughly twenty-by-twenty feet. Part of the ceiling was supported by low crude beams, part was the natural rock. The floor was also stone but covered with enough dust to show where bags had been dragged to the steps. Across the room, one of the wide grey planks they had seen the day before lay on the floor. The rest leaned against the wall. Beyond, the passage to the chapel faded into darkness.

"Well, they certainly didn't leave any for us. What is this place? A storeroom?" Juliet asked. She caught her foot on a pile of wood. "Look at this. It has carving on it. It's furniture."

Luis squatted and examined the pieces. It seemed to be a collapsed bed. He felt around on the dirty, uneven stone and found a tin can and more wooden pieces, broken glass, a loop of metal, perhaps from a cup or candleholder.

Juliet said excitedly, "I love this! Maybe somebody was living down here. Why do you think it connects to the chapel?"

Luis mused, "I wonder if this could have been a hiding place for a priest. There have been times when they were in danger of being killed—were being killed. The government has tried to wipe out the church more or less vigorously since Independence. First it was confiscation of church property, a prohibition against the church educating children, the banning monasteries and nunneries, and finally the closing of all the churches."

"The church seems to be doing okay now."

"There was a rebellion during the revolutionary

period and finally a truce, but the Catholic Church still has restrictions. It stays out of politics—or is supposed to. It can run schools, but is not supposed to teach religion. I wonder if we could find an archeologist who would be interested in this if it really is part of the anti-clerical story. I'd love to see the children in the town visiting and learning about their history. It would definitely keep the *campesinos* out too."

"The campesinos! What an adventure! Let's go get Socorro. She's going to love seeing this. Enrique and Annette too. Maybe they know someone who could tell us what we have here. But wait, Luis! How perfect this would be as my *cave*!" She pronounced the word in French. "My place to store wine!"

"Think how great your cave would be if it had such a history. You'll want your visitors to see it, won't you?"

"Oh, yes, of course. This is certainly worth a few gunshots in the night—and being ravished by the man who was supposed to protect me."

"You failed to read the small print. The protection covered only threats from the marijuana farmers," Luis said, taking her close in his arms. "We'll want to show off our find," he whispered, "and then we'll have people around us all day. Perhaps we should go back to the bedroom for a while before we tell the village."

"My workers!"

"It's still early. I'll try to be too quick."

"Anyway you like, Luis."

Later, all their friends did respond to the news, as well as the officials from the presidencia, the priest, the employees of the electrical office, those of Ferre del Mundo, and many others. The most recent use of the space was not mentioned, except to a few, but the whole town

223

likely had heard. The bricks under the chapel were removed again and everyone hunched through from one end to the other and back. It was Enrique who noticed that halfway along the passage from the chapel to the barn there was another adobe brick-filled opening. Many hands volunteered in their removal.

"Oh! Oh! This is like King Tut's tomb!" Juliet cried as she got her first look in the beam of the flashlight. There were several dainty chairs, a dimly visible statue of a figure holding the Christ child in a dusty glass case, a cloth-draped shape, stacked wooden boxes, and four *prie-dieu—reclinatorio* in Spanish, according to Enrique. Thrilled, they concluded that they had found the furnishings of the chapel.

Juliet reluctantly decreed that not even she enter. The dust made it impossible to tell how well-preserved the contents were, but it was likely that damage could be easily done. Enrique volunteered to find an expert to look the treasures over. He and Padre Ramón conferred excitedly. Zoë took flash photographs from the doorway. Everyone ended up coughing in the stirred-up dust, and reluctantly retreated. Margarita prepared a fruit drink for an impromptu party upstairs.

Eventually the house was quiet again. All the workers had departed for their break—Juliet hadn't wanted to renege on the paid vacations. The hacienda felt as if it was holding its breath, as she was, for Luis's return. He had gone home to make a promised call to his publisher, bathe and change. The night. The morning. They had been magical as their bodies engaged in the delicious labor of building a human bond. Alex had excited her until she ached. Hank had satisfied her with patient skill. But Luis had made love to her, in her, around her, and there it was— love. It had been crafted, shaped, and now had its own form, somehow tangible in its beauty and terror. Terror because it now had to be acknowledged as a thing that could be nourished or killed, respected or disdained. And it had happened before he knew of her past and present, before she knew about Zoë, or who knew what else. Never mind. There it was.

Juliet put a fresh set of linens on the bed. She pulled the bottom sheet tight thinking how lovely it would feel to entwined bodies—so lovely they *might* even notice it. She thrust the duvet into the fresh cover, and bent to smell it. Margarita had some lovely washing soap and dried the sheets in the sun. Juliet cut pink and cream roses for her dresser, put on her caftan, and contemplated a nap. Luis called and said he was working. Did she mind if he saw her a little later? No, that was perfect. She would lie down for a while. Her happy reveries hadn't yet slipped into sleep when she heard the sound of the brass bell. She ignored it at first. If more people from the village wanted to see the discovery, they'd have to wait, but when it rang a second and third time, she made her way through the house to the front door and opened it.

Alex stood on the porch.

CHAPTER EIGHT

"Juliet! What a vision you are. God, I'm happy to see you. Please forgive my coming unannounced."

"*What* are you doing here," Juliet said with a look of shocked exasperation on her face.

"Please don't turn me away until you've heard me out. Please let me come in and talk to you. I know I don't have the right to ask, but please."

"No, Alex, I don't think so."

"I've come so far, Juliet. Let me explain. We never had a chance to come to an understanding about what happened. And there're things I know you don't understand." Alex looked as forlorn as a puppy left out in the rain.

"Oh, for God's sake. Come in." Juliet trudged toward the living room, not even looking back to see if he was following.

"This house! I can't believe it. What a transformation."

"Sit down," she said wearily, gesturing to the sofa.

"Thank you. I know this is more than I deserve."

Just get this over with, Juliet thought. She sat at a distance in the chair near the fireplace. "So? What do you want to say?"

Alex sat up straight, looking earnest and contrite. "Juliet, I'm just on the verge of being able to return your money. It was horrible when my affairs went south. I was so ashamed I couldn't face you. I haven't thought of anything else since except putting things right, and I'm almost there! I know I shouldn't have come until I could hand you the check—"

"Oh, please. Don't let it concern you," she said sarcastically. He looked down in shame but forged ahead.

"When George and Mimi told me you'd bought a hacienda, I *knew* where it would be, so when I had to come here on business . . . I'm taking a chance, Juliet. You were the best thing that ever happened to me, and losing you was the worst. I think you loved me too."

"How is Aimée?"

"Aimée." Alex said her name with sadness. "I broke up with her when we got together, but I didn't tell her I had fallen in love with someone else. I didn't tell her because I was afraid of her reaction, and when she found out, it was as bad as I'd feared. I don't know it all, but I gather she was very skilled in making you believe I'd been lying. I hate to say anything bad about her, but she's got serious problems, and she's done this sort of thing before. Everybody who knows her would say the same. It's really sad." Alex shook his head, "I don't know how I can get you to believe me."

Juliet felt a twinge—was this possibly true? Would she have cared about what exactly he was doing with the six million if it hadn't been for Aimée? But Aimée hadn't sounded anything like a crazy person, and Alex *had* lied about the contract. She had been completely humiliated in front of Fred and the Nibels by her business incompetence. And here he was back with his golden tongue.

"I'm sorry if I misjudged you on anything. Don't think I don't blame myself for how things went so wrong. I was entirely stupid in accepting the terms I did on the so-called investment—"

"No! That was incompetence on my lawyer's part! I had no intention—"

"Alex, has it slipped your mind that you were *not* buying that building?"

"I had the inside track if I could show the money up front—"

"I don't want to argue about this. If there is some chance I have wronged you, I'm very sorry. I hope you can have a happy life without me because I do not want to return to how we were."

"Juliet . . . ."

She stood up. "Alex, it's time for you to go, and *please* don't ever come back."

"Honey, don't say that. May I come back when I can bring you the check? Juliet, I've made so many mistakes in my life. I felt you were the turning point. I felt I could be so much better with you. I told you my dreams. It's true I hadn't realized all of them yet but, Juliet, that was the content of my soul!"

Juliet collapsed back into her chair and put her face into her hands. His dreams. They had been lovely dreams. What if he really was trying to return the money? Oh, but there was the Garden District house, Sean Penn, his silence.

"I don't want the money, Alex. I don't want to have any more dealings with you. If I'm being unfair, accept the money as my apology. My life has moved on."

"I can see you're in a lovely place. But my life has been torture. I've been miserable. Please, Juliet, let me touch you again, let me hold you." Alex rose from the sofa and crouched at her feet, put his hands on her thighs and looked up into her face. His eyes began to tear. She twisted to the side. He caressed her cheek. "Give me another chance. Please let me love you again. I'll devote my life to making you happy."

Juliet gripped the arms of the chair. "Get out," she said, her voice trembling. "Just get out. The sight of you takes me back to a time I only want to forget."

"Juliet, please don't reject me. If you could understand how much I love you!"

Juliet made a sound of rage all the more bestial for being directed at her stupid, gullible self. "Get out!"

Finally silenced, Alex stood up. Slowly he left the room. She heard the door close.

Juliet followed him cautiously, afraid he'd still be lurking, but saw him get in his car and drive away. She locked the door, went trembling to her bedroom and paced back and forth wringing her hands. How could she have chosen Alex after someone as kind and good as Hank? Because he had been such a good lover? Because she'd been so scared of facing her responsibilities alone? Because she was a shallow fool?

Perhaps a bath would help. She ran it hot, sank slowly in, and closed her eyes. But she saw herself back in Thailand with Hank dead and Alex hovering nearby. Tears began rolling down her cheeks, and built to sobs. The shame of Alex had never completely gone away, but it had seemed to be behind her. Now he had polluted her life again. Here in her home in Mexico, for God's sake. Wanting credit for *maybe, someday* paying her back! She wept for the hopeless stupidity that had ever let him into her life. She would have to call George and tell him about Alex. Ask George to make it clear that he must never bother her again—must never make her face her shame, more like. Louise had been right. How she would gloat if she knew. But even if she were to express sympathetic sorrow, *she'd been right.* The money was blighting her life.

She had been craving Luis all through the visits of their neighbors. Her body had hummed and tingled through it all and wanted only to feel him again. He had brushed against her when he could do so discreetly; she had done the same. The bed was prepared, the room decorated. And now it was all spoiled. Her eyes ached from crying. She couldn't see Luis. He'd know something was terribly wrong, and she'd owe him an explanation.

The phone rang. Juliet climbed out of the bath and answered it—Luis, of course.

"Luis, forgive me. I . . . I have the most terrible headache. I think it's the lost sleep. Perhaps an early night would be best."

"Do you mean a night alone?"

"Uh, yes. Perhaps that's what I need."

"Darling, what have I done?"

"No, no, Luis. It's not you. It's not us. I'm feeling under the weather. Let's see each other tomorrow."

He was silent for a long time, then agreed with weighted voice.

And she did fall asleep early, escaping the headache that had come on as soon as she had made it up, escaping Alex, and escaping herself.

Alex found Joe and Judy's B&B on his first pass around the pueblo. The door stood open. "Hello?" he called.

231

"Hi there," said Judy, popping around the corner. "Do you need a room?"

"I do. This place looks so inviting. Do you have space?"

"We do. Come on in. We don't have parking, but cars are always safe here on the street."

Judy showed Alex a room, which he praised for its charm, commenting on details of which she was proud until she glowed. He washed up and went back to the patio. Judy invited him to sit down with her and Joe. "Would you like a drink? It's just us here today."

"Looks like the people here are as nice as the town is pretty. I'd love a drink."

"Vodka tonic?"

"Perfect."

"What brings you to Itzcui?" Judy asked. "I'm always nosy," she laughed.

"You sure are!" Joe called from the bar. They chuckled fondly.

"I came to visit an old friend, but I told her I'd be in tomorrow and I don't want to show up unexpectedly."

"Who's your friend?"

"Juliet Ashe."

"Juliet Ashe? We have a Juliet Pierce."

"Yes, yes, of course. Ashe was her married name. I didn't know she wasn't using it. So you know her?"

"Heavens, yes. She stayed with us for a several months when she first arrived, and we see her all the time. We just adore her."

Alex smiled. "Me too. She's found her own place I hear."

"She bought the old hacienda! She's doing a beautiful job of restoring it. We had quite a bit of excitement over there today. She found some rooms under the house, and looks like one was full of things that used to be in the chapel. That hacienda was so grand it had its own chapel! Pretty much the whole town trooped over there to see. She's going to plant vines up behind the house and make wine and store it in the underground rooms."

"Really? I can't wait to see it. Good things are always happening to Juliet."

"Goodness! With her husband gone and her so young?"

"Of course, what am I saying. That certainly wasn't a good thing." Alex shook his head. "And I was there when it happened—that's how we got to be friends. I was able to give her some support. It happened on their honeymoon."

Joe had just come to the table with Alex's drink. He froze in amazement. "On her honeymoon? We knew it was an accident, but she didn't tell us anything else."

"It was at a resort in Thailand. They were sailing. Apparently the anchor got stuck and her husband went down to free it. He was attacked by a shark."

"A shark!"

"So ironic, really. He could have bought the country, and what good did his money do him?"

"He had a lot of money?"

"More than God."

"Really? Well . . . well, thank goodness she had something when he was gone."

"It was terrible for her though. His family fought it, practically accused her of murder. I don't know how much he left her. Probably over a hundred million."

Joe and Judy couldn't get their mouths closed.

"I guess I shouldn't have said anything about all that. Of course, she's the most genuine person, the loveliest person. She's probably afraid of making people feel uncomfortable. Please don't tell her what I said. So, is there a place I can get some dinner?"

The next morning Judy was standing pensively in the street after drawing Alex's route to La Paloma in the air and saying goodbye to him. She didn't see him turn in the opposite direction. When Zoë came by, Judy was unable to resist. "Come in for some coffee, Zoë. I have some incredible news."

"What's up? I've only got a minute. I'm going to the post office and then I'm off to Mexico City."

"Listen. A friend of Juliet's stayed here last night. A *really* handsome friend and so charming. He's visiting her now. It's awful. He said her husband was killed on their honeymoon by a shark!"

"Oh, that has *got* to be a joke!" Zoë burst out. "Eaten by a shark! On their honeymoon! Please!"

"Oh, don't do that to me, Zoë. If you get me laughing . . . ." Judy began her demonstration of what happened when someone got her laughing, but soon sobered. "But it must be true. Why would he say it if it wasn't? I can't really imagine asking her about it. And then he said Juliet's husband's family accused her of murdering him! For his money, I guess. He said she had at least a hundred million dollars!"

"Holy shit. That's no laughing matter," Zoë said, eyes wide with amazement. "She's been holding out on us. Listen, Judy, let's not tell anyone else, just keep it a secret as she apparently wants it. It seems to me her friend was talking out of turn. I can imagine—well, actually I *can't* *i*magine—there could be good reasons you wouldn't want that sort of thing known."

"Oh, that's right, Zoë. I shouldn't have said anything, but I'm glad it was to you. You're right. I'll never mention it again."

234

Juliet left early to visit her vineyards. The meeting with Alex still had her shaky; she had another cry on the way, and after meeting with Señor Arce and dealing with business, she walked over to the shady area where his house would be someday, sat against a tree, and tried to come to terms with what had happened.

Would this be the last of Alex? Surely she had been firm enough. Perhaps not so much firm as hysterical, and who knew if he might interpret her outburst as ambivalence. If she could have been cold and calm it would have been better. She could put nothing past him. How awful it was that he had found her. And what to do about telling Luis? Hank, the money, Alex—did she have to tell about Alex? Eventually she drove back to Itzcui, still not knowing how and what to confess. But when she stopped the truck in front of Luis's house and he came out, her anxiety evaporated at the sight of him.

"Where have you been, Julieta? You've been gone all day and I've been worried."

"I'm sorry. I went off to town. I had some shopping . . . ."

Luis looked in her truck, which was empty, and back at her.

"Umm, I didn't find what I needed," Juliet said guiltily.

"Are you feeling better?"

"Yes, much better."

"Julieta, you must tell me if something is wrong, if I have done something wrong."

"No, no, Luis. I don't know what was wrong with me. Please put it out of your mind."

"Will you let me take you to dinner tonight?"

"Yes, let's go to dinner. I'll get cleaned up and walk

over."

"Come inside for a moment, Julieta. Let me hold you. You have left me on the verge of collapse. I need so to have my hands on you again."

"Oh, Luis, how sweet you are." Juliet reached her hand to his face. "I'll let you have your way with me very soon."

The ghosts seemed to have departed by the time Juliet slipped into her chair at La Mina Real. She and Luis had stopped at Patty and Ron's table where they had met their son, his wife, and their two spectacular, leggy daughters. They were visiting from Madrid where the son worked for Banco Santander. He and Luis exchanged pleasantries in Spanish and Patty begged Juliet for a tour of the catacombs for the family, who had unfortunately been in San Miguel and had missed the excitement the day before. The visit was arranged. Then Juliet and Luis had been called over to talk to Socorro, who was sitting with her cousin and had a similar request for his benefit. He was an elderly, impeccably dressed gentleman, and a priest. The introductions and requisite formalities went on for some time.

Dinner was a difficult exercise in proper public behavior. They sipped their wine and ate their pasta, while keeping hands and feet scrupulously apart and refraining from leaning too close, though their eyes caressed and spoke of love. Enrique joined them about halfway through, full of excitement about the discovery. He had contacted Miguel Estrada of the Museo Nacional. He could come tomorrow. Would that be convenient? Could her workers set up some lighting in the chamber? Oh, yes—he smiled with his inside knowledge—he remembered she had given the workers those days off. Juliet said she'd get someone over to run a wire and hang a bulb.

"I believe effete though I am, I could do that," Luis said.

"Perhaps I also," said Enrique.

"I'm embarrassed. I could perfectly well do it too," Juliet laughed. "I'm in danger of forgetting how to wipe a counter, never mind wiring a switch. You know we don't live like this in the U.S. We certainly have an underclass, but they get paid more than a middle class family can take on for more than brief periods. I don't quite know what to think of my builders and maid and gardener." And her farm workers and managers and yet more construction crews and Nibels and . . . . Ashamed of her comment, Juliet's laugh was followed by a frown.

"Jes," Enrique said, not noticing, "We are living here on two levels. Jou know the word '*criada*'? It is used as jou say 'maid' but it is from the verb 'to raise,' a person raised from the servants of the house, the next generation of servants. I am saying this poorly."

"Do you mean 'born to' her position?" Juliet asked.

"I think that is right. Jes, I think so."

Luis kept his mouth shut. His parent's home in the city had a crew of gardeners, a driver, who knew how many maids and *mozos* on staff. And some of them were second generation, maybe third. Inequality of wealth in Mexico was a scandal and he didn't care to be reminded. It was too easy to congratulate oneself on being a provider of jobs, and heaven knew his father and sister were directly providing upwards of seventy thousand last time he asked. Not to mention the builders who constructed homes and bridges and roads and shops and office buildings with Ferre del Mundo materials, or the jobs those businesses provided. But what about the millions who didn't hold those jobs? Who might starve if their corn plots failed. Who lived at the mercy of the rain or corrupt officials without the money for

237

the school uniforms and textbooks or a new roof or a truck? He shook his head, tried to listen. The conversation had moved on.

"I'm so excited about the idea of setting up the chapel again," Juliet was saying. "First thing, I have to get the doors repaired. The lock is broken and some of the wood is rotten. I think I'll go over to that shop in Querétaro that has the replica hardware. Or, what do you think? Should I go to Dolores Hidalgo and buy some old mesquite doors? At any rate, I have to have real security if I'm to put the things back in there. I even thought of per-manently bolting the outside door and creating an entry from inside the house. Tours would require someone to be home anyway."

"That's a good idea if jou don't mind people walking through the house," Enrique said.

"I think there should be occasions when the hacienda is on the tour—parts of it—and some day I'll have a tasting room in the barn and will want to use the catacombs for storing wine. What's the Spanish word for cave? "

"*Cueva*," Enrique and Luis said in unison.

"But you want the word *cava*. Spanish has a word similar to the French for wine cellar," Luis explained.

"*Cava*." I'm sure when I get through with my guests they'll buy wine hand over fist. And I need a chandelier for the chapel, maybe sconces. There's that place in San Miguel. I'm so glad I put in that ox-eye window. It gives great light."

"Where will you have privacy?" Luis asked.

"Hmm. In the fields? My vineyard and winery will keep me too busy to need privacy. It's a job, you know," Juliet smiled. "But, no, you're right. Opening the chapel and the house, and the tasting room—it would mean losing my home, wouldn't it, at least part of the time. Do you think I should make the rest of the north wing into an apartment where you could retreat? Instead of three bedrooms, make two and the other into a living space or office, another kitchen? What would you do Luis?"

"I could imagine a little writing hideaway in the north wing, if it were my house," Luis answered, looking at her with curiosity and hope. She had not asked Enrique.

"Poor Juliet," Luis continued. "Soon you will have your builders, and your *muchacha* and *mozo*, and your tour director, and someone pouring wine, and someone hauling cases to the cars . . . . How will you resolve your class issues?" He spoke with more than idle curiosity.

"Self-deception, Luis. It's tried and true, right?" Juliet smiled wryly and made a hopeless gesture with her hands.

The misshapen moon was high by the time Luis and Juliet walked back from the restaurant. The evening had been sweet with the band playing on the plaza, though the clarinets could still make you wince. Crickets filled the air with chatter and the stream gurgled under the footbridge.

"Let's go sit in the garden. The night is magical. We can torture ourselves for a while," Luis said, hugging her and kissing the side of her face. Juliet seemed to be as usual; he was almost convinced everything was all right. But when they were close on the love seat and he reached for her, she pushed him gently back.

"Luis, we have come so far. I have to ask. Are you Zoë's lover?"

"Did someone tell you I was?" Someone must have said something yesterday. That was it. Fool! He should have reassured her before.

"No, one said anything but you seem . . . very close. I think everyone does think—"

"Yes, Julieta. I was her lover, I must admit it. But I never was in love with her, or told her I was. It's over. It's been over. I told her so some time ago. Believe me, it is you I wanted since the day I saw you. I remember you coming to the table and Zoë leading me on into our usual play, and I thought even then how I wanted to talk only to you and not to be seen as someone who joked or flirted his way through life."

"You liked me even then?"

"Ah yes, querida. You know what that means. *Wanted.* I wanted you. You seemed so sweet and gentle and now I know that it is true. And so intelligent and interested in ideas. You are only a little sad and sometimes I think I can change that. Will you give me the chance to try? Can you forget about Zoë? My feelings for you are so different. Please forgive me."

"I guess Zoë intimidates me, Luis. She's so exotic and beautiful."

"No, you are the beautiful one. You are the fresh and innocent one."

"Oh, that is what I am not. I have things . . . in my past. I have made mistakes. I have to tell you. I will tell you." But she fell silent.

"Tell me about your husband," Luis said, taking her hand.

"We courted for four months, and we were married for two weeks."

Luis squeezed his eyes shut. "He had his accident after you were married for only two weeks?"

"Yes."

"My God. I can't imagine. What happened?"

She sighed. "We were in Thailand on our

honeymoon. Hank—that's his name, that was his name—he loved to sail. We were sailing around these islands. And he went in the water . . . ."

"He drowned?" Luis asked as the silence grew.

"It was a shark." Juliet looked at Luis, her eyes as soft and sad as any he'd ever seen. A tear ran down her cheek. Luis wiped it away with his thumb.

"Oh, that's horrible. I'm so sorry," he said softly.

Juliet shook her head. "I think I've recovered sometimes, and then I think I haven't. There's more. He was older than me. Much older."

"How much older?"

Juliet bit her lip. "Twenty-seven years," she whispered. "Lot's of people thought the marriage was wrong. He'd been divorced and he was terribly unhappy. I *know* I made him happy. He was sweet. But the awful thing is that I can't remember any more how much I . . . . Sometimes I feel so guilty. I had a hard time and I had a bit of a breakdown. He left me with money and it feels wrong. His family resents me. They wouldn't have anything to do with me, and it felt like it poisoned things. I don't know. We were going to have children, if we'd had time . . . ."

Luis sat back and sighed. "I don't know what to say, Julieta. I'm glad you told me." Best to leave his own money out of it for the time being.

"I'm not exactly your sweet little tabula rasa, am I?"

Luis smiled. "You're my sweet surprise in life."

"I want to go forward, Luis. I hope you can overlook all that? Can you? I don't suppose you'll know that for a while."

"No. I know now. I have heard a tragic story and honest self-examination. I don't want to overlook what this tells me of your character." Luis pulled her to her feet and held her shoulders. "Let's go to bed." She nodded, not looking at him, still half-afraid.

"I'll close the house," he said. "I'll be there in a moment."

Luis began to turn off the lights, each click a sign of ownership—the master of the house, the master of her body. He thrilled with too much anticipation to do more than flick his mind over what she had said. He could see why she kept her history secret, and understand that she was traumatized. But her very acknowledgement of her guilty feelings absolved her, did it not? He lit the candles in George and Mimi's candelabra—six tapers in the two heavy sculptures of silver—and carried them into the bedroom. He put them on a table near the bed where the light could play over the carved headboard and what was to come. He closed the shutters and turned off the lamp.

Juliet came from the bathroom still fully dressed, and Luis walked toward her with extended hand. She allowed herself to be led to the bed.

"Now, let me see again how lovely you are," he said, reaching toward the buttons on her blouse. He slipped it from her shoulders, looking from her breasts, half-concealed in a flesh-colored bra, to her eyes, as Juliet tried to let go, to be simply happy with this wonderful man.

She undid the buttons at Luis's neck and wrists and pulled his shirt over his head; he pushed her back on the bed and unzipped her jeans, plunged his face into the V of lacy panties the open zipper revealed, and lost himself in the aroma men are born to adore. When their clothes were a pile on the floor, Luis whispered, *"He esperado mucho este momento. Eres hermosa, dulce, extraordinaria . . . ."* The Spanish fell on Juliet's ears as though it were her native tongue. Their bodies concaved and convexed; their hands and arms intertwined, alternately gentle and urgent, until Luis's pleasure compelled Juliet's, and hers, his.

242

Luis kissed her face, her eyes and nose, lips and cheeks. "Oh, Julieta, I loved that. I have waited for you all my life and I have kept all my desire for you. That is how I feel."

Juliet made sounds of happy pleasure, nuzzled her face into his neck, let her fingers caress his arm and hip and thigh. "Luis, how sweet you are. You may do it again and again; you have permission to do it again and again."

And so shortly, Luis did it again. He moved in her slowly and for a long time, while Juliet closed her eyes and found herself unable to cease a sound low in her throat. He gave himself over to her vibrato until it seemed to take control of his being, and his life was complete.

After, they sat on the bed and drank water Luis had fetched from the kitchen. They were happy, just that. Both smiled dazed smiles, laughed, and shook their heads at their sweet state, at the miracle of man and woman.

Luis massaged Juliet's foot, head tilted, eyes down, seeming to give the pressure of thumbs on instep all his attention. "Juliet, would you think me insane if I asked you to marry me?"

Juliet started. "Is that a question about your mental health or—?"

Luis laughed nervously. "You would never know that I try to express myself well. The question properly phrased is: Will you marry me?"

Juliet found herself speechless. She opened her mouth and closed it. This might be the most perfect moment of her life, but she couldn't grasp it.

"I don't know what to say."

"Does it seem soon? It is soon, but then again, don't we know?"

"I don't know what you are thinking. Maybe you think I am a bad girl if I don't marry you after what we've

243

been doing, that you will have to give me up because you can't respect me."

Luis laughed. "What gives you that idea? No, indeed, Julieta. If you won't marry me I'll gladly live with you in sin, and be delighted to teach sin how to sin more thoroughly." He pulled her close and whispered against her cheek. "Yes, sin . . . . There is gluttony and I will consume every molecule of you. Lust. Too obvious." He leaned back on the pillow. "*Pereza*. How do you say it in English? Laziness?"

"Sloth."

"Oh, yes. Slod."

"Slo-TH. Slo-TH." Juliet laughed.

"Now she is making fun of my accent while I am trying to make love to her!" Luis raised his eyes to heaven. "Slo*th*. Isn't there an animal?"

"A lazy animal."

"Yes, I will sloth in bed with you all day and night. Sloth. That sounds quite sinful." Luis sat up and looked intently into her eyes. "Julieta, I know I'm crazy but I assure you I've never been crazy like this before. I am standing aside and saying, 'What is he thinking?' and then shrugging and saying, 'Let him do what he wants; he's a grown man. He wants you.' "

Juliet looked down. "Oh, Luis. There is still much to tell."

"What? You have not married again!"

"No."

He smiled. "Are you a fugitive?"

"No. I'm, I'm . . . ."

"Is it something bad?"

"No, not really. There's just . . . I know you don't really know me, and I'm not sure I know much about you either. Be truthful. Haven't you hidden things from me too?"

"I know I have not hidden my character from you. I have not hidden the work I have chosen for my life. I have not hidden my sexual orientation," Juliet smiled. "or my values. I am hoping you will take me for what you see. There is nothing I am ashamed of that you need to know."

"I can't believe there is, Luis. I'm grateful that you want me. I'm *overjoyed* that you want me! Let me think. Let me think. Marriage is so big."

"Julieta, should we talk about where you go on all those days you are not at La Paloma?"

She did not meet his eye.

"Forgive me. We will talk another time. I want nothing to interfere with the glow of such a night. I will let you think—and I will sneak back to my house so that Margarita will not find me here in the morning and tell the village."

"Margarita has time off, remember?"

"Well, someone is sure to come, and, truthfully, I feel I have found some great treasure chest of creativity and I want to lift the lid and run my fingers through the gems. I want to work! If you married me, I would go only to the next room and could come back to kiss you in your sleep every few minutes, but as it is . . . ."

"I *think* I am flattered that I've had this effect on you. You may go." Juliet smiled. "*Hasta mañana, mi amor.* Is that right?"

"Yes, it's absolutely right. I am so fortunate to be this man."

Luis was enough ashamed of himself not to focus on Julieta's reluctance to tell whatever she was not telling. When was *he* going to be open and honest? But of course the truth was that he wanted his pledge, wanted to successfully woo her before he confessed. He had weaseled out of her charge that he'd not been honest, but she would think back and notice, he was sure. Could he bear to risk losing her after what had happened these nights? Never had he encountered a woman who so excited him. Had she liked how he made love to her? Had he been too quick? Surely the first night. How darling she had been, playing with him and the decrepit truck. They were so perfectly attuned, their humor and their bodies. Perhaps he needed the truth of his fortune to win her. What kind of fool would not use all his assets on so important a quest?

The story of her marriage! What a dreadful event. But it made sense of her desire to have a new life in Mexico. Her husband had clearly left her the money for the hacienda and her comfortable life, but Luis greatly admired her determination to plant her vineyard and sell her wines. She seemed to say she felt guilty over the money she'd inherited; he needed to make sure that she'd never fear more guilt by confounding his own money in his suit.

Luis took stock. His time incognito in Itzcui had been the happiest since his time at Yale. No one was befriending him for his name, no one was flirting with it either. And he'd had friends and sex enough. Soon enough relinquished? What if Julieta found out how recently he had told Zoë that they were through? Would she believe that he had not slept with her since they'd met?

And then Itzcui had brought him Julieta, the beautiful, gentle, feminine, considerate object of his desire. His delight in her hadn't developed over time, though it had increased. No, it had sprung on him and wrestled him to the ground almost at first sight. They could slip into a life of companionship, of comfort, creativity, and real achievement, he was sure. He lived too much in his mind. He needed her vineyards, and wine, and laborers close by

246

him for a full life. Did she want the fanciest tractor made? More vineyards? He would buy them for her. Did she want to travel? Have old masters over the fireplace of her beautiful home? At last, something to do with the money.

But she had made a joke when he proposed. He had been precipitate, yes, but would she have him in the end? Would that dead husband and whatever pain he represented get out of the way? Surely he could best a man, even one with so many more years of experience, who could never make love to her—and she had come! He was sure. Oh, *hermosa!* Was it possible he could have such a precious partner?

Luis stayed up for nearly two hours sitting in front of his computer, but not working after all. He examined the last several days, the days of headlong pleasure, and of terror when she seemed to withdraw. He did not doubt that he wanted to marry her. Marriage to Julieta was like a literary device that miraculously manifests; a link that makes the parts of a story whole, meaningful, and satisfying; a link that makes a life whole. Luis completed by Julieta. The banal tale of Luis's life lifted to literature.

At last he went to bed and slept, and in the morning leapt up with all the enthusiasm for writing he had hoped for the night before.

He opened a new document. He wrote about a man deep asleep in the dim cold of the sea. In his dream, the mermaids are calling him down, down into icy darkness. They try to entice him with open mouths and taut, frigid breasts. He swims up and up with all his strength, but he is so very deep he begins to doubt that he will ever see the miracle above him. Just before he enters into hopeless certainty that he will drown and stay forever, he bursts through to the precious air-borne smell and hot light of woman. He was *náufrago*—castaway—in the void, and she is the miracle of the *tierra* that saves him. He crawls up her smooth, salty *playa*, and evolves from a meager, maimed fish-being to a brilliant, intelligent excrescence of thrusting desire. He buries himself in her mysterious substance— yielding, supporting, malleable, and firm. Her sand is silky, warm and dry above, cool, calming below, and lower yet, wet as his home element, and pure as the eternity of space. He will live forever within her perfect holiness. He saved the document as "Julieta."

His muchacha came and cooked a breakfast he ate without seeing. He stopped briefly and called Juliet. Her machine answered—she was likely walking her terraces— and told her he was working, and loved her.

Juliet had barely finished her own breakfast when Enrique arrived with Señor Estrada from the Museo Nacional. Short, very round, and full of enthusiasm, he pronounced the whole hacienda *preciosa*. The hidden items were *tesoros valiosos!* His inspection—by flashlight since no lights had been strung—found one of the reclinatorios to be sadly worm-eaten, the red velvet padding for knees and arms nearly threadbare, as were the seats of the matching chairs, but much else was intact.

"Ah, but this is very fine woodwork. I would guess late eighteenth century. These are all rosewood. And, let us see . . . ." Señor Estrada moved over to the large rectangle facing the wall. Three pair of hands gently turned it around and lifted a stiff piece of canvas that covered it. "Oh, my. This is very beautiful. This painting is Peruvian, I believe. School of Cuzco. That would be much older. See the intricacy of the work, the detail of the jewels, the hair, the Spanish court dress the Virgin wears? And look at the paloma that hovers above her. See, it holds the olive branch, the symbol of God's promise not to again destroy the earth by flood. Perhaps the hacienda was named for this painting. And the gilded frame! *Very* fine. It will need restoration here and here. The painting seems perfectly intact. A miracle! This must have been over the altar.

"A very charming carving here," Señor Estrada moved to the glassed shrine holding the statue. "San José without doubt. These gilded halos! Beautiful. And how rich the green robe. The *Niño* is very finely done. I am most impressed with the preservation."

And on to the contents of the boxes: A blackened chalice in heavily-tarnished silver, rather small. Lovely candelabra, also tarnished. A monstrance. A foxed and yellowed linen altar cloth with an intricate design in pulled threads. At the opening of the last box, Juliet was the one who exclaimed the loudest. It contained four bottles that looked like they could be wine! Communion wine, Señor Estrada opined. Juliet extracted a hand-blown bottle whose cork was sealed with wax. No label. She shook it lightly. There was liquid! The light was so dim that not even a level could be seen, much less color, though its weight suggested it was full. If this was early twentieth century wine, it might even be drinkable.

"Could I be permitted to send one of these bottles to the United States for analysis, Señor Estrada? I've studied wine at the University of California and I know one can tell a great deal about the contents even without opening the bottle."

"I think that would be very interesting, señora. I can see no objection and I can arrange a permit for you. Would you like me to send my assistants here to bring these things to the museum for cleaning and conservation?"

"Oh, yes, but if I can provide security to your satisfaction, do you think I could have them back to restore the chapel? What if I made it available to the public?"

"I believe these are legally yours, señora. How fine if you shared them with the pueblo."

"Do you believe these things were hidden during the anti-clerical movement?" Juliet asked.

"It is very likely. Hidden and somehow forgotten."

"Let me show you some other things in another chamber," Juliet said, leading the way down the passage.

It was nearly noon when Zoë appeared on Luis's porch, tapped at his open door, and entered without asking. He felt annoyed, but rose with his usual graciousness and kissed her cheek. "Would you like some coffee, Zoë? How have you been? Did you go to Mexico City?"

"No. I spent an entire day searching for my copy of the contract I signed with my gallery for my December show and didn't find it. We have a serious lack of agreement about the terms and I'm just certain—oh, never mind. I hate griping, don't you?"

"It is entirely unlike you to complain, and why would you? You lead a charmed life where the road rises to meet you and your contracts are to your advantage."

"I suppose it is true, though it always seemed you'd be likely to trip if the road wouldn't stay put."

Luis smiled.

"I've been realizing, however, that I'm a girl who has to work for a living."

"What has made you think like that? Isn't working on something you love, isn't that the best way to live? And don't you make a good living?"

"Well, I've been thinking what it would be like to do something you love *and* have all the money in the world."

Luis grew cold. "What kind of fantasy is this?"

"No fantasy for someone I know."

Luis sat back in his chair and stared at Zoë as his maid brought the coffee in. Zoë rose from her chair to put cream in her cup, sat back down, and watched Luis stir his coffee slowly. The smell of cinnamon filled the air.

"Aren't you curious who I'm talking about? Or do you know?"

Luis thought quickly. Should he deny it? Did he *have* deniability, or had she met someone who had told her all?

"No, I don't know," he said, rather grimly.

"You don't seem very curious. But I can't resist, it's so extraordinary."

Luis said nothing. Zoë seemed repugnant to him suddenly. She was surely the last person to whom he'd want his secret revealed. She seemed to have no inkling that he was stiffening with anger.

"The word is that Juliet is fabulously rich."

"Juliet?" Luis sloshed coffee into his saucer. "What do you mean, fabulously rich?"

"*That* got your attention. Say, a hundred million, and I'm not talking *pesos*. Judy told me after an old friend of Juliet's told her. A man came by to visit her a couple of days ago. Did you meet him? I didn't. And he also told Judy that her husband died on their *honeymoon* and, get this, he was killed by a *shark*! And his family thought *she* had killed him."

"Zoë, I don't know what to say. This sounds either preposterous or extremely private. I think I feel very sorry for Juliet that this is being said about her behind her back. Who knows what the truth may be? So, you learned about this when?"

"Yesterday."

"Why did you decide to tell *me*?"

"Ah, Luis. Circumspect as always. Well, sorry, I couldn't resist. I thought you would want to know."

251

"Why is that?"

"You've been keeping her company, haven't you? And we don't keep secrets, you and I. Maybe she's a black widow, and you should be careful. Or maybe it would be worth the risk?" Zoë gave him a cool smile.

"Zoë, this is such a small place, and we have too much gossip already. Wouldn't it be kind *not* to tell people this?"

"Yes, you're right. I won't tell anyone else. But admit that you acted like it was the news of the century."

"No, I'm not going to admit that. And now, my lovely Zoë, you must forgive me. I was actually working, and my muse is tapping her foot waiting for me to get back to her."

Zoë rose and moved toward the door. "Don't pretend you're just going to forget what I said and go straight back to work. But I do apologize for interrupting you. Who knows what priceless prose has been lost forever. *Hasta la proxima.*" She danced down the steps and disappeared in a flash of color and a cascade of black hair.

Luis's head spun. He jumped up and paced. If Julieta had money, if Julieta had *real* money, then the issue would be moot! If she accepted him, it would be because she loved him. Oh, let it be true, he thought. What should he do? Tell her he knew? Respect her privacy until she was ready to tell him? Surely better. Since the part about the honeymoon and the shark was true, likely the part about the money was as well. Should he go ahead and confess to her about his situation? Yes. Definitely yes.

Zoë walked up the hill toward the plaza feeling an unfamiliar prick of guilt. What if Luis was right and the truth was other than Judy had told her? Perhaps it would be only fair to tell Juliet that these rumors were going around.

Let her deny or quash or ask for secrecy. It would be interesting to see her reaction in any case. Zoë stopped, turned and went back down the hill. She chose a path that took her to the hacienda without passing Luis's open doors. For some reason, she didn't want him to know she was visiting Juliet; hopefully she wouldn't find that he had run over ahead of her.

"Juliet! Juliet!" she called when she reached the door.

"Annette?" Juliet's voice came faintly from her office.

"No, it's Zoë."

"Hi Zoë. I'll be right there." Juliet shut down her computer and slid a stack of papers into a drawer, which she locked. Zoë was looking out into the garden when Juliet entered the room.

"Hi," Zoë smiled. "Mind if I visit?"

"Of, course not! Have a seat. How about some tea? Weren't you going to Mexico City?"

Zoë told Juliet about the contract problem, but with full she-said, they-said details. There had been no sense going to Mexico City until she found it. Juliet told about Señor Estrada's visit.

"Was it true that there was marijuana down there?"

"Oh, my God. Tons. They came to get it in the middle of the night, and there was shooting, and I was hiding in my room, and then they drove away with this colossal load. Who told you?"

"Enrique. Weren't you scared?"

"Yes, as a matter of fact, I was, but now it seems like a great adventure."

Zoë looked down and fiddled with the fringe on her rebozo. "Juliet, there's something I need to talk to you about," she said at last.

253

"Oh?"

"I thought it would be kind to tell you that there's a rumor going around about you."

Christ! Did everyone know she'd slept with Luis already? "Oh?" she said again.

"Frankly, the rumor is that you have a very great deal of money."

"How much is a great deal? I have *some* money."

"They say a hundred million dollars."

Juliet blanched, tried to laugh. "That's a nice round number, but ridiculous. Who is *they*?"

"It seems a friend of yours stayed with Joe and Judy."

"When was that?"

"After the discovery of the chapel things? He told them."

Alex!

"If this person is who I think it is, he's one of the all-time champion liars," Juliet said. "More like a sociopath. Nothing he says can be believed, that's for sure. My husband left me some money. If I'm careful and can develop a successful wine business, I'll be okay. That's all. Who knows about this?"

"Well, Joe and Judy, and me, and Luis."

"Luis." Juliet tried to stay calm, and failing that, tried to appear calm. "I'm surprised he didn't mention it."

"Yes, I know you two are close." Zoë peered at Juliet, trying to read her face. Zoë's finesse—Luis had had about a ten-minute window to tell Juliet what he knew— had dropped a bomb, not an eventuality she had been careful to avoid.

"I guess not that close," Juliet said softly. And how closely did Zoë know about her and Luis? "Thank you for telling me this. I hope you'll say that the news of my riches is greatly exaggerated, if people ask." She made a brittle sound, not quite a laugh. "I wish!" Was that convincing enough?

When Zoë had gone, Juliet bolted the doors, went to her room, and lay on the bed. Tears rolled down her face unchecked onto the duvet. *He had known. He had known.* Caring attention, a seduction, a rushed proposal, and all the time he had known. And he was Zoë's confidant as well as lover—perhaps former, perhaps not.

The tears dried. The heart hardened. She lay for an hour; the phone rang twice, each time making her angrier at the thought of Luis and his excuses. Later the phone rang again, and shortly after, someone knocked on the door. Knocked again more loudly. Luis. Part of her longed to speak to him, to let him make it right, whatever that would mean, but she would not. Let him wonder why the door was locked.

An idea had hovered at the back of her mind for some time: A plan to give away the money. There had always been the idea of creating a foundation—world health, micro-loans to women, assistance to doctors studying family medicine, mosquito nets . . . . The problem was that she would need to be so intimately involved with programs and management. It was daunting, choosing truly useful and well-run programs and competent staff—a full-time job. She couldn't do that and her vineyards too, which were where her heart lay. She would give the money to someone who would use it well.

How much should she keep? A million? It might take that to fully equip Las Fincas. Two? She would keep all her other vineyards in the U.S. and Mexico, and her investment in Quinta da Agostinho, and some cash or liquefiable assets, and she would be nearly a normal person again. Blessed, not cursed.

In the hour after her cry, Juliet set her decision in motion. She would give the money to a proven team—the Jim and Melody Jordan Foundation. They were devoting their enormous fortune to world health, education, women's issues. She went to her office, found a contact online, and called. She told the woman who answered that she was Juliet Ashe and that she wished to talk to Melody Jordan about making a gift to the foundation in the name of her late husband, Henry Ashe. Would Mrs. Jordan call at her convenience to arrange for the foundation to meet with her financial team in San Francisco to discuss the transfer? Juliet mentioned a figure, and was graciously treated, not surprisingly. Mrs. Jordan would call tomorrow at the latest. Juliet gave her number and explained that she would be traveling and might be intermittently out of touch until the day after that. Melody Jordan called back in ten minutes.

After their conference, after a warm and emotional meeting of minds, Juliet called for a plane to pick her up in Querétaro to take her to San Francisco. One last time for a private plane, she thought, and pulled out her suitcase to pack. In the next hour she phoned Enrique to say that she had been called away, and to ask him to oversee the transfer of the chapel furnishings to the Museo. She told Margarita that a month's wages were awaiting her, asked her to arrange a watchman until the artifacts were safely removed, and to empty the refrigerator. She tucked one of the communion wine bottles in her suitcase. Then she closed the house, ignoring the buzzing telephone in her purse, and drove off in the pickup. As she passed Luis's house, he saw her and raced toward the door. She did not glance his way.

Luis collapsed in his chair. Something had happened. It had to be Zoë. He took out his phone and dialed her number.

"Zoë, good afternoon. Forgive me for intruding, but did you by chance talk to Juliet about what you told me?"

"Well, yes. I decided you were right and it would be best to tell her of the rumor."

"Did you tell her that you told me?"

"Yes. She asked who knew."

Luis paused. "I am sorry to ask, but did you suggest that we were lovers?"

"Really, Luis, I didn't think it relevant. Am I missing something? Don't you want to know what she said?"

"No thank you, Zoë." He snapped the phone shut with more force than was necessary.

Luis realized that he had approached the ramifications of the news from his point of view only. He hadn't considered the possibility that Zoë might tell Julieta, and what Julieta might think if she learned that he had been told. But, no, how could it be a problem? He had fallen in love and told her so. Had he said it properly? But he *had* asked her to marry him, *without* knowing! If Julieta had the same fear he did, if she was living as secretly as he was, she nevertheless would realize he could not have been thinking of her money. Whatever Zoë might have intimated, surely Julieta would have believed him that it was over. Wouldn't she? But something had happened.

Luis crossed to La Paloma. All the windows were shuttered, both wings. He walked around the barn and, looking over the wall, saw that the back gate was bolted and the doors on the porch shuttered too. He pushed at the door that led to the garden. It did not give. Julieta was gone. He had done something terribly wrong. Maybe he had been a fool to leave her last night. Did it appear that he had just had sex with her and left? What had been so

257

important about writing just then and what made him think a woman would put up with such a thing? And how could he find her? He had her cell number of course. He dialed yet again and got her message yet again. "Julieta! Julieta! Call me!" How many times had he called today? What if she were going back to the U.S.? He had no idea where she would be.

Luis walked dejectedly up to the plaza, to the restaurant. Elena brought him a beer and sat down to chat. She and Silvio wanted to stock better wines, she said. Did he have any favorites—good value for money? She wanted to talk to Juliet too. And she'd been thinking about the chapel museum at La Paloma. She wanted to put up signs. Perhaps Juliet—or better the presidencia—could print up brochures for the tourists. Luis grunted, mumbled. He knew why she was talking to him about Julieta and wine and the hacienda. People were noticing, and here he was terrified that there was no longer anything to notice.

Margarita passed on the street, and he jumped up to intercept her. Where had Juliet gone? She didn't know, but she had the month off. A month! *En la madre*! He pressed his fingers to his brow. He had blown it.

CHAPTER **NINE**

Juliet didn't reach San Francisco until after two in the morning. She collapsed at the Pacific Heights house and drove to Napa the next afternoon. When her father got home from the winery he found Juliet on the porch swing. She jumped up and gave him a hug.

"Julie! What are you doing here? Are you locked out? Where is Shirley?"

"Doesn't matter. I was having a lovely sit. I've come running back, Daddy. I've messed up again."

He joined her in the swing. "What's happened?"

She confessed. She had gotten involved with a Mexican man and had now run away from him. She told the true story of how she and Alex had broken up, and how Alex had shown up at her new home. But, the same thing had happened again—she'd found another lover with bad faith.

"I fell for him, Daddy. Why does this happen— Oh, never mind. I know exactly why this happens to me."

"Did I meet him? Was it Raul?"

"God, no."

"Is it Enrique?"

"Not another older man, Daddy. Just nine years older. Christ, that's bad enough. No, he was out of town when you were there. He goes to Mexico City a lot. Who knows what he does there."

"Oh, baby. I'm so sorry. What are you going to do? Are you going back?"

"I can't even think about that. But here's what I am going to do, Daddy. I'm going to give the money away."

"What! Julie, that's crazy. You're one of the luckiest people on earth. You can do anything!"

"Don't worry, I'm plenty spoiled. I'll keep some, and I'll keep my vineyards. I *want* to make a go of my wine. I *want* to work. I just don't want to work on my damn portfolio. It's full-time, Daddy, and I'm still doing a lousy job. Actually, the truth is that it isn't full-time and it should be. As soon as I got online down there my inbox filled up with pleas and requests, and the Nibels are always recommending sell this and buy that. I never catch up with the work. I'm thinking of giving a million to my friend in Willits for his 'self-sustainable' work. Most of the rest I'm giving to the Jim and Melody Jordan Foundation. They do great stuff and that's *all* they do. They support all the causes I believe in."

"I see. I understand. You were keeping a lot of people employed up here, Julie. Hank's financial team isn't going to be happy about losing their meal ticket."

"No, they're not, but I'm trying to give up being responsible for so many livelihoods. I'll keep Fred on for taxes and bills and the like. What do you think, Daddy? The vineyards? Enough to finish building Las Fincas? My interest in Quinta da Agostinho? I was thinking of buying you a nice house here in the valley—with a cottage for me, if you don't mind. Maybe a couple of million in securities.

And then an article in the papers about how the Ashe estate has made an impressive donation to Jim and Melody Jordan, and all the fortune hunters can take note and leave me alone."

"When are you doing this?"

"I have a big meeting with the Nibels next week in the city. It's going to be awful. I'm going to need all my courage to face those guys. We have to figure what goes in the package to Jordan, how we transfer it, my tax issues. I only have the vaguest idea how it works, but the Jordans are sending me the CEO of the trust. She'll be arriving in San Francisco tomorrow, and Fred and I are meeting with her. I hope she's a good hand-holder."

"Julie, this breaks my heart to see you so burdened." Sheldon put his arm around her shoulder and pulled her close.

"Daddy, I think this is the answer to my problems. I'll still be rich enough to feel shame anytime I want, but *this* amount is like a black hole trying day and night to suck me into oblivion. I don't want to be a rich heiress. I don't."

"Is this partially about the accusations that you married Hank for his money?"

"Yeah, I guess. I never had the chance to prove I didn't, and somehow when he died it was like confirming I did. No one in his family has spoken to me since the funeral, and it wasn't very pretty then. Part of me feels ashamed. I know it's not logical, but I do. If I give the money away that proves I'm a decent person, right?"

Sheldon sighed and squeezed her shoulder. "Baby, you have to quit torturing yourself over this. There was never a more decent person."

"Thanks, Daddy. Though I don't suppose giving the money away is going to make things with his family any better."

"I dare say not. But that Louise . . . . A life without her is a life well-lived." He paused. "Julie, was this also about what I did to your mother?

"What do you mean?"

"I always thought that you married Hank in part because I failed you, and your mom. Mostly your mom. No, mostly you, because she couldn't live, hard as she tried. That maybe you were looking for the support I hadn't . . ."

Juliet sighed. "I was angry and hurt, it's true. And I was . . . awful. I was awful to you. I'm so sorry. But I can't be superior about life choices any more. I love you. I want you to be happy, and I'm not going to say how that has to look."

"Bless you, baby." Sheldon kissed her cheek.

"When I'm through with the Nibels, we'll go look at houses, okay?"

The Ashe Mansion was profoundly silent, emptier than it ever had been in its existence. Juliet stood in the cold central hall where you saw the enormous parlor to the right and the library to the left. The hall continued past the base of the curved steps, past the formal dining room, past the oval ballroom with ladies' and gentlemen's retiring rooms hidden in the spandrels, past the less formal sitting rooms, and on toward the pantries, kitchen and servants' quarters. It was time for it to go; it had been sitting unused for a very long time. Once she had considered renting it, but the prospect of storing the contents was one of those daunting issues under whose weight she had fallen. Now she had come to choose some things for her dad's new house and the large guest cottage behind—the closing was tomorrow—and others for shipping to La Paloma, along with the boxes of books in the basement. Then an offer of the parental home, including the remaining furniture, the

Sargent paintings, and Hank's mother's jewels—among them the necklace she had worn to that ball—would be extended to Hank's family. If they didn't want all or some of it, an estate sale and the open market awaited.

When she entered the silent plush of oriental carpets, silk brocade drapery, and rich upholstery, Juliet was almost overwhelmed by sadness. If it weren't for the studio portrait of Hank on the Steinway, resembling a youngish senior statesman, she would hardly be able to remember what he looked like and how he had moved through these rooms. Upstairs in the master suite there would be their wedding photo—more like the bride and her beaming father. Juliet could no longer recapture what she had been thinking. Had she been such a moral coward as to try *not* to think? These rugs— Serapi, Herez—did she have any right to them? But, if not her, who? She had made a deal with Hank to try to grow into ownership, to share in the disposition of the fortune. They had planned to move toward philanthropy. Certainly Hank would never have let go the reins, as she was doing now, but still she was keeping faith, wasn't she?

Juliet suddenly remembered hiding her rings in the library. Hank had shown her the copy of *Pepys' Diary* that contained the combination to the safe hidden in the master bath, and she had taken off her wedding and engagement rings some time after he died and left them in the hidden compartment in the book.

The shelves were largely filled with leather-bound decorator copies of the classics, but there were a few others: *A Perfect Storm*, some Patrick O'Brien, James Lee Burke, and Robert Ludlum. Hank's impressive collection of charts was kept in a special cabinet. The most valuable book was a signed first edition of *Two Years Before the Mast* by Richard Henry Dana, Jr. In it was a reference to the ship

Ann McKim of Baltimore on which one Nathaniel Ashe had reached California in the 1820s. The family story was that his leg had been crushed by a loose water-cask, and he'd been put ashore in San Francisco where he'd recovered. He'd opened—what else—a hardware store.

Just as she was rich because Hank had been rich, Hank had been rich because Nathaniel had established his store a few short years before gold was discovered in northern California. Some of the men who came in the rush found gold, some did not, but all needed something he had to sell, and many of them filled their needs at his store.

The Ashe family was able to believe in its exceptionalism because Nathaniel Ashe had let loose a cascade of money that had flowed down through the years. Subsequent Ashes had only needed not to be profligate to have the wherewithal to invest and increase. It was rather like the endless self-congratulation of the U.S. whose people failed to note the accident of being first off the mark in exploiting the oceans of oil fortuitously located beneath its waves of grain.

She found the Pepys where she remembered and opened it. The star sapphire surrounded with diamonds and the pavé wedding band beside it gleamed importantly in the dim room. Juliet slipped the sapphire halfway down her finger and marveled again at the depth of the blue and the sharp bright points that held their own within the brilliant diamond surround. It had been on her hand as she reached for Hank's white arm in the bloody sea. The shark swam back into her memory, looking at her with its dead Cretaceous eyes.

Juliet hurriedly replaced the rings in the book and put it on the desk. She would never wear them of course, but it would be wrong not to keep them. Perhaps they could go to a son for his bride? And what son was that, she thought sadly.

Looking around the library, she saw nothing that would suit the new house in Napa, or La Paloma. Hank had said the house had been mostly furnished by his grandmother, and later, his mother and Blaire. The decor didn't represent his taste—not that his taste had been her own taste. But she would keep some of the less formal carpets, the enormous Chinese pottery horse in the dining room, and a fine painting of a Napa vineyard upstairs. A collection of Victorian majolica would be right in La Paloma, too. Hank's portrait. A contemporary sofa from the bedroom and a couple of armchairs would furnish her living room behind her dad's house, and an old sea chest had always appealed to her. She wandered from room to room for two hours, remembering, tagging pieces for the movers. She'd take the lovely Frette linens, the cookware, an oak table from the breakfast room. The ormolu; the faux-, or perhaps not, Louis IV; the silver tableware, tea service, serving platters—no. Nor the Limoges, nor the collection of porcelain birds, though they were exquisite. She had understood that Blaire got quite a settlement in furnishings, as well as houses and money; Juliet wondered again what on earth she had taken that all this stuff had been left behind.

Later, after the movers had packed and delivered things to the new house in Napa, after other items had gone to storage to be shipped to Mexico, after the nautical charts had been sent to George, and after the future of the house had been settled, Juliet returned to say goodbye.

She sat at the bottom of the stairs in the echoing entry hall where the marble floor protested the loss of its rug with a frigid glare. Twisting to look up and back, she saw the stair top where she had stood while Fred and Alex talked in the library. And now Luis. She had been broadsided. So gentle and polite, so careful of her presumed pain. Those little daily visits, cups of coffee, lunch on the plaza. The laughter, the lovemaking with more *love* in it than she had ever known. Did it have to matter that he knew about the money? Juliet's eyes each squeezed out a tear. It did.

Luis, the Man of Mystery. He treated everyone as he treated her, didn't he? Had he ever said an impolite word in his entire life, she wondered? Was he emotionless to the core? Did a mind all too clever know just how to play her? Juliet had no idea how she would achieve distance. To return to Itzcui was to re-enter an intimate sphere of society: Joe and Judy, Annette, Socorro, Enrique, Elena— Zoë. Even she was interesting company. She was not likely to find available men after she had firmly put Luis into the category of . . . of . . . could one go back to *acquaintance* after what had happened? But why not, with that formulaic way of interacting he was so good at? She'd encountered the master, hadn't she?

She wasn't really depressed, she told herself, not like after Hank and Alex. The future would be different. There was much to be excited about: her winery, the new plantings on the terraces behind the house, the chapel, her lovely La Paloma, and even the free time to read and think. Her responsibilities were reduced a thousand times, down to just what she loved. Should she report to Luis that the money was gone, or perhaps just say that she was not ready to move on from the past, and, also that it was too painful to discuss it? She was sorry, but she had realized . . . something.

It seemed it would be impossible to hate him even if her money had been a temptation. But if he had lied about Zoë? Perhaps not then. She'd know if he went back to Zoë, though he might be mad at her for telling that he knew about the fortune. Oh, this was crass. At least with his refined demeanor, an unpleasant confrontation would be out of the question.

Fred had contacted Paige and David, Louise and Evelyn, to say that Hank's house and many of its furnishings were available. Negotiations had ensued and just this morning, she and Evelyn had agreed to a price of $34.25 million. It would be added to the Jordan package, about which the family as yet knew nothing. Juliet had thought hard about whether her obligation was to give the money to Paige and David, but she simply didn't want to. Fred had told her that Paige was in divorce proceedings after an embarrassingly short marriage, and David had just required a full court press to get him out of a cocaine possession charge. The money would do more good in the Jordans' hands.

When she stood, she caught her reflection in the gilt-framed mirror. She wore her San Francisco clothing—a crisp blue business suit with white-edged lapels that she'd put on for the negotiations that morning. It had been extremely civil. Thank God it wasn't Louise buying the house. But her memories were as cold as the marble floor. She put three sets of keys on the side table. It was nearly over.

Sheldon was amused at finding himself in his spacious new house and content to think Juliet had tied down another million or more if she should ever need it. The guesthouse would be her residence in the States and she would pay the taxes on the whole.

Bill, up in Willits with his family, his foundation, and his internet community of visionaries for the new energy-strapped world, was beside himself with Juliet's generosity. He'd make her proud, he vowed. He was sorry she wouldn't accept a place on the board.

At Davis, Juliet had been warmly greeted by two of her old professors and had thrilled them with the bottle of communion wine from Mexico. They would get right on it, they said, showing her how a syringe could be slipped down alongside the cork, and discussing the chemical and other analyses that could be made on the extracted wine. They chatted about a recent hoax involving wine bottles reputedly belonging to Thomas Jefferson, supposedly found walled-up in a cellar in France.

And in a few weeks, they had reported that the wine was definitely older than the 1950s when atmospheric nuclear tests had started. Its color was a red so deep as to be nearly brown, with heavy sedimentation and an alcohol content of 11.68. The cork had been imported from Spain, but the seal, composed of chalk, shellac, and turpentine colored with cochineal, was Mexican, as was the hand-blown bottle apparently made from the lime green glass manufactured in Puebla, the ancient center west of Mexico City. DNA testing had matched the content to the Listan Prieto grape, grown in sixteenth-century Spain, which had recently been identified as the so-called "Mission Grape" brought to California by the Franciscans.

Juliet took back her bottle on a return trip to the lab. Maybe someday there would be an event important enough to open it—with backup at the ready in case its flavor wasn't up to the occasion.

A month passed and more. As her affairs fell into place, Juliet regained her balance. The Jordan Foundation and the Nibels had reached agreement. Vines for the terraces were ordered and ready to be shipped; vans and brokers were standing by. As she drifted into sleep, her mind was often pleasantly occupied with Las Fincas and the new vineyard. She would be getting to her life's work at last.

But she couldn't pretend that there wasn't lots of pain and apprehension when she allowed herself to think of Luis. At first his e-mails had bombarded her inbox. She had deleted every one unopened, and recently they seemed to have stopped coming. His too-sweet protestations of love were all spoiled, but someday she'd find someone right, and with the money gone, she'd never have to go through this again.

The press release from the Jordan Foundation appeared and was commented on everywhere: A generous gift of $10.3 billion by Mrs. Henry L. Ashe in honor of her late husband's interest in health and environment. Mr. Ashe's connection to Home Base was recalled. Also noted was the even larger amount given by investor James Winslow the previous year. The Jordan foundation was reported to have an endowment of $58 billion, down approximately $7 billion in the recession.

CHAPTER TEN

La Paloma was as still as the Ashe Mansion had been when Juliet let herself in the front door. She was so used to the sound of her builders, of Margarita clattering in the kitchen, or sweeping the floors that it hardly seemed like home, but she trusted that word was going out this minute that she'd been sighted driving through town, and before long everyone would be here to greet her and start work again. She had left so quickly that she'd had to wire wages to the community savings and loan for the boys to pick up, since she hadn't wanted them to find permanent work elsewhere, or think she had skipped out on their severance pay. She had been able to keep her phone and electricity paid, too.

Juliet put down her suitcases and walked from room to room, throwing open the shutters on the windows and doors. From her bedroom, she looked toward Luis's house. It had been closed up when she went by—not an unusual sight—but Juliet had the sinking feeling that he might be gone. And had a day gone by without her thinking of him?

The phone rang.

"Juliet, is that you?" Judy cried.

"Hi, Judy! How did you know I just walked in the door? How are you?"

"How are *you?* Joe saw you drive through the plaza. Come on over for dinner, okay? We've missed you terribly."

"Sure, great. What time?"

"Come at five. We'll watch the BBC."

"Lovely. See you then. I'll tell you about my trip."

Ah, but would she? Now was the time to figure out what she was going to say. Should she just come clean? Yes, I was blindingly rich, and now the Jordan Foundation is? She imagined the looks, the billion-yard stares. No one got over it.

Joe and Judy soon reminded her of all she loved about Itzcui as her vodka tonic was set before her and the latest gossip was elaborated into hilarious tales. But soon it was her turn.

"We didn't know what had happened to you, Juliet. We were so worried."

"I'm sorry, Judy. I was thoughtless. I went to see my dad."

"Is he all right?"

"Yes, he is now," she said evasively, but it was time. "Judy, we need to talk about that rumor about my 'fortune.' Zoë told me that you had heard about it."

"Oh, Juliet. I was so afraid I'd done a bad thing."

"Judy, you were taken in just as I once was. You heard it from Alex, right?"

"Yes. He seemed so nice."

"Well, he's not. When my husband died, Alex got the idea that I had lots of money and he came after me. I'm

272

sorry to say that I fell for him and was considering marrying him when I found out what sort of person he is. He was back trying again. Look, I don't have a hundred million, nothing like it. My husband had children from a previous marriage, and he left me some money too, but I've run through most of it. Please, don't let people think I'm rich. It would make everything weird. Will you tell people the truth, if they ask? Please?"

"I'm so ashamed, Juliet. I should never have told Zoë. I'm sorry."

"That's okay, Judy. I told Zoë it wasn't true. I don't know if she believed me. She had told Luis. I haven't actually seen him since, I was called away so suddenly. Is he around?"

"He came by here and asked if we knew where you were," said Joe. "We haven't seen him lately either. He hasn't been at any parties since I don't know when. There was quite a bash at Randall and Peter's last week."

"Too bad you missed that party, Juliet." Judy raised her hands to heaven. "They had the place fixed up like you wouldn't believe. They served a salmon with scales made of thin, thin slices of radish. They must have had two hundred candles, and these swags of white cloth draping down from the ceiling on either side of the doors, like the place was the Cirque du Soleil. Lord knows what they spent. Everybody was sad you weren't there. You know Alfonso and Uli? They were asking about you."

"Wow. I really missed it," Juliet sighed. "Well, now I'm back. My vines are coming in a few days and I'm finally going to get my terraces planted. Oh, and I found a vineyard over near Ezequiel Montes that's for sale. I think I might buy it. That will keep me busy."

Ease into honesty. What would friends think when they wanted to see her little vineyard and saw instead the

273

huge plant she was building? I've lived with lies so long I can't seem to stop, she thought. It was humiliating that for fear of exposure she hadn't entertained the family that owned the winery Las Fincas was partnering with, even though she'd been invited to several events including the daughter's wedding. This has to stop. And yet she lied to Judy and Joe again.

Luis stared blankly at the expansive lawn from the solarium in his parents' home. He had just called Enrique and found that, at last, Juliet had returned.

"My friend," Enrique had said, "I have let you try to pretend that each time you call me, and even from Cordoba, that it is not about Juliet, but you are doing a poor job of hiding it. What is it? Are you in love with this girl?"

Luis had been silent.

"*Bueno?*" Enrique prodded again.

"Yes, *amigo*, that is the situation."

"But something has separated you?"

"Yes."

"Perhaps that can be remedied. Has there been a misunderstanding? Of course, this is none of my affair. I do not want to intrude. But I can see why you would love her."

"Enrique, forgive me if I do not tell you more. I am very unsure what the problem is. I thought we had become close and then she went away and we have not spoken. I will come back to Itzcui tomorrow and see if I can sort it out. I'll see you soon, and thank you."

The situation had partially clarified itself to Luis. Julieta must indeed have a great deal of money and had been hiding it for reasons that were, to him, crystal clear. She, being under the carefully induced impression that he was of very modest means and must suspect him of having an interest in the money rather than in her. Everything hinged on when she thought he had found out. It was no good that he had proposed before Zoë had brought the news, if Julieta didn't know that. This "friend" of hers had apparently been in Itzcui several days earlier, so she must be thinking that her secret was revealed to him at that time. Who *was* he anyway? Luis remembered how strangely depressed she had sounded after the night of campesinos and love, after the morning sweetness, and the discovery of the treasures. How frightened he had been of losing her—but she had recovered and received him again. They had shared even deeper intimacies and he had asked her to marry him. How could she think he learned of her money and then proposed? Didn't she know him at all? Hadn't he been wooing her for months? Had he sounded less than serious? Surely not. It made no sense.

His sister, Sofía, breezed into the solarium and planted a warm kiss on each cheek. "Mami told me you were back. I've been looking all over the house for you. When did you get here?"

"Last night."

"You look miserably jetlagged. How was Spain?"

"Spain was lovely, but I was very dull. My writers were rather dull too. I don't think the seminar went well, though some were kind enough to say that it had been stimulating. Oh, and I visited Villarrubia. It's become a sort of bedroom village for Cordoba. I found a tile there for Papi. I think he'll be pleased. But, how are you? Mami tells me the business has been worrying you."

"Yes, I must face the Home Base problem. We're losing a lot of business since they descended on Mexico. I'm hopeful we'll get some of it back as their stocking problems become apparent to the customers. They're really doing a terrible job in some of their stores. I've threatened

275

my managers with death if they don't implement our restocking guidelines to the letter. I've been off on a round of inspections. How dreary were some of the towns I've seen."

"Poor girl. And while I indulge myself in Cordoba."

"No, I don't mean to complain. Listen, Luis, here's my plan. I'm going to start an outreach to each and every *municipio*. I'm going to offer cost plus nearly nothing for local projects, and play on their patriotism, as well. There will be certain other incentives to officials who use Ferre del Mundo, I suppose."

"Like what?"

"I could extend the municipal discount for some private projects."

"Aha."

"*And* I'll give bonuses to local managers who develop good contacts and give good service. I bought nearly two hundred new trucks this past month! I love it. It's a fight to the death! I'm going to make Home Base go home!" Luis smiled distractedly.

"So you're going back to Itzcui?" she asked, pulling her black hair to the top of her head and lifting her legs onto the love seat.

"I have an appointment with my editor tomorrow, then I'll go. I've just heard that a friend has returned to Itzcui and I want to see her."

"Wait a minute. What's this? A *woman* friend?"

"Yes. I met somebody."

"Oh, Luis! You haven't said this before. Who is she?"

"She's an American widow."

"Is she older than you?"

"No, she's very young. Only twenty-six. Her husband died shortly after they were married. I don't know why I'm telling you this, Sofi. I think I've ruined the relationship. This is very ironic. I believe she had the idea that I wanted her money."

"How much does she have?"

"I'm not sure, but perhaps something like us. I Googled her and found an obituary for her husband, the *billionaire,* Henry Ashe—survived by Juliet Pierce Ashe. I know her as Juliet Pierce."

"I can't believe this!"

"I know. And I think she's living like me, in secret. At least, that's what I believe is the situation. I haven't been able to talk to her in a month. Something happened and she ran away. Sofía, I asked her to marry me."

"Luis! What did she say?"

"She said it was too soon. But I thought it could happen. And then she was gone."

"Have Mami and Papi met her?"

"No, I didn't want to show her our life until she agreed to marry. I didn't have any idea about her money. I think I was very foolish."

"My darling brother! She will never resist you in the end. What is she like?"

"She is beautiful and intelligent, and she is starting a vineyard in Itzcui, and will make wine. She has a degree in wine-making. And she loves books. She reminds me of you."

"Luis! This is so extraordinary. Shall I come and tell her how pure your motives are, how fine you are? I will make her understand you."

"That is very tempting, Sofi, but I think I must find a way myself. Don't talk about it, please. Not even to Alejandro. Certainly not to Mami and Papi. This may not turn out well." Luis sat forward with his head in his hands.

"I am so honored that you told me, Luis. I will be

277

waiting night and day to embrace my sister. Does she speak Spanish?"

"She's learning, but . . . . Do you think it would be a big problem?"

"I suppose we can all speak English. Though, of course, Mami's isn't very good. Will Mami like her?"

"I think Mami would love her. She has a very sweet manner. Should I go buy her an enormous diamond? To convince her I do not need her money?"

"Is she the kind of girl who wants a diamond?" Sofía glanced at her three-carat display piece.

"She presents herself very simply. I suppose it would be the last thing she would want, nor anything that would serve the purpose to show the obsceneness of our wealth. What could I give her? I once thought I might give her a very fine tractor. Ah, but I don't know if she will even talk to me."

"Luis! Sofía! Where are my darlings?"

"Here, Papi!" Sofía called.

"Shall we ask him if you can give her the Velázquez?" Sofía teased.

It was late afternoon when Luis reached his house in Itzcui. He could see that the hacienda was open. Margarita was sweeping the porch and the pickups of Juliet's crew were parked to the side. He unlocked the heavy doors to his sitting room, carried his suitcases inside, and opened the double shutters in the bedroom and the kitchen. In the living room, he put his computer on the table, lifted the iron hasps on the window shutters, and threw them back. He caught sight of Zoë's photograph, took it from the wall and frowned at the image of lovers kissing on the steps of a pyramid at Palenque. He imagined dashing it to the floor, glass shattering around the room.

Uttering a short laugh at this uncharacteristically violent and satisfying fantasy, he hid the photo behind the book-filled ropero. He might not be prepared to smash it, but he surely wanted to put reminders of Zoë out of sight. I'll wait until the workers go home, he thought, and then go talk to Julieta.

Luis opened his laptop. He'd check e-mail, stare into space. The book was off to his editor. What would come next he had no idea. He'd hoped that the writing seminar in Spain would have been a good time for his unconscious to begin the next project, but his brain had largely occupied itself with Julieta. He felt at the moment that writing books was one of the great futilities, one of the major prevarications, and that his life was a complete failure. All he wanted to do was be close to that energetic, sparkling girl. He was in terror that this isolation from her would be a permanent state. He had been on the verge of a trip to California, or hiring a detective, or both.

At last, the pickups drove past. Margarita walked along the road carrying a plastic bag.

"*¡Margarita! Buenas tardes. ¿Cómo estás? ¿La señora está en casa?*"

Yes, she was at home. He picked up the bottle of *vino negro*—the red wine so dark it was called black—that he'd carried from Spain, squared his shoulders, and headed out the door. When he called into the house, Juliet walked into the entry with a sour little smile.

"Hello, Luis." Her kiss didn't quite contact his cheek and she said nothing more. This was as bad as he feared.

"Julieta, Julieta. May I come in and talk?"

"Oh, thank you. Where did you find this wine?" There was no warmth in her tone.

"I've been in Spain and thought this was special

279

enough to bring back to you." Juliet led Luis to the living room, put the bottle on a side table, and sat in the chair near the fireplace while Luis took his usual end of the sofa. It was the same seating arrangement as during the talk with Alex, she thought, and the parallel darkened her mood still more. Luis sat up on the edge of the sofa, just as Alex had, and looked unhappily at her.

"Julieta, it is clear that our relationship has fallen apart and I don't know why it has happened. Will you tell me? Why didn't you answer my e-mails?"

Juliet looked away. "I didn't read them. I suppose it's true that I'm not ready for a new life," she said at last.

"Are you telling me that you cannot move on from your marriage?"

She didn't answer.

"Did your departure have anything to do with what Zoë told you?"

"How do you know what Zoë told me?"

"I asked her."

"How did you know to ask her?"

"Because she told me, too."

"It may have had something to do with it."

"Julieta, look at me! Are you going to talk to me? Look! It's me! I love you. Don't you know that? What did your departure have to do with what Zoë said? What are you thinking?"

"Luis, I have decided to . . . I just can't go on with you. I am not available to . . . be your partner."

"Oh, Julieta." Luis sagged. "How can you do this to me? I never loved anyone like I love you. Do you think my love is insincere? Do you think I want your money?"

Juliet looked at him sharply. "It's not about money. Which I don't have."

"But what else makes sense? We were so happy,

no? Don't tell me you weren't happy. It isn't believable that you are so shackled to the past that you cannot move on, is it? You must have thought I wanted this money, whether it is real or not. Tell me the truth."

"Luis, I don't have but enough money to get my winery going."

"Something happened, Julieta. You have never been open with me. There have always been secret things. I can believe that you could want to hide having money—"

"Luis, I find this discussion—"

"Julieta! I know about this! My family is one of the richest in Mexico!"

Juliet sprang to her feet. "Oh, please! You couldn't want my money because you have so much money? That's perfect!" Her face twisted. Next he'd have a mansion in the Garden District. She wanted to scream.

"I hid it from you and everyone in Itzcui. It's why I live here. No one knows about my family."

Juliet paced in front of the fireplace. "I feel very upset, Luis. I wish you'd go. Please. Everything is just getting worse."

Luis stood and opened his palms to her. "My dear, you are being unfair. I have told you the truth. Listen. My family owns Ferre del Mundo. Whether you do or do not have money is of no possible consequence to me. I have tried to live my life to escape its burdens." He threw up his hands. "Its responsibilities as well."

"And you tell me this convenient thing only now because you've been afraid I'd want *your* money? Is that it? That's rather insulting."

"Just as insulting as your fears about me, I say with no pleasure," Luis murmured softly.

"Clearly neither has trusted the other nor does now. That would seem to be a poor basis—"

"You understand the motivation though, don't you? Admit it. Be honest with me," Luis pleaded.

"You talk of honesty when you didn't tell me what Zoë said? When you live like a monk and supposedly have all the money in the world?"

"When did I have a chance to tell you what Zoë said? And what does Zoë's rumor have to do with anything? It came from that man who came to Itzcui, right? We were staring into each other's eyes for a long time before that, weren't we?"

"There was no marriage talk before, Luis. I don't think I believe that Zoë wasn't or isn't more important—"

"Stop! I do not even *like* Zoë. How could I like someone who was so very careless about her kindness to you— and to me, for that matter."

"There! Luis, you are *glib*! I'm sure—*I'm sure*—Zoë has no idea of these *true* feelings, if that's what they are. And I don't want to hear any more pretty talk."

"All right. You may be right. I disguise my feelings. I think I understand that, but I didn't disguise my feelings toward you."

Luis and Juliet stood, color high and breath quickened.

"Please go, Luis. I hate so much to argue and accuse you, but I think we went through the last open door. Please go."

Luis stared at her, his jaw working, then dropped his eyes, and walked across the room. He stopped and turned. "One thing, Julieta. Please don't tell anyone what I told you about Ferre del Mundo."

"Ah, yes. Your wealth is a secret I'll take to my grave." Juliet made a dismissive gesture and looked away.

"Thank you."

She heard his steps in the entry and the closing of

the door. After pacing around the sala, the kitchen, and the dining room, she finally sank into a chair, put her head on the table and cried.

CHAPTER ELEVEN

Two weeks later, Joe took a fall. After too many vodka tonics, he lost his balance on the little step up from the patio to the arcade. Judy had gone to bed, but heard the heavy thump and cry, and ran out to find him lying in the patio, rocking in pain. She phoned Enrique's house, but he didn't answer. Next, she called Randall and Peter who lived closest, before remembering that they were in San Miguel. Then Luis. He came immediately, bringing his car in case it was needed. Inside he found Joe lying on the paving stones.

"I'm fucked, Luis," he said.

"Don't say that, Joe," Judy cried, "You'll be fine! Luis, we have to get him to the hospital."

"We'll call the ambulance at the Centro de Salud. Where's the phone? Get him a pillow and a warm blanket." He found the number in the little book Enrique had made for the town. No one answered. Judy gave a groan as Luis hung up.

"I'm going to the driver's house. You keep him warm. I'll be right back, Joe."

"Thanks, Luis," Joe said through clenched teeth.

"Judy, call Juliet to help you," Luis said as he ran toward the car.

Luis returned with Enrique, and the ambulance soon followed; the driver, Felipe, and Enrique had been on the plaza. At the same time, Juliet drove up in her truck. In a moment, they were all clustered around Joe.

"Sorry about my bad manners," he laughed grimly. "I've fallen and I can't get up." Joe's leg lay at an unnatural angle.

With equipment from the ambulance, Enrique checked Joe's vitals. "He should go to the hospital," he said, preparing a shot for the pain as Felipe came in with a hand-carried stretcher—this was no gurney, and Joe was heavy. It was going to be a struggle.

"Joe, how do jou feel?"

"Hey, what did you give me? Great stuff."

"*Bueno.* We try to put jou on this side where does not hurt? And then push jou on the stretcher? Very gentle."

Joe moaned and cried out once. Judy cringed in sympathy. Juliet held her while the three men maneuvered Joe onto the canvas sling and conferred about ways to get him to the ambulance. They lifted the foot end of the stretcher, put a bench under the handles and hoisted the head end in the air. Juliet and Felipe were told to each take a handle at the foot; Juliet faltered and Judy ran to help her lift. They shuffled out to the ambulance and slid him in.

"Do jou want to come in *la ambulancia*, Judy?" Enrique asked as he climbed in beside Joe.

"I'd better get dressed and pack some things, don't you think? He's going to be all right, isn't he?"

"He will be okay to the hospital, I am sure," Enrique answered evasively.

"I'll drive you, Judy," Luis offered. "Are you going

to Santa María?"

"No, I believe is better San Javier in Querétaro. Better equipment."

"Fine. We'll see you there." Judy and Juliet blew kisses to Joe as Luis closed the doors. Felipe pulled the ambulance into the quiet street and soon rounded the corner toward the plaza. Judy turned to find that most of her neighbors were standing quietly in a group behind her. They came one by one, wishing God's blessings on Joe, taking Judy's hand and looking into her eyes with infinite sympathy. It was more than she could take and she burst into tears.

All the way into Querétaro, Luis talked gently to Judy, even getting her to laugh a bit, while Juliet remained silent in the back seat. Juliet was sure Judy was in denial about the seriousness of the situation; Joe's circulation had been getting worse and worse. One glance at the edema in his legs told you that. His heart *had* to be weak. How was it going to stand the repair of his hip? It probably wasn't.

They reached the hospital after midnight and found Enrique waiting for them in the lobby. He took them to a cubicle off the emergency room and introduced them to a frighteningly young female doctor. Joe was propped up on a narrow bed, apparently somewhat sedated. He opened his eyes when Judy, Juliet, and Luis came in, and smiled his big smile.

"How are you, old girl?" he asked Judy.

"How are you, sweetheart? How was the ambulance ride?"

"Enrique took good care of me. Dr. Cruz wants to have a conference with us. She has some ideas."

"We'll wait in the lobby, shall we, Juliet?" Luis said.

They took seats on either side of an artificial bird-of-paradise in the empty lounge. After an awkward minute,

287

Juliet asked, "Do you think he'll make it?"

"I have my fears. I believe his heart is very bad. I think a fall is often the thing that can push people over the edge."

"That's the way my grandmother died."

"Yes, mine as well."

They were again silent. Both were sad and extremely uncomfortable. This was first time they had been alone since the terrible scene in the living room, and both were aware of it.

Luis stood. "Excuse me, Juliet. I need to make a phone call."

He doesn't call me Julieta, she thought.

Luis returned after a time. Judy and Enrique joined them shortly after.

"They want him to fly back to the United States," Judy said, shaking her head. "I have to find out what those evacuation planes cost. I always told Joe we should get that supplementary insurance, but we never did."

"Won't Medicare pay for it?" Juliet asked.

"I don't know. I haven't any idea. I think I'd better call the consulate in the morning."

"So why don't they think they can treat him here? Did she say?"

"Dr—what's her name, Enrique?"

"Doctora Cruz."

"Dr. Cruz thinks its going be difficult with his heart problems."

"Is Joe settled for the night then?" Juliet asked.

"They're keeping him near the emergency room. I think they hope he'll fly out in the morning. I really don't know what I'm going to do." Judy twisted her hands and looked around the waiting room, tears starting in her eyes.

"I have a friend who has a house here in Querétaro

who has offered the four of us a place to sleep tonight," Luis said, looking into Judy's face with kind concern. "He has a large house. Why don't we say goodnight to Joe and go over there. We can make some calls."

Juliet awoke with a start to find Judy sitting on the side of her bed.

"I'm sorry to disturb you, Juliet. I wanted to say goodbye. The ambulance is taking Joe to the airport now. We've got a Gulfstream to take us to Houston. I have to get out to the airport right away."

Juliet bolted upright. "It's all settled? Why didn't you wake me? What did you figure out? How's Joe?"

"He came through the night fine, but he's pretty grumpy this morning. I talked to him on the phone. I'm just so relieved we're going to the U.S. I'm sure they'll fix him up."

"I'm sure they will, Judy. The plane—is insurance covering it? If there's a problem, I have enough money to take care of it."

"No, I don't need it. How much help can one person get? I wish . . . . Okay, give me a kiss. I'm off. Will you close up the house for me? It's anybody's guess when we'll be back. Here's the key. Can you please give Rosa some money? I'll pay you back."

"Of course. Keep in close touch, Judy. Let me know how to reach you right away. Wait!" Juliet grabbed her purse from the bedside table. "I have a little pocket money. Look—1500, 1700 pesos. You can change it at the airport. No! Take it."

"I don't need it, Juliet. You and Luis and Enrique. I don't know how to thank you. I'll call." Judy rose heavily and left the room. When she was gone, Juliet put her face in her hands. Judy and Joe. It was going to be hard if that team was broken up. Perhaps they *would* save him. If Medicare didn't cover Joe's evacuation, she could take care of it later. Maybe he'd need private nursing too.

Juliet looked around her room. In the small hours of the morning, she had been only dimly aware of the opulence. Now she was astounded at her surroundings—sixteen-foot ceilings and antique furniture to scale. She got up and looked out a window that gave onto a quiet pedestrian street, then studied the oil paintings in their gilt frames, and the wooden carvings of saints on the low cabinet that extended nearly the length of one wall. Her bathroom was also antique, but well-appointed.

When she was dressed, she went out to a wide interior balcony that circled around an atrium. Two sets of stairs joined at a landing to finish their descent to the first floor. Three ornamental palms reached up past the balcony and on toward a stained glass dome. She heard the distant clink of silverware and went downstairs. On one side, French doors with etched glass opened to a dining room; an elderly man was placing settings on one end of a grand table.

"*Buenos días,*" Juliet greeted him. "*¿Está aquí Señor Zaragoza?*"

"*Buenos días, señora. Los dos señores están en el aeropuerto. ¿Gusta usted un cafecito?*"

"*Sí, gracias.*" They were all at the airport. She wished she was getting to say goodbye to Joe.

Juliet took a seat in an alcove off the dining area where the morning sun fell on an arrangement of Empire furniture. The coffee was brought in a silver pot with matching sugar bowl and creamer, and served in a bone china cup. A plate held two miniature croissants, butter, and marmalade. The silverware was heavy with baroque embellishment. Luis's friend certainly had one of the grandest houses she'd ever seen.

She leafed through a picture book of henequen haciendas on the coffee table and saw the one that had given her the idea for the ox-eye window at La Paloma. A man appeared in the atrium and opened a tap that put water into the planter that held the palm trees. He bowed to her when he saw her watching him. She was offered breakfast and moved to the table for *pan francés*—French toast— sausage and fresh juice. She asked the old gentleman if the owners of the house were at home, which it seemed apparent they were not; he said that they were in Mexico City.

Luis and Enrique still hadn't arrived when she'd finished breakfast so she wandered back to her room and took a shower, but when she came out on the balcony, she heard their voices in the dining room.

"There jou are, Juliet," Enrique said as she joined them.

"Did they get off?"

"Jes. Very difficult. Very uncomfortable for Joe. The plane was too small inside. There was a nurse and Judy sat with the pilot."

"How did it work out with hiring the plane?"

"It will be paid for," Luis said.

"Oh, thank goodness. How much was it?"

"$16,500."

"Yikes," she said, keeping in character. Reasonable, she thought. "Where will they fly to?"

"Houston. Their daughter lives there."

"Oh, good. Where are we, Luis?"

"This house? It belongs to a friend. It's very fine, isn't it? Have you looked around?"

"No, but I wanted to."

"Let's do the tour before we go back. I'm done with

291

my breakfast."

Juliet nodded. Just because Luis had rich friends, it didn't mean that he was rich. It hadn't meant that for Alex.

Rosa was close to hysteria when Juliet was dropped off by Luis at Joe and Judy's house. She had heard the report from the neighbors, and knew about the ambulance taking Joe off in the night. Juliet told her that Joe and Judy had flown to the other side—the U.S.—and that the situation was grave. Did she know if there were any bookings for the guest rooms? Judy had forgotten to mention it. There was a book; Juliet checked and found two dates: four people for the following weekend, and two more three days after that. Their names all suggested that they'd be English speakers. Juliet promised to come over and help Rosa greet them. She put a message on the machine that directed inquiries to her number, and told Rosa to come by La Paloma for her wages.

In a few days, Judy called from Houston to say Joe was having a stent put in to strengthen his circulation for the surgery on his hip. A week more and she called to say he hadn't yet regained consciousness after the stent procedure. The next report was of pneumonia. He died five days after that.

Joe's death hit Itzcui hard. All their friends had discussed each bulletin, all had tried to cling to hope, and all were devastated when Joe passed away. Would Judy return, they wondered? Annette called her to say how much they all hoped she would come back and to tell about how much love and support she had received in Itzcui after her own husband died. Juliet hadn't had her husband long enough to presume to understand Judy's loss, but she also begged her to come back. "Who will I laugh with, if you aren't here?" Luis apparently was in touch too, since he was the one who found out that Judy was returning with her daughter in a couple of weeks.

Juliet's vines were putting out their first buds. Drip irrigation had been installed, and the new gardener—Samuel—had been trained to keep the system functioning. Juliet had found a chef and manager for the tasting room and restaurant at Las Fincas. On a trip to Guadalajara she ordered chairs and tables, wine racks, and corn-husk sunflowers. In Tequila she bought used barrels to be cut in half to be used as planters.

She was less social in Itzcui, because all this kept her busy and because there was Luis to be avoided. Time and again she looked over at the red house, saw him go in and out, leave town and come back. They spoke only of mundane things whenever they found themselves face to face.

But she thought about the mansion of Luis's friend and replayed what he'd said about Ferre del Mundo. When she Googled the hardware empire, she learned that the owner was Miguel Angel Villarrubia Reyes, not Zaragoza, that the family was second or third after Carlos Slim in Mexican wealth. And there apparently was no son because a daughter was said to be taking over the company. Had he found out about Home Base and made up the Ferre del Mundo connection because of that? Crazy. It was making her crazy.

"Enrique, who owns Ferre del Mundo? Is it a Mexican company?"

"Oh, jes. The Villarrubia family. Very rich, I believe. I think one of the most rich families in Mexico."

"Do you know them?"

"I? No, of course not. I do not know such people."

293

She missed Luis more as time went on. One day she checked to see if her leftover antidepressants were still in the back of the drawer in the bedside table; she almost took one. What if she apologized? Would he still want her? Had she been too ugly in the way she'd sent him away for there to be any going back? Why didn't he come over and try again? At least she hadn't seen him with Zoë.

The things from the San Francisco house arrived. The sheets made her sad; she'd slept on them with Hank, and never would with Luis. The carpets were too grand. The Chinese horse didn't know what to make of its surroundings. Perhaps she'd carry it back to her father's house someday. At least the majolica was content. Hank's photo was placed with a collection of family pictures in the living room and Juliet lovingly arranged the books on the shelves. That's what a house needs, she thought, as she realized that the quality of the sound in the rooms had mellowed.

Spurred by the report on the communion wine, Enrique had tracked down more history of the hacienda. Doña Joaquina Sánchez, ninety-eight years of age, said the family had originally come from Cholula. She knew that they had been very religious and might well have guarded the chapel relics or hidden a priest.

She remembered when Guadalupe Sánchez had gone to the other side and had ended up fighting in World War II. When it was over, he stayed in California, and all his brothers and sisters went, one by one, to join him. The cattle had been tended by renters for a time. Finally, the herd was sold and the place abandoned. Jimmy Sánchez, some grandson or great-grandson—Doña Joaquina wasn't clear which—had come, perhaps five years ago, and put the hacienda on the market. She said with wonder that he spoke almost no Spanish, as if describing a bird that had wings but didn't know how to fly.

"It will be great that the *inauguración* of the chapel will be after Judy comes back," Juliet said to Annette. They were working in the chapel, trying to decide where to place a pedestal Annette had found for the San José and Santo Niño in the glass case.

"When does Judy get in? I think it should go opposite the window where the light is better."

"We could direct one of those spots wherever we want it," Juliet said.

"I guess that one isn't doing much," Annette said, looking up.

"I'll get Chango to bring the ladder. Judy's supposed to get here not this Friday but next, and the blessing is on the following Sunday after mass. God, that's twelve days. I've got so much to do."

The re-upholstered furniture, repaired picture frame, and cleaned chalice, monstrance, and candle sticks had been returned by Señor Estrada. Juan Diego had made a grand new chapel door—one that looked anything but new and was adequate for a fortress. He had also made a balustrade that stretched across the chapel to prevent visitors from approaching the altar too closely. A section opened for the privileged.

"Margarita and I decided on the food yesterday. She'll get her sister in to help."

"Do you think this wall looks too bare, Juliet?"

"Yes, but what can I do? I don't want to buy new things for the chapel, do I? Don't we just want to show the things that were here? Not that your pedestal is going too far, and of course I'm using my Puebla vases."

"Why not paint an account of the discovery on the wall? We could ask Luis or Enrique to write up something

295

in Spanish. Maybe English too? In *dos mil nueve* below the hacienda discovered themselves these treasures *de la época* of the persecution *de la iglesia Católica*."

They laughed at Annette's Spanish parody. "I like that. With a painted frame and curlicues? We could have an English handout. Do you know anyone who can do that kind of work? Maybe we should have a fancy dado around the whole room."

"Oh, absolutely. Maybe Father Ramón knows where to find the guy who touched up the church. Oh, God. I saw a church in Veracruz last year that was painted with a different pattern on every angle of wall and column and ceiling. I took a lot of pictures. Shall I try to find them?"

Word went out that Judy and her daughter, Jan, had arrived, spurring an impromptu "welcome home" pot luck to materialize. Juliet ran across the patio to give and receive hugs, to meet Jan, and to shed tears with Judy. "This is so wonderful and so sad," Juliet said, wiping her eyes. Jan, you look just like your mom."

"Yeah, but she's all Joe." Judy gave her daughter a fond look. "She's sweet to come down with me, isn't she?"

"My company was sweet to go out of business just when I was needed." Jan laughed a very Joe laugh. "Mom and I have some serious adjusting to do but we'll make it, won't we, Mom."

Judy made a what's-one-to-do face and sat down resignedly at the iron table. "How about a vodka tonic?" she suggested.

"I'll make 'em. You too, Juliet?"

"Sure," Juliet said glancing at the only slightly lengthened shadows across the patio. She'd probably get a headache, but it seemed right to drink with Judy. The older woman looked so drawn and sad, had aged so much in two months.

"What did you bring us, Juliet?" Judy lifted the lid of the casserole dish. "Ah, enchiladas. I haven't had Mexican food since I left."

"Margarita made them. Have you heard that the chapel is being blessed Sunday?"

"Yes, Luis told me. I think that's so great."

"When did you see Luis?"

"He picked us up at the airport."

"Wow! What a nice guy," Jan called from the bar near the kitchen.

"I thought Enrique—"

"Judy! My dear!" Randall called from the doorway. His hugs and condolences were barely started when Zoë sailed in, radiant in red and white embroidery. Judy teared up again and everyone fussed around her. Soon, Enrique and Annette had come, and Judy was on her second drink—saying repeatedly how grateful she was to have such friends. Rosa brought out plates of guacamole and quesadillas. Tequila and wine were poured. Peter arrived with a platter of crostini topped with roasted red pepper. Silvio and Elena provided an enormous tray of lasagna. That being Joe's favorite, a toast was raised and eyes moistened.

Before the night was over, it seemed as though half the town had come to see Judy. More bottles of tequila appeared and were emptied. More wine was poured. Judy recounted the trials of Joe's fall and decline. Jan revealed to Juliet that her former employer had run a wine club. They nodded over qualities of vintages—Jan was impressed at Juliet's Quinta da Augustinho connections—and shook their heads at the world-wide cutbacks in discretionary spending. Juliet wondered if she should offer Jan a job. Luis

297

arrived late and kept himself across the patio from Juliet, but when she left, he soon followed her out. She walked home without knowing that he was behind her, trying and failing to think of what he'd say if he caught up.

Jan came by early to help at the inauguración of the chapel. Fearless with her high-school Spanish, she soon was laughing in the kitchen with Margarita, Margarita's sister, and her mother. Marcelino set up folding chairs borrowed from the senior center on the porch facing the chapel and its wide-flung doors. The Peruvian Virgin in her opulent gown gazed down on the preparations. Candles waited to be lit. The ruby-colored glass vases held white hydrangeas. Jan and Juliet took a moment to sit outside the kitchen on the porch to rest and drink glasses of lemonade. Nearby, a small fire descended to coals that would be used to burn copal incense.

"How's your mother doing, do you think?" Juliet asked.

"I think this place is so what she needs. She's going to be sad wherever she is but I think she'd find it impossible to go into a depression here. So many great people."

"It's a sweet village, isn't it?"

"Mom said you'd lost your husband, too. I'm really sorry."

"It wasn't easy, but we'd had nothing like your parents' forty-seven years. I can't imagine what she's feeling."

"I think it will be good for her to run the B&B, don't you? She'll be able to use the money too."

"Was the evacuation flight covered in the end?"

"That angel Luis paid for it."

"He did?"

Jan looked shame-faced. "Oh, jeez. I think I wasn't supposed to say that. He's pretty secretive, right? I guess my mom said he didn't want anyone to know. Forget it, okay?"

"Oh, sure," Juliet said weakly.

"*¡Señora!*" Margarita called. "*Los mariachis están aquí.*"

"Uh, oh," Juliet said, laughing nervously and jumping up "The mariachis. I'm not sure whether I'm supposed to break out the tequila, or hide it."

The opening went perfectly. The chapel was thoroughly blessed. Most of the town was fed on pulled pork, beans, rice, and a salsa suitable for removing the top of your head. Eight kilos of tortillas were consumed. Ten dead tequila soldiers, somehow upright, stood on the colonnade. Uli and Alfonso presented Juliet with an antique painting on tin that recounted a miraculous return of a lost goat after a farmer prayed to San José. Señor Aguilar, who had sold her the bed and much more, came to see the chapel and the setting for his antiques. Her partners in the Las Fincas project visited the hacienda at last. The mariachis gave a magnificent and deafening performance, following which Enrique played his cello in a corner of the living room. Luis had not come.

Looking elegant in a black and white embroidered Oaxacan tunic over a long black skirt, Juliet emerged from the chapel with late guests, and directed them toward the food inside. She lingered on the porch, turning for yet another glance toward Luis's house. This time, she saw him. He was almost unrecognizable in his suit and tie, and was arm in arm with a woman whose beauty and elegance were clear even from a distance and in fading light. Juliet's heart sank. Too late.

It had been at the moment that Jan said Luis had

paid for the plane and wanted it to be a secret, that she had known that what he had told her had all been true. She'd been watching for him all through the afternoon, dreading and hoping for his arrival. It was painful when she thought he had not chosen to attend, but this was worse. She watched the perfect couple approach and waited for the blow.

They reached the bottom of the stairs. "Juliet, good evening. How are you? Please allow me to present my sister, Sofía Villarrubia Zaragoza."

"What a pleasure!" Smiling, Sofía climbed the steps and took Juliet's hand.

Juliet looked into her beautiful face and mumbled something unintelligible. She remembered vividly that Villarrubia was the name of the Ferre del Mundo family.

Sofía smoothly continued. "Luis has told me very good things about you and I have hoped to meet you. We are so distressed to be late. Unavoidable, but very embarrassing."

"But . . . Sofía Villarrubia Zaragoza. Does that mean that Villarrubia is your father's name and Zaragoza your mother's?" Juliet asked.

"Yes, it is my mother's name that I use on my books. And forgive me. Sofía, this is Juliet Pierce Ashe.

"Oh, Luis." Juliet squeezed shut her eyes.

"Please, Juliet. May we see the chapel?" Sofía asked, somewhere in the far distance.

"Of course." Sofía's arm slipped through hers. Gold and silver shone richly in the candlelight. Dark red cushions, the frieze in burgundy and ocher, the Virgin, each of the painted pearls on her dress gleaming—all was perfect.

"Exquisite!" Sofía breathed. "Truly exquisite."

"I didn't know about the wall painting," Luis said.

"It's a very fine idea."

"It was only finished the day before yesterday," Juliet said, avoiding his eyes.

"Luis has told me that he was with you when these treasures were discovered. That must have been very exciting."

Before Juliet could speak, their neighbors the Acostas appeared on the porch. "With permission, Julieta. Many thanks for this wonderful event. Luis, *buenas noches.*"

"Hector, Elena, may I present my sister, Sofía Zaragoza?"

"A pleasure."

"Equally, Señora Zaragoza. We like very much to have your brother here with us. Your family must be very proud of him."

"Very proud. And he says how much he loves this beautiful pueblo."

"Goodnight, Julieta. *Mil gracias.*"

Again, the three were left alone on the porch.

"So, Julieta. Will you show me your lovely home?" Sofía squeezed Juliet's arm and urged her toward the door. She threw her brother a smile over her shoulder.

Sofía had a trained eye. She commented on the carpets, the majolica, the finer pieces of furniture. As they stood before the huge fireplace, their backs to the room, Sofía whispered to Juliet, "My brother loves you very much. I hope you will consider his heart."

Juliet had to fight not to cry. "Thank you," was all she could manage.

They rejoined Luis on the porch where he was exchanging pleasantries with departing guests. He looked on nervously as Sofía kissed Juliet goodbye. "We will meet again very soon," she said, "I know it. Please forgive me for my brief visit."

301

"Juliet, I will see Sofía to her car. May I talk to you after that?" Juliet nodded, her eyes moist.

Sofía and Luis crossed the yard toward a large car waiting in front of Luis's house, their heads close in conversation. The last of the guests departed behind them. Juliet could hear Margarita and her mother laughing as they tidied the house.

Luis was coming back. He knew about her, had introduced her with Hank's name, had introduced his sister with the compound surname that included both father and mother, confirming Villarrubia entrepreneurial colossus and explaining Zaragoza nom de plume. Juliet could not remember why she had lied, why she had refused to hear Luis's explanations. Now, the truth of their bizarrely parallel lives seemed so simple and obvious.

Intent on emptying the house, she went inside, thanked her helpers and told them not to worry about the rest until the morning. Having been hurried to the door, and buoyed with a generous tip, they crossed the yard, laughing and talking. Their voices merged into the night. Juliet hoped Luis was listening to hear them go.

In the chapel, the votives lining the railing had gutted, leaving the shortened tapers on the altar as the only light. Shadows crept toward the last glints reflected from the treasures. The Virgin smiled at her with a compassion she had never seen in her face before. How satisfying it would be to believe, to fall on one's knees and pray: *Queen of Heaven, open my heart to the beauty of love and life.* With tears pooling in her eyes, Juliet used a long-handled snuffer to extinguish the remaining candles, and with them, the sight of the Virgin's sweet visage. She closed the first door without effort; the other always caught on an uneven tile. There was the sound of footsteps in the dark. Luis stood again at the bottom of the stairs. He had taken off his jacket and tie and opened his blue shirt at the neck.

"Julieta?"

She left the door and sat on the top stair. Luis sat beside her. Together they looked out into the night, their shoulders just touching. A trumpet began playing somewhere in the village, practicing the solo from "El Niño Perdido," The Lost Boy. All else held its breath.

"I'm sorry we were so late. A funeral in Querétaro. A colleague of my father." Luis paused. "Will you agree that we have managed our love affair very badly?"

"That would seem to be the case, yes."

"Do you think . . . do you think we might try again?"

"So it was true about Ferre del Mundo and hiding in Itzcui."

"Entirely true. And it was true that you were also pretending and hiding."

"Yes, but I did give most of the money away—though that doesn't matter." Juliet turned to face him. "I wasn't kind to you, Luis. I'm so sorry. I don't know why you want to have anything to do with me."

"I know about money twisting things. I'm sorry to offer you the same problem again, if you will have me."

"Luis, I feel scared and superstitious. Does it ever stop? What if you die? I don't know if I can face trying again."

"Nonsense. Of course you can." He touched her cheek. "You are so alive, you can't help yourself. It will be good—better than good. I want to watch you grow your winery. I want to watch you grow our children. Don't condemn me to live without you. Help me find my way out of my convolutions and my obscure and useless ideas. Julieta, I need you."

"Oh, Luis, when you are near, I remember how

303

sweet life can be." They leaned into a long and soft kiss, then another.

"Come, help me close this door," she said, rising to her feet.

Luis crossed to the chapel door and began to ease it up and over the uneven floor. He stopped. "One condition, querida: I'll close this door for you if you'll agree that we keep all the others open. All our lives."

"Luis, I love you more than I can say."

"And I too, more than I can say. But I will dedicate myself to finding the words."

Acknowledgements

My thanks go to my editor, Katrina Robinson, and to María Lorena Hernández Yáñez for Spanish language handholding. Douglas Fir translated my cover vision into photographic reality. I consulted Robert Frank's fascinating sociological study, *Richistan,* and paraphrased from Juan Rulfo's *Pedro Páramo*, as translated by Margaret Sayers Peden. The characters Joe and Judy are partly based—the best parts—on John and Anna Honan, true bon vivants who brightened my early years in Mexico, but any other resemblances to actual persons are coincidental. I was able to depend, as always, on my husband, Jonathan Kingson, for aid, patience, and encouragement.

About the Author

Carolyn Kingson was born in New Orleans and spent thirty-seven years in northern New Mexico. She and her husband now live in a small Pacific-coast village in Mexico.
www.carolynkingson.com